TAKE ME APART

VITALE BROTHERS
BOOK 1

BREA ALEPOÚ

SKYLER SNOW

Cover Artist: Cosmic letterz Charli

Editor: Kate

Formatting Brea Alepoú

WARNING AND TRIGGERS

Triggers:
Death, violence, detailed torture, Parental abuse, parental neglect, former drug abuse, mild knife play, light dub-con.

Author's Note:
The mention of autism in this book is not indicative of ALL people with autism nor is it a way to vilify them. My writing partner has based the character on me and my attributes. Neither of us are mental health professionals so let's just stow that before it starts, kay? Kay! This is a work of fiction. Neither of us are cops and know how they work besides the research that was performed. Happy reading!

Please note, we are not experts on the mafia lifestyle. The purpose of this book is for romance entertainment **only**. This is a work of fiction. Enjoy your time out of reality.

One
TEX

MY HEART SQUEEZED IN MY CHEST AS MY LUNGS TIGHTENED. The fuzzy dizziness that filled my brain made my fingers feel numb. Still, I kept my gun poised, my back straight, and my feet planted. The cool October air was filled with an electric charge as if, everything would go up in a blaze at any moment.

"Steady," Rourke mumbled beside me.

"I'm calm," I muttered back.

He nodded. "You take the back. I'll take the front."

We split apart without another word. I swept to the left, and he made his way up the front steps. We'd chased the perp a good six blocks before he ducked into this house, but now everything was quiet. Too damn quiet. We weren't exactly in an upscale part of town, yet there wasn't a baby crying, a tv blaring, or a radio going. It was as if the entire house had fallen into a pit of nothingness. My stomach turned.

Fuck. Only god knows what we're going to find in there.

I ducked past the windows and traveled through the alley to the back gate. The thing was barely intact, hanging on by a thread as its rusty tops jutted into the air. I searched the yard, my eyes sweeping back and forth as I tried to pick out any subtle movement.

Nothing.

"Shit," I swore under my breath and reached over the gate to open it.

It scraped against the rough concrete. I winced, my shoulders going up around my ears as I glanced around again, praying no one had heard that. When there was still no movement, I shoved my body through the gap I'd made. It was just wide enough but tugged at my uniform as if trying to stop me from going inside. Ignoring the feeling that I should turn back, I moved forward.

As much as these moments unnerved me, they made me too. The thrill of sweat-slicked skin as adrenaline coursed through my veins was better than any trip I'd ever taken. It was more intoxicating than sex. The fear mixed with excitement was the reason I loved my job.

I moved onto the cracked and lifting steps of the back porch. They creaked beneath my boots, making a loud noise. *Shit.* I kept moving. Leaning up against the peeling blue paint of the wall, I reached out and wrapped my hand around the dented, silver doorknob. I sucked in a quick breath. As soon as I turned it, the door flew open.

"Fucking pig!"

I ducked back as the first shot rang out. Something whizzed by my face. My feet shifted, and I threw myself at the side of the porch, launching my body over the railing and falling into a patch of dry weeds and dirt. My shoulder slammed against the ground, and intense pain shot through me, making me grit my teeth.

"Put the gun down, Carl," I called. "You're only making this worse for yourself! Drop the goddamn weapon!"

"Fuck you!"

I shook my head. So, aside from armed robbery, Carl seemed desperate to tack on attempted murder or, at the very least, assaulting a police officer. He'd already resisted arrest. The man was digging a hole for himself and probably didn't even fully know he was doing it. I'd seen the shit he was on when we searched his car. That much glass? He was riding high and mean as a viper right now.

He squeezed off another shot, and I scrambled to my feet. My left arm was useless now, dangling by my side as my shoulder and neck tingled. *Damn, it's gotta be dislocated.* I shoved myself against the side of the house and gripped my left arm.

Great. I was fighting a meth head with a gun while I was down one arm and trying to blink the black spots out of my eyes. Those odds were uneven as hell.

Everything went still again, and the hair on the back of my neck stood on end. I felt like a predator was stalking me. My gun was thankfully still gripped tightly in my right hand, so I waited, my breathing coming in quiet gusts as I focused every bit of my attention on listening to the sounds around me.

There. A branch snapped, and rocks shifted. He was taking his time, sneaking around the corner. I had two options; I could run and possibly get shot in the back or I could stand my ground and try to shoot him before he shot me. As he rounded the corner, I picked option number three.

I dropped to the ground and squeezed the trigger. His shot rang out, aimed at where I had been only moments before. But mine was already ripping through his leg. He let out a strangled yell and fell to the dirt.

"Drop the fucking gun, Carl!"

"You shot me," he shouted. "Oh fuck, that hurts, man. Fuck!"

I dragged myself to my feet and jogged over to where he sat on the ground, dazed and holding his bleeding leg. Blood had already soaked through the jeans and was making a sticky mess. While he was distracted, I took the opportunity to kick the gun away.

"I'm surprised you can feel anything, considering how much meth you're on."

He blinked up at me. "What happened?"

"Hands behind your back. Now," I said as I kept my gun trained on him. "Rourke!"

"Right here," my partner called as he rounded the house and joined me. "He had his girlfriend tied up in there. She's a mess." He stared at me. "What's wrong with your arm?"

"Dislocated. Can you cuff him?"

"Shit," Rourke said as he took out his handcuffs and walked over to Carl. "On your stomach, come on."

Rourke made quick work securing Carl and called in for an ambulance. Once the call was in, he shushed Carl and took off his belt. Working fast, he tightened it around the man's leg.

"You're fine, drama queen," Rourke told Carl, giving his leg a little slap. "The bleeding is already slowing." Rourke rose to his feet, a grin stretching his lips. "How the hell did you manage this shit?" he asked as he waved a hand toward me. "You always have to choose the path of most resistance."

"You told me to take the back, asshole, remember?" I nodded to Carl. "Is he gonna be okay?"

"Yeah, he's good."

"Fuck you! He shot me!"

Clearly, Carl disagreed. Rourke ignored him and checked out my arm. He whistled as he took it in and grimaced.

"Can you pop it back in and stop staring at it?" I asked.

"They say you're not supposed to do that, you know? Protocol is to wait for the ambulance."

I was going to put one of my boots right up Rourke's ass. He knew damn well I wasn't going to wait around until the ambulance showed up just to do the same thing. I stared at him until he caved.

"Alright, stop pouting, princess. Brace yourself."

I holstered my weapon and leaned against the wall of the house. Rourke took hold of my arm more securely, examining it closely. I closed my eyes and waited, bracing myself. Just when I opened them to yell at my partner, my shoulder cracked as he popped it back into place.

"Oh, fuck you!" I bellowed. "You... goddamn..."

"I know," Rourke said. "Hurts like a bitch, doesn't it?" He walked over to one of the windows and peeked inside. "Girlfriend's still there. I'm going to go in and question her soon as they get here."

The distant sound of sirens was fast approaching. I rolled my shoulder, pulling a face at the lingering throbbing that had been left behind. It felt a lot better, but it was definitely going to swell up and be a pain later on. That was a problem for future me.

"I'll stay and—"

"You're not doing shit," Rourke interrupted. "Backup is

on the way, and I can handle a little questioning. Go home. It's not like you have plans tonight anyway."

"I'm fine," I argued.

"Go. Home. Don't make me have to talk to the Sergeant."

I glared at him. "You're a little bitch."

"Love you too," he teased as he waved at the paramedics jogging down the alley. "Get out of here."

Groaning, I gave in. As much as I wanted to stay, I had to admit that the fun part was over. Now came questions, paperwork, and bureaucratic bullshit. While I didn't love it, sticking around and doing everything right was a great way to continue to get noticed. And I *needed* to be noticed if I wanted to make detective.

"DIDN'T ROURKE SAY YOU WERE GOING HOME?"

I glanced up from the computer and stared at my Sargeant. Rourke was still out, but I'd gone right back to the precinct. I'd been on my way home, but I got that urge in my belly to go back and see what else I could get into for the day. My shift wasn't technically over, and my arm was fine. I wanted to work.

"I was going to, but I feel fine," I said as I stood up and followed her to her desk. She dropped a stack of folders and sighed. "What's all this for?"

"Huh?" She looked up at me like she was only seeing me for the first time and frowned. "Oh, something I'm working on for the chief. Did you put everything into your activity log?"

I nodded. "First thing I did when I came back." I picked up a file. "These are so old. What are you looking into?"

"The Vitale family again. Chief wants a big bust. Taking down a crime family? It doesn't get much bigger than that."

I whistled. "Shit, no one's been able to get anything major on them in like twenty years."

"Yep, that's the problem," she muttered.

"I bet if someone did figure out what's going on with them, he could probably make detective a hell of a lot sooner..." I trailed off.

Sergeant White stared at me before her eyes narrowed. "Not this shit again. You just became a cop two years ago. Why are you trying to move so fast?"

"We both know I want detective."

"Yes, but you get there through busting your ass and doing the work," she said as she plucked the file out of my hands. "Not by taking shortcuts. I don't want to see you nosing around these. Go do some work."

"But—"

"I don't want to hear it, Caster," she said shortly. "Focus on what's in front of you."

Fuck that. I was already two years in. By now, my father had been a detective and had started receiving accolades. He was hailed as the best of the best, and I was left standing in his shadow, a fraction of the man that he was.

"Sargeant White? My office," the chief called.

She sighed. "I'll be back." She scooped up the files and dropped them into her filing cabinet before shutting it.

I nodded and watched her go. The office door shut and my hands moved before my brain could keep up. I'd shoved my leg against the file cabinet just as it closed. Sure enough, it hadn't locked the way she thought it did. I pulled it open and reached inside. Taking out one of the folders, I scanned the info and moved to the next one.

The Vitale family was like a ghost story to a bunch of

camp kids when it came to cops. An old crime family, they ran New York and what they got into was nothing short of shocking. Guns, drugs, prostitution; you name it, they did it.

I flipped through and stopped. One of their known clubs wasn't far from where I lived. I looked at the clock on the far wall, and a grin tugged at my lips. Okay, I probably wouldn't find anything. But it was worth checking out, right?

Glancing around, I made sure no one was watching as I snapped a picture of the page and shoved my phone back into my pocket. I closed the drawer and went back to the desk.

Seems like I have plans after all.

Two
Enzo

THE SOFT FEEL OF PAPER AGAINST MY FINGERTIPS' PADS AS I turned the page was soothing to the soul like a scalpel slowly slicing through warm flesh. The words were beautiful poetry that sang to my soul every single line, a piece of the author that could never be taken back.

"What are you reading now, Enzo?" Giancarlo asked, effectively bursting the bubble around me.

He knew how to ruin a perfectly peaceful moment. I should be used to it working with my half-brothers for so long. Giancarlo's sense of personal space needed work.

I attempted to engross myself in the book once more to surround myself with the world of fiction, but no such luck. A shadow was cast over the pages obscuring the pure poetry I'd been reading. A heavy sigh slipped from my chest and out of my mouth.

"Let's se—" Giancarlo attempted to snatch my book away.

Don't touch my things. Agitation settled in the pit of my stomach and fizzled out just as quickly. Holding onto anything was nearly impossible for me.

The moment his fingers came within an inch of the book, I had a knife out and pressed firmly against his exposed wrist. He went still as our gazes locked. One wrong move, and he'd be decorating our oldest brother's office in red. And after the last incident, I doubted Giancarlo wanted to pay for another renovation.

"Is that necessary?" Giancarlo asked through gritted teeth.

Is breathing necessary? I blinked slowly at him before retracting my knife and placing it back in its hidden pocket.

"Why must you bother him, Gin?" Benito waltzed into the office, and I promptly closed the book.

"I was bored."

"Don't have me send you back to the hospital. It's nothing but a call away," Benito said as he took a seat.

The paper on his mahogany desk was neatly organized. The moment his hand touched it, I forced back the urge to put a bullet in his head. Benito moved things around, ruining the perfect organization that I'd created.

I looked away from the ruined perfection and met my brother's hard gaze head-on. He knew what I'd been thinking. I glanced away and stood up, moving closer to his desk now that he was there. The Blues music that filtered through Benito's speakers was turned down, and the mild thumping of the club under us could be heard through the walls.

"You can go home and have your peace once you check on a few things," Benito said.

"Fine." There was no use arguing. I'd ultimately do it.

"I get to go home, too, right?" Gin asked.

Benito didn't even look up from his paperwork as he answered. "No, you have been slacking off, and I'm not going to clean up your shit."

"Neither will I." I shook my head at my brother as he tossed his arms up.

He acted like a child on a good day. Still, Giancarlo was the second to Benito in our family.

"Enzo, there have been two busts lately of my warehouses. Find out who's leaking the information." Benito passed over two yellow folders, and I grabbed them.

He did everything the hard way, making it nearly impossible for the cops to keep track of our movements or even place anything on us. I opened it, and four cops' faces and addresses were on the papers. I scanned each one, committing them to memory.

"They were recently removed from the police force. Looks like they had a clean-out day. Take care of it," Benito said.

He never liked loose ends. Something close to excitement sent little sparks dancing over my fingertips. I'd get to touch a scalpel soon or, better yet, a saw this time. My shoulders dropped as I imagined what I'd do to my next project.

"Don't draw it out, Enzo. I want it clean." Benito's words cut through my momentary excitement like a serrated steak knife through the hand.

"Consider it done." There was beauty in a clean kill. Still, it was nothing like the chaos I indulged in when I was untethered by other orders.

"Gin, I need you in that meeting with ACTI developing."

"I get boring meetings?"

Benito glanced up. "Don't start, we both know your

talent is best used there." He passed over the card to the company. "Get it done. I want them no matter the costs."

A knock at the door stopped any more talk of plans as it opened. One of our men stepped in and brought over a tablet. He placed it down on the desk before retreating.

"The night is never ending," Benito said. He rubbed his chin as concentration came over his face. "How long has he been here?"

"He just stepped through the doors ten minutes ago."

"Who?" Gin asked. He walked around Benito's desk and peered over our oldest brother's shoulder. "Is he stupid or ignorant?"

"Has he made any moves?" Benito asked.

The guard shook his head. "No, sir. He's standing at the bar right now."

Benito put the tablet down, and the screen drew my full attention. His slender nose, pitch-black hair, strong jawline, and blue eyes drew me in further. His chest was impressive, from what I could tell through his clothes. What took the cake was the look in his eyes. I wanted to know more instantly.

"He's only been on the force two years, getting rid of him shouldn't be hard," Gin said.

My chest clenched, and I found my hand moving toward the tablet before the thought fully formed. I turned it around, absorbing all his information. Tex Caster. Twenty-five years of age, six-foot-two, one hundred and seventy-five pounds. Even his police academy test scores were there.

"Wouldn't be a good idea. He's a retired detective's kid." I turned it back around and showed Benito, sparing Tex's life for now. "His father is the one who took down the Revello family thirty years ago."

"Yeah, but we aren't the Revellos," Gin argued.

"Right, we don't make reckless mistakes," Benito cut in, looking between us. "However, I have run into his father once. Leave the cop for now. Enzo, since you pointed it out, you keep an eye on him." Benito passed the tablet back to the man who was waiting, and he slipped back out the door.

"Don't fuck it up, Enzo."

I nodded and slipped the files into my suit jacket. They pressed firmly against my ribcage, a constant reminder I had targets to take care of.

I braced myself for the inevitable. The moment I opened the door, I was prepared for the onslaught of music. The heavy base pounded in my ears and resonated through my body until it was a part of me. My teeth were set on edge for the first five seconds as I forced myself to endure it.

Each step increased the volume and the feeling of glass being shoved into my ears. The pain soon numbed me from the inside out. I stopped the moment I made it to the ledge, taking in a deep, controlled breath. The smell of sweaty bodies, mixed perfumes and colognes, and alcohol clogged my airways.

The dance floor was full of bodies pressed against each other, moving to the beat of the music. A group of women danced in a circle. Next to them was a couple thrashing against each other oblivious to the people around them. It was a normal night at one of our clubs, the music blaring over the speakers as people let all their inhibitions go and flung themselves headfirst into inebriation.

How simple it was for them to give up that control. One sip, and they were willing to hand their life over to chance. People never ceased to fascinate and disgust me.

Tingles ran up my spine as pinpricks danced along the side of my face. I'd know the weight of someone's stare any day. Turning, I caught those same startling blue eyes. Even far away I could feel the intensity, desire and ambition that swirled in them.

The corners of my lips turned up, and I smiled at him. His eyes widened. No doubt he thought I wouldn't even pay attention to him. I wanted to see those gorgeous eyes up close.

Benito had placed me in charge of watching him. I might as well get a better look. I slipped back from the banister and made my way downstairs.

Fixing the glasses on my face, I stepped down on the bottom floor. People moved out of my way even while drunk. I stopped at the bar, and one of the girls hustled over to me.

"Yes, sir?"

I never ordered a drink. To lose any semblance of control outside of my allowed moments was against everything my brother had taught me growing up. His words flashed through me. *You keep it locked up, and I promise I'll let you have your fun, but only when I say so. If you don't listen, you'll never get to do it again.*

I'd only been seven when my mother saw it fit to drop me off on my biological father's doorstep. Benito took me under his wing and never once went back on his word.

"That gentleman over there, what has he ordered?" I pointed to Tex. He was looking out to the dance floor as he sipped his drink, but I could still feel his eyes on me.

"A gin tonic," she said, giving me the information instantly.

"Send him another. Place it on my tab."

She nodded, her bright pink hair falling over her face as strands slipped out of the ponytail. My fingers twitched at my sides. Sweat dripped down the nape of my neck as the urge to fix her wrapped me up in a thick blanket. The air grew thicker with every breath.

Control. I needed to find something to break the cycle of chaos that wasn't mine. I pressed my thumb against my finger until the pop echoed through my hand. I did it five more times each finger cracked with the right amount of pressure. Each one brought me back down.

"I don't think I asked for a drink."

A smooth voice broke out over the pounding music. I'd been so wrapped in my head I'd missed Tex getting up. This was why I hated being at the club. Everything about it was out of order and a constant reminder of how displaced I was.

"Now you have one. Consider it an invitation to come back." I turned on my heels and headed for the door. I'd have one of my men watch over Tex for the time being. Leaving took priority.

A calloused, hot hand wrapped around my wrist. Heat traveled up from the point of contact and sent sparks along my flesh. The fine hairs on the nape of my neck stood to attention, kickstarting my flight or fight instinct.

I twisted around, rotating my hand and breaking the hold. I gathered both of Tex's wrists in my hands as I slammed him against the wall next to the door.

"Don't touch me."

Tex's eyes were far bluer than the picture had captured. Flecks of baby blue mixed with cobalt, making his eyes look more like a gorgeous piece of glass.

"But you can touch me?" He arched a brow, not pushing back on my hold, although I saw it in his face. He wanted to shove me away. The muscle in his jaw ticked along with the twitch in his hands.

I moved close, and my beard brushed along his smooth

face. "I can do as I please. If that's a problem, then I suggest you stay far away from me."

He attempted to break my hold, and I pulled back just enough to twist him around and slam him against the wall. Tex was not only bigger than me in muscle, but he was also taller than me by a few inches.

I enjoyed taking people by surprise when they underestimated me. They saw the glasses, groomed facial hair, and the nerdish look that made hunting more fun. Someone like Tex was my ideal prey.

"Be good," I whispered just loud enough for him to hear over the music. I applied pressure between his shoulder blades, and he winced. Tex went still, and his right hand started to tremble.

Oh. I moved my hand over and pressed hard. *I wonder how much he can take.*

Sweat beaded on the back of his neck as he tried again to pull away. I shook my head. I couldn't get carried away, especially not here. I reluctantly pulled my hand away and watched as his hand dropped. He reached for the arm that was clearly in pain.

The door was opened for me, and I walked out of the bar. The moment the October air hit me and a chill settled over my agitated flesh, I calmed down a bit more. My ears still thumped with the music annoying me to no end. I'd have to find a more pleasing sound to drown it out.

One of the men pulled my car up to the curb and handed me the keys.

"It's not a problem," Tex said, stopping me in my tracks.

I glanced at the rookie cop as he answered what I'd previously said. *I can do as I please. If that's a problem then I suggest you stay far away from me.* His pupils were dilated, and the way he licked his lips gave me all the answers I needed.

"Get in." I slipped behind the wheel, and only a second passed as Tex looked back at the club and ran over to my passenger side.

He opened it up and hopped in. His foot instantly bounced once he was in a confined space with me. Tex's large hands rested over his crotch. The moment he realized where I was looking, he stopped hiding the evidence of his arousal.

"Don't get scared now."

Tex whipped his head toward me. "I'm not. Don't be a disappointment."

Something close to laughter tried to break free, but I swallowed it down. *This one is going to be fun.*

I started the car, and Tex put his seatbelt on. I watched his every move waiting for him to grab his badge or point out the fact he was a cop. I pushed my glasses up on my nose before dragging my gaze up to meet his eyes.

"Don't ask."

I cocked a single brow at him.

"I'm a grown man. Yes, I know what I'm doing. This face of mine may look soft, but I can handle more than you think."

Did he think I'd let him slip away? He'd already walked into the cage with free will. There was no leaving, not till I set him free.

"Bold words. Hope you aren't all talk."

"Same." Tex grinned at me, showing off his pearly whites.

Cute. It was like looking at a kitten. Teeth and claws, but in the end, nothing more than prey.

Three
TEX

I'M IN OVER MY FUCKING HEAD.

The entire drive I felt agitation flowing through me. Every flicker of his gaze that came my way, every little smirk he pulled, felt like he was holding some inside joke that I was on the outside of. The sleek leather seats of his car were cool, and I thanked everything that they were so I wouldn't melt into a goddamn puddle.

Beside me was a monster. His face was well-known to most of the police force but for me, it was especially prominent. I remembered my father looking at these case files in the basement, pouring over them as he tried to find some way to unravel the Vitales. I would know that dark hair and those chocolate brown eyes anywhere. Although, he'd gotten older since those pictures, more mature and refined.

Shit. Will you shut up? I glared at my rebellious cock as it stood at attention. The rush, the danger, and not to mention the hot as fuck man beside me was enough to get my blood pumping. I hadn't gotten laid in so long that I was almost afraid I would bust a nut in his fancy car.

My arm throbbed, but I ignored it. The drink at the bar had made more blood rush to it. At first, it hurt more, but now it was becoming a fading, background kind of pain. Hopefully, if I needed to, I would be able to kick his ass if he tried to kill me. But why would he? As far as he knew, I was just some guy he'd hit on in his bar. Enzo had no idea I was going to be the one who lit the match and incinerated his worthless family.

The car stopped, and I glanced up at a tall building. "A hotel?"

Enzo looked me over as if he was dissecting me. "Yes. Is that a problem?"

Yeah, it's a big problem. I'd been hoping to get back to his place, see what I could find, or at least know the location so I could return when he was out. A hotel was a problem. It showed me nothing about who he was or what he'd been doing.

Maybe I can still use this. Get close to him. He doesn't have to know who I am.

I grinned at him. "Nope, not a problem at all," I said as I grabbed the handle and let myself out.

Looked like I was going to have to play the long game. He rounded the car and dropped the keys into the valet's palm. The young man jogged off, but not before Enzo passed him what looked like a huge tip.

"Are you coming?" Enzo asked.

I stared at the building and then at his retreating back. He wasn't waiting for me, as if he was much too busy and important and didn't give a damn if I went with him or not.

It felt like a leash had been looped around my throat, and I followed him, my feet moving on their own.

What was it about him that intrigued me?

"Good evening, sir," the woman behind the counter smiled at him. "Your laundry has been delivered to your door, and your dinner will arrive in an hour. Is there anything else I can do for you?"

Enzo shook his head. "That'll be all. Goodnight."

"Goodnight, sir."

I whistled as we waited at the elevator. "Are you some kind of big shot or something?"

"Or something," he answered shortly.

I examined the side of his face, but he gave nothing away. He didn't so much as glance at me, but I felt like he was watching my every move. Reaching up, he adjusted the black-framed glasses that were perched on the bridge of his nose.

How the hell is this man in the mob?

Most gangsters had an air to them; tattoos, greasy hair, thick accents, and too much damn bravado. He had the last trait, but the rest? Enzo looked neat and clean, like a professor who worked at a top-notch college. Even the long, blue jacket he wore seemed tame and unassuming. But I knew the truth behind that innocent facade. His family was responsible for countless atrocities, ones that we couldn't prove. No one in the Vitale family was innocent.

Enzo gazed my way finally and held it. He didn't say a word, his eyes running over me before he stared at me intently. There was a slight tilt to his head as if he was asking and answering questions that never left his thin, pink lips. There was something else, some burning inferno in the depths of those brown eyes that made me want to squirm. My lungs burned, and I realized I was holding my breath.

The elevator dinged, breaking the spell that had been cast over us. Enzo waved a hand, all gentlemanly as he gestured for me to step into it. Just like that, the flickers of danger I'd seen in his eyes were gone.

"After you," he said.

I stepped onto the elevator and refused to look over my shoulder. The way Enzo stared daggers into my back, I felt as if that's what he wanted; to see some kind of fear on my face. However, I wasn't going to give that shit to him. I turned around, and he stepped beside me. He pressed the P button, lifted a black box, and typed in his password quickly before he let the box shut and the elevator began to ascend.

5135. I need to remember that.

Enzo turned to me, and I raised a brow. "What? Is there something on my f—"

His hand crashed against my mouth, covering it while the other shoved into my pants. My eyes widened as he stroked my hard, aching cock through my boxers. The soft fabric rubbing against my erection was almost too much to take. My body responded instantly, my hips jutting forward as he stroked me while gazing into my eyes.

"Cum for me," he demanded. "Before this elevator reaches the penthouse, I want your boxers flooded."

My heart leaped into my throat. *What the hell?*

He grinned, the unassuming facade breaking just for a moment as I saw the devil in his eyes. "If I'm going to fuck you, I'm not interested in you shooting your load and getting tired before we even get going. You'll cum before we start, or you'll leave."

My back slammed against the wall. In the mirrors of the elevator, I groaned at the image of him stroking me inside of my jeans like it was nothing. Enzo slipped his hand free and opened them up, coaxing my cock out before he stroked me harder and faster. *What am I doing here?* My thoughts were forced back to reality quickly as Enzo's fingers toyed with me.

"Mmm, fuck," I moaned against the heat of his palm. "You're insane."

"No talking," he demanded. "Cum or get the hell out of my sight."

My eyes drifted to the numbers on the elevator as it rose. We were fast approaching floor thirty. When my eyes met Enzo's again, he tilted his head.

"There are only forty-seven in the building," he answered without me even having to ask. "You're running out of time."

Shit. The fact that he was imposing a time limit only made it that much worse. My cock throbbed in his expert grasp as my heart pounded so hard it was all I could hear. The ache in my balls overtook the ache in my arm as Enzo held my gaze and stroked me right to the edge.

"—uck!"

My breathing stopped as my eyes rolled back, and I slumped against the wall. The feeling in my legs disappeared, and I knew I was going to hit the ground, but I forced myself to stay upright. Had it really been that long since someone had touched me? Pleasure traveled up and down my spine, and I knew the answer to that was hell yes, it really had been forever.

I peeled my eyes open as Enzo pulled his hand away and examined the sticky mess I'd made on his palm. There were splotches of my cum on his pristine coat as well. His brows furrowed, an irritated expression coming over his face as he released my mouth and looked at his clothes disdainfully.

"All over me," he muttered.

I groaned. "It's not like it's my fault," I countered. "You were the one jerking me off, remember?"

"Yes," he said shortly, an exasperated sigh following. "I suppose I got carried away." He looked at my still semi-hard cock. "Really? How old *are* you? Nineteen?"

"Twenty-five," I mumbled, shoving my cock back into my jeans as the back of my neck and cheeks erupted into flames. "It's been a while," I snapped when he continued to stare. "Oh fuck off," I added when he raised a brow at me as if I was lying.

Enzo's grin returned, and it was as if he was back in a good mood. He shoved his hand out toward me. "Clean this up."

I blinked at him. "No way. I'm not tasting my own cum."

Enzo's right hand twisted into my hair, and he shoved his other hand over my lips. I stared at him, my mouth falling open in disbelief. He took that chance to smear cum into my mouth. I recoiled at the salty taste, the fact that he was so damn hot made it go down a hell of a lot smoother.

If he wasn't in the mob, I would be back fucking him every night.

The danger alone was enough. But the way he took control and made me question every single thing I knew to be true was fun as hell. It felt wrong and intoxicating all at once.

He pulled his hand away as the elevator dinged, and we were let out into a small hallway with a door. Enzo collected his dry cleaning and let himself inside as I trailed him.

"Would you like a drink?" he asked.

"Sure," I said. I had no intention of drinking more than a sip, but I could use it after the whole elevator thing.

I followed behind him and glanced around. There wasn't a thing out of place. Every picture was generic hotel art. All of the furniture was high-end, but neutral tones of sandy brown and white, all of it accented with chrome appliances and gray pops of color. It said nothing about him.

Shit. Is this a waste of time?

Enzo shrugged off his jacket, draping it over the back of a chair as he walked to the bar. He took out two glasses and filled them with clear liquid from an expensive-looking crystal decanter. Enzo passed one over to me after dropping an ice cube into mine, the same way I'd had it at his club.

"Thanks," I said.

He nodded, silent again as he stared at me over the top of his drink. Like he hadn't just jerked me off in the elevator and was now casually staring at me. I sipped, enjoying the burn of gin as it coursed down my throat. Honestly, I hated the shit, but I liked the way it burned, and my father never could handle it. But I could. Just like I was going to handle Enzo Vitale.

"Take your clothes off," Enzo said.

I blinked at him. "Just like that?" I asked. "You don't want to talk?"

"What would you like to talk about?" he countered as he rounded the bar and walked into the living room. Enzo sat down, removed his shoes carefully, and placed them out of the way on the side of the couch. "I thought you wanted to be told what to do. That's why you followed me, isn't it?"

My throat tightened, and suddenly, I couldn't swallow. Enzo's grin widened. Every instinct in me screamed to turn and run the hell out of there before he could get his hands on me. Still, I stayed where I was.

One, I wasn't going to flee when I needed to do this to get closer to him and figure him out. I still had to scope out his place and see if there was anything here. If not, then it looked like I would be fucking him more than once until I was given access to his real place. Two, I was mesmerized. Everything about Enzo screamed danger in big, pulsing red lights. I wanted to see more.

Focus on the mission. Get dirt on him, take the Vitale's down, make detective.

"Hey." Enzo snapped his fingers just once, and I awoke from my stupor to stare at him. "Clothes. Off. I told you once that I would do what I please with you. Strip."

My cock jumped, and I reached up to unbutton my shirt. Enzo sipped his drink, his eyes following every move I made. *Am I really doing this?* I paused for a second, only for Enzo to give me an impatient look. I continued.

This was no different than going undercover. I had to keep my composure. I was going to prove to everyone at the precinct that I was not my father.

I was better.

Four
Enzo

Fabric fluttered to the floor, and I glared at Tex as he dropped his clothes carelessly. His fingers hovered over the button of his jeans.

"What?"

I looked from him to the mess he was creating. Tex rolled his eyes.

"Really?" He yanked them up and looked around before tossing them onto the single couch.

"No."

"What do you want me to do? Hang them up?" Tex sounded exasperated.

"The closet is through those doors on the left."

"You can't be serious."

"Hurry up," was all I said.

Tex stared at me for another second before he yanked

his stuff up and made his way to the bedroom. I let him go alone, knowing there was nothing there.

I sipped the gin in my cup, listening out for Tex. He was taking longer than necessary, but he was no doubt looking for something.

"I don't like to be kept waiting."

Tex emerged from the room half-hard and fully naked. I'd been right. His body was magnificent. His chest was huge and looked good enough to bite. Varying tattoos littered his torso, none of them standing out to me. However, I committed every single one of them to memory.

His dusky-colored nipples were pierced with black bars. I'd been hoping they were and was glad to see that was the case. All he needed now was matching bars through his cock and lining his taint.

"You're still dressed," Tex pointed out.

"Good observation skills. You should be a detective," I said.

Tex flinched but quickly covered it up as he moved closer to me. *So adorable.*

"Turn around," I said.

Tex rolled his eyes, but his cock jumped at my command. He turned around, and I took in every detail, mapping it all to memory.

What the fuck is that?

A poorly drawn duck with a cowboy hat on holding a gun was tattooed on his right ass cheek.

"You like it?" Tex asked with a smirk.

"Hardly."

He laughed. "I can tell by your face." Tex shrugged. "I was fifteen, and my friend was an aspiring tattoo artist. You know how it is. Reckless teens."

"Not at all." I snapped my fingers and pointed to the floor in front of me. "Hands and knees."

Tex's mouth fell open, and I waited him out. He shook his head, seemingly making up his mind as he sauntered over. Tex lowered himself in front of me, his gaze unwavering as he got on his hands and knees.

"Turn around."

I was once again faced with that horrid tattoo, but the rest of Tex made up for it. The knife hidden under my pant leg was sharp enough to skin the blemish off in one swipe. It would be nothing more than a small nick.

I rolled my shoulders back as I forced the thought to the furthest part of my mind, focusing on Tex for now. I coated my fingers in lube, pressed one against his hole and worked it in. "Stay still," I warned as Tex tried to take more of my finger into his hot body.

A visible shudder wrecked Tex's body. "You're gentler than I thought."

"I don't like breaking my toys too fast."

"Wha—" Tex's words were cut off as I added another finger stretching him. I spread them, opening his hole and pulling a deep groan from him.

He squirmed, his hole clenching down on my fingers as he tried his hardest not to thrust his hips back. My fingers danced over his prostate, steadily applying pressure in a pattern until the muscles in his back tensed. I changed it up before he could cum.

Sweat rolled down his spine, making his naturally pale flesh glisten under the lights. I eased my fingers back. His hole clenched around them, begging for me to stay, but nothing came out of Tex's mouth.

Can't have that. I wanted to hear him beg, to break under me.

I teased his prostate again and lightly stroked his cock, not enough to truly stimulate him. A growl emitted from Tex as his shoulder blades bunched. He seemed quite irritated with me.

Toying with his body, I worked Tex up once more. His cock was hard between his thighs, begging for more than the light caresses.

"Fuck," Tex growled. He turned his head, and his blue eyes were glazed over like a car window in the rain. "Please let me cum."

I thought about it for five seconds. "Tell me the passcode to get to this floor." I stroked his cock with a faint touch, only stimulating him for a few short seconds. Nothing that could get him off.

Tex shook his head. "I don't know."

"Then I guess you don't need to cum."

"Fuck—"

My fingertips stroked along his prostate again, applying the perfect amount of pressure as I stretched him to accept another finger. He was up three, going on four.

I eased my fingers out again and rested them against his fluttering hole. "Ready to answer?"

Tex panted, the muscles in his legs flexed every time his toes curled. He looked ready to give in.

"No, give me another question." He glanced back at me, his lips wet, and drool slid down his chin.

He was a mess, but it was one I'd created. There was nothing more beautiful, except maybe if there was a splash of red decorating his smooth flesh.

I grabbed a fistful of black hair and yanked. Tex's head tilted back, forcing him to lift his hands off the floor. "I asked a question, and I expect an answer."

"Shit if I know!" Tex kept his gaze steady, but his fingers twitched, and his body fidgeted. He was a decent liar.

My eyebrows lowered, and I allowed Tex to see the displeasure on my face. Fear flickered in his blue eyes as he tried to shrink back. I doubted he even knew the response he was giving, so high on pleasure.

I tightened my hold on his hair, and he sucked in a breath through his teeth as his eyes watered. The silence built as I stayed still, imagining all the ways I wanted to punish him.

Tex licked his lips, opening and closing his mouth like a fish out of water. I released him, and he fell forward, sucking in a breath as if he'd been holding it the entire time. I removed my glasses, folded them and placed them to the side.

"Lying is one way to make me upset." I let the full weight of my stare rest on Tex just like I would do any target my brother sent me after. A familiar prick of ice crept through my veins, making goosebumps rise over my forearms. My lips turned up in a smile.

"What are you going to do?" Tex asked. His voice shook slightly.

"I've answered that already." I moved around to face him and lowered myself to a squat. "Whatever I want." I slipped my knife out of its holder and pressed it against his cock.

The tension in the room thickened. Where others would have a hard time relaxing, I felt at home. The trickle of ice that always took hold of me when I held a weapon consumed me.

A drop of precum kissed the blade, and more was to follow as Tex stayed still. His cock jumped as I moved the knife lower.

"You've lost your fucking mind." He reached for me.

"Hands down."

Tex flexed his fingers before dropping his hands at his sides. His breathing was erratic. His chest was coated with a light sheen of sweat as his gaze stayed glued to the knife I had pressed against his cock.

I cupped his balls, and Tex's eyes widened as an unfiltered moan dripped heavily from his parted lips. His cock was an angry red, begging for a release I hadn't granted.

A whimper broke free the moment I let his balls go, and it made me smirk. He was a greedy thing. Even now, with a knife so close to him, his body was begging for more.

I moved the knife down further until it rested at the base of his cock.

"It would be a shame to cut this off." I stroked Tex's cock firmly for the first time since the elevator.

An undignified whimper bounced off the walls from Tex.

"You wouldn't," Tex said.

He met my eyes finally, and I let him see just how serious I was. A toy without a cock wasn't exactly ideal, but I'd still be able to use him.

Tex's Adam's apple bobbed. To make sure he knew how serious I was, I dragged the sharp blade over his flesh using hardly any pressure. Blood bubbled up to greet the knife mixing with the precum already dirting it.

"Fuck," a strangled moan left Tex.

"Don't move," I commanded.

Tex bit his lip but went still. I saw it the moment he gave in, unable to hold out. "Five... One... Three, five."

Disappointment and pride warred inside of me. I hadn't been sure for a second. He'd paid close enough attention, but my little rookie cop was proving he was a lot smarter than his test results showed.

The small drop of blood was nothing more than a tease and my instincts screamed for me to keep going. To spill more of the beautiful crimson liquid.

I pulled the blade away, and Tex sagged instantly, resting his ass against his calves. His pupils were blown as he took in shaky breaths.

"You deserve a reward, don't you agree?" I got up and opened the closet closest to the door. Tex's gaze followed me around the room as I grabbed everything I needed.

By the time I made it back over to him, he'd calmed down again, no longer on the edge of cumming. His eyes were a bit clearer as he stared at me.

"Lift up and turn around."

Tex gave me no trouble, no doubt anticipating his reward. He turned around and sat up on his knees. I admired the shape of his firm ass and contemplated for the second time tonight carving the hideous tattoo off his ass cheek.

I opened the box, and the sound of cardboard tearing echoed around us. Tex's head began to turn, and I fixed it, forcing his head back the other way.

"Peek, and we will be done."

Tex sat up straighter, his back stiff with how hard he was holding himself up. It would be laughable, but I was sure if I did, he'd turn, and the fun would end before I was ready.

I didn't bother adding lube to the wireless prostate massager. The little black device was no bigger than a finger and a half.

"Spread yourself."

Tex's fingers were trembling as they grabbed each cheek and spread. His hole still glistened with lube, begging to be fucked. Soon. My cock pressed firmly against my pants, but I prided myself on my control. And with Tex, it had been tested repeatedly.

I rested the tip of the massager against his hole, teasing the puckered flesh, drawing a moan from Tex. I leaned over his shoulder to watch the side of his face as I shoved the massager in. His mouth opened, but no words came out as I acted quickly.

My arm wrapped around his neck and my legs around his waist as we fell back against the floor. I pinned Tex's hands behind his back between our bodies. Even through my clothes, I could feel the heat radiating off his flesh.

I wove my other arm behind his head, still clutching the remote. Tex instantly struggled, trying to escape my hold, but it wasn't breaking as he lifted me an inch from the floor and slammed us back against it. A laugh rushed out of me as the pain added to the shockwaves of pleasure crashing through me.

"You're still hard, although I could kill you right now." My leg brushed against Tex's weeping cock.

I pressed the button on the remote, turning the vibrator to the highest setting. A choked-off groan came from Tex, and he started fidgeting around in my hold for a different reason. I applied more pressure, counting the seconds I could hold him.

The air around us got thinner until I was left panting. Six, seven, eight... Tex's body jerked, and the hot splashes of cum soaked into my pants. I released him a second later.

Another second passed, and Tex sucked in a gasping breath. I rolled him off me and sat up. My hair fell from the careful style I'd put it in. My heart was beating erratically as I stared down at Tex. He slowly blinked at me, and I smiled. He didn't move as I snatched the prostate massager out of his hole.

I unbuttoned my pants and pulled the zipper down. All sound was drowned out by my heartbeat. I couldn't wait to sink into him. To ruin him even further.

"I'm not done with you yet." I rolled Tex over onto his side, his cloudy blue eye focused on me even now as he tried to take in deep breaths.

He was watching me. I'd always liked observing but being observed had never felt so good.

A smile broke out over my face as I relished in the new sensation coursing through my veins. I slipped the condom over my cock and hooked one of Tex's legs in my arm before I sank into him.

Tight wet heat strangled my cock as I plunged inside of him all at once. A strangled moan came from Tex, and I wanted to hear it again. It was too close to a cry.

The moment I thought about him crying, my cock jumped inside Tex. *Tears spilling down his face. I bet they'd taste like heaven.* I pulled back until only the tip of my cock rested against his hole. I snapped my hips forward. The clash of our flesh together resonated around me and was accompanied by the wet suction of Tex's lubed hole sucking me in. It was nearly as pleasing to listen to as the sound of internal organs slipping free of a body and splattering to the floor.

A shiver trickled down my spine alongside the sweat. It made my shirt cling to my skin, but even that irritation wasn't enough to make me stop.

My hand wrapped around his cock, and Tex whimpered. "Cum for me again."

He shook his head slowly, his eyelashes fluttering as I fucked him relentlessly. I tightened my hold on his cock, stroking him in time with my thrusts.

Electricity danced up my spine, and with every thrust, I

grew closer to climax. My breathing was erratic as I stared down at Tex. His cock grew hard, and he whimpered as a single tear slipped from the corner of his eyes.

My orgasm hit me like a sledgehammer, and I fought to stay upright as I filled the condom with my cum. My irritation at not filling and marking Tex was a small flame in the back of my mind as spots danced before me.

Tex's back arched, and his hole clenched around me, drawing out my orgasm as he came again. Only a few drops slipped free from his cock, and I was half tempted to keep stroking him. To see more of those tears. *One isn't enough.*

I stood up on shaky legs and stared down at Tex sprawled out on the floor. Cum decorated his torso and chest. His eyes were closed, and his breathing was heavy.

"You made another mess." I clicked my tongue and let out a sigh as I accepted the mess before me. "I'll have to punish you for it later."

Tex murmured in his sleep, and I took that for consent. I couldn't take my eyes off him. "You really should be careful of the monsters you seek out."

I forced myself to walk away and get cleaned up. A thorough shower and a fresh change of clothes later, I was set. I made quick work of straightening everything back up, even moving Tex to the bed and cleaning his body. I checked over the files in my coat and glanced at the time.

Benito said to keep tabs on the cop, and I would but in my own way. I put my number in Tex's phone, knowing he'd call. I checked over the penthouse, making sure nothing was left behind. I rarely kept anything there besides a change of clothes.

I left water on the nightstand and made my way downstairs. Each number that lit up on the elevator felt like a reminder of what I was leaving behind. A body I'd lost myself in.

Don't worry. It will happen again. I reminded myself of that, closing my eyes momentarily. The ding of the elevator had me shoving everything away and sinking back into the numbness I surrounded myself with for day-to-day life.

"Mr. Vitale," the front desk woman greeted.

"I'm checking out."

She nodded. "Shall we leave it vacant?"

"Yes."

Her slender fingers flew over the keyboard before she lifted her head. "All taken care of, sir."

I didn't step away, and she patiently waited for me to say what else I needed. "Breakfast and wake up call at five thirty."

She didn't question me as she typed in the note. "Consider it done, sir."

Stepping out of the hotel, the crisp night air chilled me further. I fought the urge to glance back at the hotel. There was no way he would be up yet. If he was I wouldn't mind playing with him a little longer. Although if I didn't get started on cleaning up the crooked cops dropped from our payroll, Benito would put a bullet through my skull.

As much as death was beautiful and alluring to me, I didn't have a death wish.

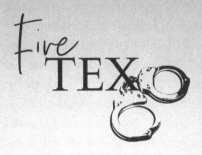

Five

TEX

RINGING. CONSTANT, ANNOYING, RINGING. IT INFILTRATED THE dream I was having and I groaned as I reached out, slapping at the nightstand and searching for my phone. Instinctively, I picked up the receiver and pressed it to my ear.

"What?" I mumbled.

"Good morning. This is your five-thirty wake-up call. Breakfast will be up in twenty minutes. Can I get you anything else?"

I peeled open an eye. *What the fuck is going on?* Shifting in the bed, my legs brushed against sheets that weren't my off-brand, bargain bin kind. Everything hurt. I pushed my fingers through my hair and rubbed at my eyes, trying to make my brain function.

"Sir?"

"Huh? No," I muttered. As I glanced around, the night raced back to me. "Shit!"

I hung up as the woman asked if I was okay. All I could think about was the fact that I was in a strange hotel room. And the most horrifying truth of all.

I'd fucked the enemy last night.

Reaching back, I touched my ass and hissed. It felt like I could still feel him inside of me, stretching my hole and fucking me into a haze of stupidity. The scent of his cologne lingered, and I felt his knife pressed against my cock, dragging over my flesh as he stared at me with those deep brown eyes. There was a throbbing around my neck where he'd choked me until I was sure I was going to die.

Shivering, I forced myself out of his bed. I realized I was still holding onto a pillow and I tossed it away, flinging the scent of his cologne up into the air. My cock twitched involuntarily, and I bit back a groan. Last night hadn't gone the way I planned at all. Somehow, Enzo had gotten into my brain and turned me into an empty-headed bitch.

That thought made my balls ache.

"Fuck!" I snapped.

I looked around for my clothes and remembered they were hanging up in the front closet. I stormed to it, snatched them down, and left a pile of hangers on the floor before making my way to the bathroom.

"I am so stupid," I muttered.

I flipped on the light and stared at my reflection. How the hell had he gotten into my head like that? How did he know I remembered the code in the elevator? There were a million questions I had about Enzo, but I couldn't think beyond the constant, aching throb of my asshole.

Before I could do anything else, I needed his scent off of me. It lingered, infiltrating my nose and making me want to scratch him off of my skin. The shower heated after I flipped the switch. I sought out the little complimentary bottles of hotel soap and shampoo once I stepped inside.

I didn't even get any info. I planted my hands against the cool tile of the wall and thought about what to do next. The risk had been worth it, but the reward was not. But now that I had Enzo Vitale in my sights, I couldn't even imagine letting it go and walking away from him.

He was mine.

My hands ran over my body, and I pushed memories of him out of my head. As my fingers slid against my hole, I could feel him pressed up against me, the heat of his breath fanning against my ear as he rutted inside of me with the same sure, precise manner that he held himself. Part of me wanted to unravel it, to watch him lose his cool and laugh at the result.

I stepped out of the shower before I allowed myself to go too far down the rabbit hole. Once I was out of the steam-logged stall, my mind calmed, and I focused on the task at hand. Tossing on my clothes, I walked out and started looking. I searched every inch of the place, but just like I'd suspected, there was nothing. No photos, no notes, no technology to snoop through. Enzo Vitale was thorough.

"Shit," I muttered.

The sound of knocking made me go for my gun, but I remembered I'd left it locked in the glove compartment of my car. No way would they have allowed me into Blu with it. I cautiously made my way to the door, the hair on the back of my neck standing on end.

"Room service!"

My shoulders dropped a bit. I looked out into the hallway and found a man there with a rolling cart. Sighing, I gripped the doorknob. *Will you calm down? Everything's fine!*

I told myself that, but I was still on high alert. Slowly, I opened the door, and the man smiled at me.

"Your breakfast, sir," he said. "Would you like it inside?"

"Sure," I muttered, completely lost for words. "I didn't order this, though."

"Mr. Vitale arranged it and has already taken care of everything," he said as he poured a cup of coffee. "Is there anything else I can do for you?"

I blinked at him. "Enzo did this?"

He nodded.

"Okay," I said slowly, picking up the white mug and frowning. "And where is he now?"

"Gone," he said shortly.

I raised a brow. "Gone where? Does he come here all the time? Is this his place? Or is it just somewhere he stays the night from time to time?"

The smile stayed plastered onto the man's face, but his eyes changed. For a brief moment, his gaze flickered around the room as if he was waiting for someone to jump out. When he looked at me again, I stared him down, waiting for an answer.

He shifted from one foot to the other. "I'm sure Mr. Vitale can answer any questions you have for him."

Right. I wasn't going to get a damn thing out of this guy. Nodding, I stared at him until he exited the suite as quickly as humanly possible. Shaking my head, I doctored up my coffee and looked at the feast that had been left for me. I didn't want to eat the shit Enzo had ordered, but my stomach cramped and growled, making it apparent that it didn't give a damn what I wanted.

I plucked up a piece of toast and went in search of my phone. It was right where I'd started, sitting on the bedside table like I'd put it there, but I was damn sure I hadn't. *Did Enzo do that?*

I snatched my phone up and looked at the time. "Shit. Gotta get to work."

Rourke was going to kill me if I was late. I ignored the slight pounding in my head, jogged to the breakfast cart, and secured myself a plate. Climbing into the elevator, I requested an Uber while I shoveled eggs and bacon into my mouth like a starving person. When the doors opened, a woman stood in front of them and pulled a face at me. I wiped my breakfast off my face, smiled with stuffed cheeks, and mumbled an apology as I shuffled past her.

I dumped my plate on the check-in counter. "Sorry, I don't know where that's supposed to go. If Enzo Vitale comes back, can you give him a message?"

The woman blinked at me. "Um, yes, sir."

"Actually, I should write it down."

She slid me a sticky notepad, and I scribbled out a quick message. When I passed it back over, she ripped it off and stuffed it into an envelope. I had to admit; I was impressed she didn't read it. I would have.

"Will that be all, sir?"

"Yep. Thanks," I said.

The entire ride back to my car I couldn't stop thinking about Enzo. He was a weird, neat freak, asshole, but damn, I couldn't get him out of my brain. My cock begged for another round. He was a dangerous, wild thing that had no social norms to adhere to. Yet, I couldn't think about anything else but his hand on my hip and his voice growling in my ear.

"Oh, get the fuck out of my head already!"

"Excuse me?" The driver looked up into the rearview mirror, his eyes narrowed.

"Sorry, talking to myself."

The man frowned. "If you're on drugs right now, I'm putting you out of my car. I'm not dealing with that shit again," he muttered.

I groaned inwardly and apologized profusely until he stopped glaring. Great, I was starting to make people think I was crazy. Maybe I was losing my mind because how else had I ended up in this situation? From tracking Enzo Vitale to taking his cock, when had I decided that was a good decision?

Get him out of your head. That was the first and last time that's going to happen.

I shoved all thoughts of Enzo Vitale far, far away from me as I jogged to my car. Time was ticking by, and I needed to focus. I parked haphazardly, rushing into my apartment after I glanced at the time on my phone. I pulled on my uniform, scratched my cat Penelope behind his perfect ears, fed him, and ran out of my place like my ass was on fire.

Twenty minutes later, I was in the precinct. I clocked in and climbed into the passenger seat of my squad car, panting. Rourke glanced over, his dark brow raised as he looked me up and down. I shut my door and stared right back at him.

"What?" I asked.

"You're late."

I groaned. "Don't start. I had a late night."

Rourke grunted. "I can see that. There's a mark." He pointed to his neck with his pen. "Right there."

I stared at him, horrified, for all of one second before I snatched up my phone and stared at my reflection in the camera. He was right. It wasn't a hickey or anything like that, but a red line that stood out against my skin. It was right where Enzo's arm had wound around my throat, those suffocating, terrifying moments when I thought he was going to kill me, only for him to release and fuck the life out of me. My cock twitched again.

Down, boy.

"Where *did* you go last night?" Rourke asked, making me shut off my phone and glance at him. "I know you came back here after I told you to take your ass home."

"There was no reason for me to go— Ah! You son of a bitch," I ground out through clenched teeth as Rourke's fist slammed into my shoulder.

"Yeah, that's what I thought," he said. "Idiot."

"Oh, fuck you," I shot back. "I can still do my job."

"Until someone grabs your damn arm the wrong way, and you piss yourself in pain and end up with a bullet in your head."

Rourke was a good friend and a great partner, but sometimes I wanted to slap him. He was so uptight and rigid when he wanted to be.

"I'm fine," I stressed. "Yes, it hurts, but I can work through the pain if I really need to. Okay?"

Rourke grunted and started up the car. That was as good as I was going to get, and I knew it. I pulled out my phone and checked over my messages before I pulled up a notepad and started typing. Enzo Vitale. Neat. Strong. Notices things. Crazy as fuck. It was a good list, but a short one. I needed more to go on. I had to meet up with Enzo again.

I thought back to the note I'd left him. It was short, precise, and to the point. Just two words.

Fuck You.

Six

Enzo

THE SOUNDS OF THE CITY WERE MUTED OUT IN THE SUBURBS. One could almost believe they were in a whole different universe. There were no blaring horns, the fog of pollution, or blinding neon lights. In another life, maybe I'd live in such a calm place. But that hadn't been my fate. The constant noise and smells were home, one I'd grown accustomed to.

I pushed open the back gate, the wood freshly painted black and the bushes surrounding newly trimmed. Someone had a lot of time on their hands.

Toys littered the yard, a pogo stick, a firetruck near the swing set, and a shovel in a sandbox that had sand spilled around it. My eyes twitched as all of my focus was drawn to the uneven sand. It wasn't important, and yet I walked over to the small box.

I needed something else to focus on, something familiar

that wasn't out of place and that didn't drive my need to fix it or tear everything apart. I reached into my coat, and my fingertips brushed along the cool metal of my staccato 9mm. It was familiar and perfection.

My hand wrapped around the gun and pulled it free. The moonlight glinted off the top of it, even the sky was mesmerized by its beauty. I took in measured breaths, remembering step by step how I'd taken it apart and cleaned it. My fingers twitched along the gun as if they were moving with my memory.

I felt more in control by the second and turned away from the distraction and to the house. The back porch light turned on as the door opened.

"Just taking the trash out."

The man I was there to see stepped out of his house. As if he sensed a predator in his presence, he went still, his gaze sweeping over the yard until his eyes fell on me. There wasn't a need for me to introduce myself. Recognition surfaced in his brown eyes the moment ours met.

"Don't do this here," Johnny McDowell pleaded.

I was a monster, but I wasn't a sloppy one.

"Don't worry. I don't plan on splattering your blood on your freshly cut lawn. Tell them you have to go."

Johnny made his way to the trash and dropped his bag in. I still held my gun out, but he made no move to run. He knew better. His family would be used as collateral, and Johnny wasn't a man to place his family in harm's way.

He walked back to the door, his shoulders set back and standing up tall at his full six-four height. If he wanted, he could fight me and run. However, we both knew how that would end. I'd been known to take men down twice my size.

Johnny opened the door, keeping his body outside as he shouted inside. "I'm headed out, babe."

"At this time of night, Johnny?" Her high-pitched voice scraped against my eardrums.

I put my gun away, no longer needing an anchor so I could deal with mild annoyances.

"Don't start, Linda."

Johnny stepped back and glanced over his shoulder. Our eyes met briefly before he let the screen door close and headed for the back gate. Footsteps came from inside the suburban home before the back door was slammed open.

"When will you be back?" Linda shouted. Her bright green eyes landed on me, and understanding clicked. Her pink-painted lips pressed together in a fine line. "The boys—"

"Linda, get back in the house," Johnny snapped.

She looked ready to argue, her pleading eyes never straying from me. "Boys need their father."

If she thought she was pulling at my heartstrings, she'd be sorely mistaken. I wasn't sure I even had one.

"Linda, go back in, please."

She stared at me for a bit longer before she turned to her husband. Heartfelt goodbyes were another thing I didn't understand about humans. She knew this day was coming. Even if it wasn't me bringing death to her door, it would be something else. A car crash, a heart attack, anything.

"Johnny." Linda's voice broke, and Johnny glanced my way.

I showed nothing, neither caring if he drew this out or hurried it along. Either way, his end was near, and it would be at my hands.

He turned and marched over to her and pulled her taut against him. He was a good foot taller than her. Where Johnny looked as if he was in his mid-forties, Linda still had the youthful look of a twenty-year-old. I was nothing more than an observer. She clung to him, desperation in her eyes as he continued to peek at me.

She whispered to her husband, but it meant nothing. Johnny knew the result. He'd signed the dotted line. And I was there to collect.

Johnny pulled away and cleared his throat. "Get back in the house. I love you."

Linda sighed and covered her mouth. Tears rolled down her cheeks and disappeared behind her hand. She turned away and hurried into the house. The door slammed shut, and Johnny let out a heavy sigh of his own. He stared at the house for another second before he turned away and headed toward the back gate.

He stopped and looked at me. I knew he would make some kind of demand. They always did.

"My family stays out of this."

"That's up to you," I answered truthfully.

He turned and stared at me. Maybe if I was a child, his hard look would have scared me. But he was nothing more than a man who was used to having power and was now powerless.

"Let's get this over with," Johnny said.

We headed toward his car, and I slipped into the passenger seat. There'd been a reason I'd chosen him first out of all our informants. Johnny had been the best. If it wasn't for his partner slipping up, he'd still be on the force. I didn't suspect him of being the rat, but Benito wasn't going to take my guess as a sure answer.

I directed him where to go. The further away we were from the city, the more the cold electrifying excitement tingled under the surface of my flesh. Johnny didn't bother with small talk, and for that, I wouldn't slice his throat and watch him bleed out. I could be merciful.

"Here," I said.

We pulled up at one of the many abandoned buildings we owned under a few aliases. Johnny grunted and threw the car into park. His fingers drummed on the steering wheel as he made no move to get out.

Don't be a runner.

"My family..."

"Depends on your answers."

Johnny nodded and got out of the car. I followed suit, sucking in the stale air of the night. The stars sparkled in the sky, a sight that wasn't available in the city or even the suburbs. Too much light pollution.

I admired them for another second before walking behind Johnny. My phone vibrated, and I sent the confirmation to my men. They'd be there exactly in fifteen minutes. Having a set time over my head made all the tension bleed out of my body. There was something about being confined in an organized square of time. I wouldn't go past or end it too quickly.

"Have a seat." I pointed to the only chair in the room.

He looked around, and I knew his eyes caught on some of the men already there. They walked around quietly, staying out of my way.

"I never mentioned my deal," Johnny started.

"I know."

His shoulders sagged as he sat down on the metal chair. The hole in the ceiling was perfectly placed over his head. Moonlight shimmered down on him as if death was there to greet Johnny and welcome him to the afterlife.

"Doesn't change that you were dismissed from the force."

Johnny scuffed. "Dismissed? More like fired. They

couldn't stick anything heavy on me but allegations. I was a damn good cop."

"If that was true, I wouldn't be in front of you right now."

Johnny's fists balled up on his thighs, and he glanced away. It was the truth. Why was he acting as if what I'd said was so wrong?

"My partner confessed to overlooking a few cases." Johnny shrugged.

His partner had already been dealt with. Arnold Keys died from a self-inflicted gunshot to the head.

"Who's looking into my family?"

Johnny shrugged. "All task forces were shut down after the fiasco two years ago. No one wants a blood bath. Too many innocents died with no justice." The muscle in his jaw ticked as he averted his gaze from me.

That word held little meaning in this life. Revenge is what he meant. He was all about justice, except when it came to needing help with his sick son. Then all of a sudden, justice wasn't so important.

I hate cops. They're the worst kind of human trash. Tex's face flashed before me, and my stomach twisted in discomfort. *Maybe not all cops.* It was one night and a toy I wouldn't get to play with again. Deep down, I hoped that wasn't true.

"What can you tell me?"

"I want my family to receive two months of what you guys were paying me," Johnny shot back.

"All your kind does is take."

I could make him talk, but Benito said no playtime. And right now, I might lose myself to the blood, missing any information he may or may not hand over.

"One." I held up my hand, stopping his negotiations. "It's already being generous. Unless you're willing to sell your wife to us, I'd stop negotiating for more money they won't be able to pay off."

Johnny shut his mouth and nodded. He let out a sigh as he leaned back. The scrape of the chair against the concrete floor echoed around the room as he pushed it back.

"There were whispers about the new mayor wanting to bring down a crime family in order to get re-elected." Johnny shook his head. "Fucking politicians. As far as I know, the chief shot down the idea of a task force for now."

I stared at him, waiting to see what else he had for me. Johnny's tough-guy act dropped as the minutes ticked by.

"The last bust on Bedford Ave? The tip came from some junkie. He was cracked out on meth. We let him go, but I heard he was picked back up."

"Name," I demanded.

Johnny looked everywhere but at me. It was like he could tell his time was nearly up. His leg began to bounce.

"I don—"

"Think. Remember, your family's lives depend on your answer."

He stopped moving and finally met my gaze. Anger flashed in his eyes as his brows dipped and his lips turned down in a frown.

"It was Carter, no, Clark, maybe Carl. It started with a C."

I nodded, and two men moved forward at my signal. Johnny attempted to jump up, but they held him down. He'd put on a brave face only to chicken out now.

He was a disappointment, but they all were. I pulled my Staccato XC 9mm out and aimed for his head. Johnny gritted his teeth and met my gaze, his mouth opening, but no words could be heard over the bang of the bullet leaving my gun and piercing the air.

My hand snapped back slightly from the recoil, and I steadied once more before lowering it. Johnny's head flopped back before rolling forward. Empty eyes looked back at me.

Blood dripped from the hole in the middle of his skull. The bead slid down around his slender nose and over his thin lips. It was mesmerizing as more joined it creating their patterns on his face before falling to his clothes or the ground to be soaked up.

I watched, basking in peace for another second before I went about the cleanup. We had people who did most of the work, but I preferred to make sure there was nothing left behind.

Sound trickled in. It was like a bubble had popped, and I heard the men around me talking and moving.

I stripped out of my clothes and wiped my face clean, getting rid of all evidence. One of our men walked in, holding a fresh pair of clothes. I'd prefer to shower, but it would have to wait. I'd have to deal with the way my clothes clung to my sweat-slicked skin and the way the warehouse stench wafted off me.

"Send it to the butcher," I said as I slipped the beige slacks on.

The material wasn't new, yet it grated against my flesh with every touch, setting my teeth on edge. *This is not right.*

Irritation settled in the pit of my stomach, turning over and over again as I forced myself to push past it. The shirt was no better, a light blue button-up I made sure to tuck in. I was handed the Aosta Italian melton topcoat and glasses that I normally wear.

Everything that normally made me feel calm was doing the opposite.

"Sir?" one of the men called.

I turned to see what he needed. A tiny voice in the back of my head screamed for me to rip my clothes off and burn them. I audibly swallowed and ignored as much as I could.

"Wife is calling."

The retired cop's wife. I sighed. Taking the phone, I forwarded the call.

"Make sure she knows to keep her mouth shut."

He nodded, and I broke the phone handing it back over to him. A million ants were crawling up my arms and legs as needles poked my back and torso. I needed out of these clothes. I could feel them too much.

"And deliver the remainder of the money."

Johnny had been bought for his kid's surgery, and the Vitales always kept their end of the bargain. There was a reason no one ever ratted on us. Fear alone wasn't enough to rule the streets of New York.

Johnny's car would be returned to his family once it was thoroughly cleaned. Benito didn't take chances, and neither did I. My car waited for me on the side of the road. Although everything in me screamed for me to run toward it and hurry the fuck up, I kept my movements controlled and measured.

The drive was quick, and I made it back to the hotel. I'd planned to go home, but for some reason, my on-fire brain decided the hotel would be best. I marched through the doors, and the bright lights assaulted me. I squinted through it, swallowing back my discomfort.

"Mr. Vitale, your guest left a message for you," the receptionist said.

She didn't question why I was back so soon. Normally when I closed the room out, I stayed away for a month or two. However, even if she'd asked me I didn't have the answer.

"Has he been back here?" I asked, forcing every word out. I wanted nothing more than to stay silent and disappear into a quiet area.

"No, sir. Not that we have noticed."

I stared at her, working on voicing the question. Words twisted, and my tongue rested heavily in my mouth, determined not to move.

"He questioned a server about you but nothing more. The breakfast was half eaten before he left in an Uber," she supplied.

I turned away once I took the note, disappearing toward the elevator. My control and patience were that of a saint. Yet, the piece of paper burned against my fingertips, demanding I open it right then and there. It momentarily distracted me from my discomfort but the moment the elevator dinged and opened I ran to my door. All control went out the door as I snatched the clothes off my body. My flesh was itching and burning all at once.

Taking them off wasn't enough, and I frantically moved to the bedroom. I tossed the note on the bed and started up the shower. I didn't wait for it to warm. The ice cold was a reprieve from the overwhelming heat threatening to consume me. I knew it was all in my head, but it changed nothing.

Once I was fresh out of the shower and dressed, I made my way over to the bed. The envelope was still there, taunting me. I picked it up and opened it. A single little note fluttered onto the bed.

Something close to laughter broke free as I shook my head. I stared at the piece of paper with a smile on my face.

Fuck you.

ENZO: *RAY LENDS TAKEN CARE OF.*

I sent the message to Benito and ground my molars as I placed my phone in the cup holder.

Another unsatisfying kill. It wasn't enough, and I felt the edge of chaos closing in on me. Tension built between my shoulder blades, and the feeling of a needle piercing my flesh repeatedly grew tiresome. No amount of reading or meditation was helping.

I found myself on the other side of the city where a certain rookie cop lived. I checked my messages, and Tex was working. Five days since I'd last seen him, and strangely thinking about him and the night we'd had calmed the whirlwind of insanity inside of me. However, the memory was getting old, and I needed to do something about it soon.

Keeping tabs on him was my job, but I'd stayed away from him. He was the kind of toy I'd end up breaking too fast. Or get fixated on, and the last thing I needed to become obsessed with was a cop.

I knew it wasn't a good idea, and yet I got out of the car and walked right up to his door. The apartment was easy to break into, boasting two simple locks that wouldn't keep a teenager out. Then again, looking around, there wasn't much to steal. Anyone breaking in would either have to be desperate or obsessed with Tex.

Jiggling caught my attention, and an orange Maine Coon came out of a box that was far too small for it. I hadn't taken Tex as a cat man, but lo and behold, the beauty sauntered up to me and meowed. I crouched down and scratched behind his ears, grimacing at the hair that clung to my fingers.

He needed to be brushed and bathed.

"Since I'm here, let's see what your owner has been up to."

I stood back up and let my gaze wander, but it looked as if Tex lived like a pig. Clothes were thrown everywhere, a few dishes in the sink, and a wet towel on the bathroom floor.

My need to fix it took over. Before I knew it, I was cleaning the entire apartment. To my surprise, there was nothing here that indicated Tex was even a cop. No badge or files lying around. Not even his police academy workout clothes. If I didn't know who he was, Tex could almost come off as a regular guy.

Almost. Those startling blue eyes flashed through my mind, and I shook free of the hold he had over me.

Ringing cut through the peaceful moment, and I sighed as I pulled my phone free of my pocket. Benito's name flashed on the screen. I knew I had no choice but to answer it.

"Where are you, Enzo?"

Telling him I was at Tex's place wouldn't go over well, but lying to Benito never ended well, either. I didn't answer him, choosing to stay silent as I pet the freshly cleaned orange Maine Coon on my lap. The kitten purred and snuggled up closer.

"I need you in Manhattan. Two of them tried to run," Benito said.

Without seeing his face, I knew he was angry, although my brother was always angry. I couldn't remember a time when he wasn't. Maybe Giancarlo did because they'd been together from the start.

"Make them regret ever trying to run."

The line went dead, and I sighed.

I picked the cat up. Its body was long, the back paws nearly to my knees.

"You be good."

I sat him down and moved around the place. The dryer beeped, and I folded the towels I'd used but kept them separate from all the others. They were now the cat's towels. I took one more look around, contemplating putting cameras and microphones around but nothing compared to seeing Tex in person.

As if he knew I was talking about him, my phone vibrated in my pocket. I smirked at the update about Tex. He was on his way home. Too bad I couldn't stay and play with him tonight. I took the note he left me, adding my own and placing it on his bed.

Maybe another time.

Seven
TEX

My feet hurt so damn bad I wanted to cut them off and toss them into the dumpster. I trudged up the walk to my front door and let myself inside, the mail in my hands as I sorted through it and ultimately tossed the entire stack onto the kitchen counter. Fuck bills. I didn't want to think about how depressing it was that I made so damn little I was struggling in the city.

"Meow!"

Reaching down, I scooped Penelope up into my arms. He rubbed against my face, whiskers and fur going all over. I swiped the mess off of my skin, spitting it out of my mouth and groaning.

"Yes, thank you, Penelope. Thank you." I carried him into the living room, which was really just an extension of the kitchen, and froze. "What the fuck?"

When I left in the morning, my dirty apartment had

been put on the list as something I needed to deal with when I returned. There were clothes strewn all over the floor, trash everywhere, and something that smelled suspicious somewhere in the kitchen, but I hadn't been able to find it in the three minutes I had before snagging my coffee tumbler and bolting from the door. Now? It was pristine, like the day I'd moved in. But better.

The smell of bleach burned my nostrils as I walked through my apartment, and I crinkled my nose. Dropping Penelope off on the couch, I ducked my head into the bathroom and found the source of the offensive aroma. My bathroom was probably cleaner than it had ever been. I stormed into my bedroom next, anger and fear coursing down my spine in equal measure.

"What the fuck?"

There, on my pillow, laid neatly as if I was in a hotel room, was a note. I snatched it up and stared at the bold, straight lettering. *Maybe next time.*

My stomach lurched. I reached out, my hand grabbing for something to stabilize myself with. Instead, it flew into the dresser, knocking off a plethora of old memories to the floor below. I sucked in a deep breath as the truth dawned on me.

Enzo had been inside my home.

A crazy, murderous, blood-thirsty mobster had been in my goddamn *home.* The fear was quickly replaced as fire coursed through my veins. I snatched up my laptop and typed on it, logging into the program connected to the cameras I'd installed.

Clicking through a few times, I finally stopped when I saw him walking into my place. Penelope hopped up beside me, purring and brushing against me with his long, fluffy tail until I gathered him into my lap and glared at the screen. A familiar scent tugged at my brain, but I brushed it away as I watched him.

He'd been all through my apartment, cleaning, straightening, and moving stuff around like a damn psychopath! The camera feed cut in and out. It hadn't even alerted me that he'd been inside! My grip on Penelope tightened, and I ground my teeth as I watched him pick up my cat and disappear into the bathroom. Twenty minutes later, he came out with Penelope wrapped in a towel, drying him off. I stabbed my finger onto the space bar and shoved that same finger against my eyelid.

I was going to *murder* Enzo Vitale. The bastard had been invisible for almost a week. In all that time, I'd glanced over my shoulder and worried that I would run into him. Every tall, dark-haired man that eclipsed my vision made me think it was him back to fuck with me, but it was never him. So, why the hell did he suddenly pop up now?

I looked Penelope over, my stomach still twisted into knots. He could have hurt him. Okay, Enzo hadn't done anything to my cat, but he *could* have. And even if he didn't, he had violated my space without a second thought. And for what? To clean?

Goddamn crazy person.

I kissed Penelope's head and shoved a hand into my pocket, searching for my phone. As soon as I had it, I stabbed the contact name of my old friend and waited for her to pick up.

"Yo, Texas! How the hell are you?"

I grimaced. "No one calls me that but you," I muttered.

"Yeah, I know. It still gets under your skin, doesn't it?" She chuckled, and I heard the familiar sound of her fingers flying over the keys. "What's up?"

I pinched the bridge of my nose. "You still doing security?"

"You bet your sweet, plump ass," she said. "Why?"

"I need someone to install a security system in my apartment. I'm renting, so I don't need a bunch of wires and shit, and my landlord can't know about it. Think you can do it?"

"Piece of cake," she purred. "When do you need it by?"

"Tomorrow?"

Chelsea choked, and I imagined it was on one of those energy drinks she liked to chug. "Tomorrow? That's short notice. You know it'll cost you, right?"

"I thought we were friends?"

"My friends call me more often," she said. "And do shit with me. This sounds more like a client needing a last-minute job. It'll cost you," she repeated.

"How much?"

"Fifteen hundred."

"Shit," I swore. "Why is it so much?"

"Because my shit is good, and I'm better," she said. I could hear her smug grin. "And I know you, Tex. You don't want that cheap internet crap you slap up on a wall and only half-records when it wants to."

"You're right, you're right," I searched my brain, trying to figure out if I even had that much money to spend. "What if we go out? Grab something to drink? Do you think you could shave off...five hundred bucks?"

She was quiet for a minute. "I could use a wingman. Meet me at 7th Circle in an hour?"

"Blu," I said quickly. "Let's go there."

"Bet, Blu it is. See you in an hour."

We hung up, and I turned back to the laptop. Enzo had been on a mission, looking over my stuff and then getting to work like he lived here. I hadn't seen him in days, but at that moment I could swear I still smelled his cologne.

I STOOD AT THE BAR AS MUSIC PULSED AROUND ME. MY HEART was throbbing a little too hard, pounding in my ears and drowning the music out. *Why the hell did I come back here?* There were a thousand clubs in New York, but I'd picked the one that housed Enzo Vitale.

There's something wrong with me.

"Tex! Over here!"

I cringed as she shouted my name. My head whipped around as I tried to see if anyone was looking at me, but everyone was in their own worlds. I glanced back at Chelsea. Her dark purple hair was up in two round puff balls on either side of her head. Even in the dark, her piercings glowed a neon green. We'd had matching piercings at some point, but I'd taken mine out before I joined the academy. I missed them.

"There you are." She grinned at me. "Hey, can I get a Sidecar over here!" she bellowed toward the cute blonde behind the counter. "And an uh…"

"Beer," I supplied. "Whatever you've got in a bottle. Surprise me."

The woman pulled a face as if I'd just asked her to spit on me. I didn't give a damn. I didn't need a fancy drink right now. What I needed was something to take the edge off and was within my budget. If there was one thing I knew about Chelsea, it was that she was going to make this hurt. At least I'd get a great security system for a steal.

We took our drinks and moved away from the bar. Not that there was much room to move. We slid through the crowd together until we were in an area with a little more space. Chelsea sipped on her Sidecar, a smile on her face as she adjusted her dark red dress and pushed a springy curl of hair out of her face.

"You look good," I said.

Chelsea lit up and shoved dainty fingers against my chest. "Awww, thanks, Texas. It's been a while since I've gone out. I wasn't even sure if any of this." She gestured to herself. "Worked."

I grinned. "Have you seen you? Trust me, it's working."

Her bright, beaming grin made me feel better about the bullshit I was currently dealing with. Chelsea had always been able to drag a smile out of me. We'd grown up together since middle school. And while I had chosen law enforcement, Chelsea stuck to what she knew; technology, security, and selling information to the right people for the right amount of money.

She was a badass. I admired her.

"What do you think about the blonde?" she asked, nodding toward the woman behind the bar. "Short hair, nice build. I bet she has a hell of a grip."

I groaned. "To choke you?"

"Just a little!" she said. "Come on, look at her." She stared at her prey, a dark gleam in her eye. "I bet she's got a twisted side."

Laughter rumbled out of my chest, and for the first time tonight, I felt like I wasn't going completely insane. "There's something wrong with you." I pointed out to her. "Seriously wrong."

"Don't act like you're not into some messed up shit," she said, grinning at me. "I was there for your high school whore days."

My face flushed, and I rubbed the back of my neck while

she cackled. She wasn't wrong. Back then, I was all about falling into whatever bed was the closest. Men, women, folks in between and outside of those classifications altogether, they were all ripe for the fucking. I'd slowed down since I entered the academy. Things were hard enough trying to work without mixing in messy entanglements.

"You talk about me like you're not just as bad," I pointed out.

She grinned. "I never said that. Being whores is one of many reasons we get along so well." Chelsea elbowed me fondly. "I missed you."

"I missed you too. Sorry my head's been up my ass."

"No big deal. I know you've had a lot of stuff on your plate." She shrugged. "We both have."

I pulled her into a hug and forgot about the weight on my shoulders. She wrapped warm arms around me, and I wanted to stay just like that, feeling comfort for the first time in years. When we pulled away, she tilted her head at me, reached up, and swiped at my eyes.

"Are you okay?" Chelsea whispered. "You're...crying."

I quickly dragged my arm over my eyes and made the tears disappear. *Fucking embarrassing.* Tilting up my beer, I drained the rest of it. Maybe this was why I didn't hang out with my friends anymore. They made me vulnerable where I'd built a wall around myself to protect me from all the crap in my life.

"Long day," I answered shortly. "Now, what about the bartender? How do you want to do this?"

Chelsea searched my face, and I saw the way her eyebrows drew together. The concern on her face made me shift from one foot to the other. I prayed she would let it die. Something must have made her come to the conclusion to let it go because she didn't press me.

"I want to talk to her, but she's working." She frowned. "Do you think it'll be enough if I stare at her all night and wait until she gets off?"

I groaned. "You can't pick someone else to go after? There's a ton of other women here."

"Yeah, but I'm already staring at her."

I grinned and shook my head. "Fine, we'll wait around. Okay?"

Chelsea lit up, her big eyes sweeping to the bar and back. She glanced up, and then her eyes settled on me. "Um, I think someone's staring at you."

"Me?" I asked. "No thanks, I'm not into it."

She nudged me. "He's still staring."

I turned around to see what she was going on about and froze. Standing above me was Enzo Vitale. The look on his face wasn't the calm, collected expression I'd seen last time. It looked like he was getting ready to burst a blood vessel. Our eyes locked, and he didn't glance away even for a second.

Something inside of me stirred.

"Let's get out of here, Chel," I said as I turned back to her. "We'll come around another night. Hopefully, it won't be as busy, and you can talk to the bartender."

She sighed. "Yeah, you're right. It's crowded as shit in here." Her gaze flickered up to Enzo and back to me. "Sure you don't need to take care of that?"

I grinned. "I thought I'd want to, but you know what? It's better to leave it where it is." I draped an arm around her shoulders. "Let's go to a little hole in a wall somewhere and get fucked up. Tomorrow's my day off."

She rolled her eyes. "You just want free work."

"Am I that obvious?"

"Hell yes!" She frowned. "But I *could* use another drink."

"Atta girl," I said. "Let's get out of here."

We moved through the heavy crowd together while the hair on the back of my neck stood on end. Even without turning around, I knew Enzo was staring me down. Everything in me screamed to glance over my shoulder, to take one last look, but I forced myself to keep moving.

I needed to get that security system installed. And then I needed to take Enzo apart piece by fucking piece.

Eight
Enzo

AGITATION AND ANNOYANCE FILLED ME AS TEX LEFT WITH some woman under his arm. I'd watched him the moment he stepped in, facing the pounding music to lay eyes on him.

"Oh, what's that face," Gin asked.

His finger was poised to jam into my cheek. I gave him the barest of glances before I watched Tex's retreat. He was gone the next second, and I couldn't place the strange feeling stabbing me in the side.

"What's wrong, Enzo?" Gin asked, his tone changing, coming off more serious.

"Nothing."

He grunted and crossed his arms over his chest. Gin moved closer, his six-five height towering over me. "It's not nothing."

Drop it. I tilted my head back just a little to meet his gaze.

He didn't falter. I knew no matter if I were direct or not, Gin would keep pushing.

Bastard.

"You won't tell me, will you? I can always guess." He leaned over the railing, looking down at the crowd.

The one thing that had held my attention was no longer there. I turned away.

"I know it's not the music bothering you." Gin was right on my heels as I retreated toward the back of the club. I needed to leave. To hunt down Tex and see what he was up to.

Gin's arm draped over my shoulder, and his mouth was near my ear. "Is it that cute cop?"

Cute? Every fiber of my being reacted to my brother's words. I twisted toward him as I wrapped an arm around his wrist. I used his body weight against him as I flipped him over my back and onto the floor.

My knife was in my hand before I even thought about it and sliced through the air toward Gin's chest.

"Fuck!" Gin's hands wrapped around the steel blade stopping its descent. "Are you crazy?" He shook his head as blood dripped down, staining his white button-up. "Never mind. I know that fucking answer."

I blinked slowly at him. Gin had said Tex was cute. It was clear my brother needed to go. I wouldn't let him take my toy away.

"Enzo, I'm not going to fuck with your latest obsession," Gin growled. "Now, back the fuck off."

I stared into his eyes for another second before I eased back. He let my knife go, and I pulled out a cloth to clean it before putting it away.

"Fuck, my hands are ruined." Gin glared my way, but I saw no issue.

We stood up, and Gin caught the eye of one of the men standing in the back. He had his hands wrapped in the next second as I contemplated what I should do to the woman who'd been too cozy with Tex.

They'd touched each other in a familiar way that grated on my nerves. Only I should be allowed to touch him, to draw out whatever reaction I wanted.

"You have crazy eyes right now," Gin said, holding his cut hands together. "I have to get glued because of you."

I stared at him for a long while, and he sighed.

"It was a *bad* thing to attack me, Enzo." He shook his head, chastising me like I was a child. "Your new fixation is dangerous."

My brows dipped. Was I truly fixated on Tex already? Had he grabbed so much of my attention before I knew it?

"You tried to kill me all because I said the man was cute." Giancarlo raised his bandaged hands. "Don't start your bullshit with me. Benito will have both of our asses."

I didn't put it past my brother. He'd lock us up and toss the key into the river if we went too far.

"You have this under control?"

"Yes," I said through gritted teeth.

Gin looked skeptical, looking at his hands and then at me. "Yeah, I don't believe that shit. Maybe someone else—" His words died off as he met my gaze.

Maybe it was the pure rage coursing through my veins or the need to kill, but Gin dropped the idea of switching me out as soon as he looked at me.

"You have to be careful. Benito isn't going to like this."

I knew that, and nothing would come of Tex. "I need to get him out of my system."

Gin's head tilted to the right as he stared at the ceiling. "You could kill him."

I'd explained why that was a bad idea already, but now the thought of killing Tex made my stomach sour. I wouldn't be opposed to having him on a table and cutting into him but killing him made my neck itch.

"I'm not done with him."

"Of course not." Gin shrugged and turned away from me. "Don't fuck up."

I never did, but I hadn't fixated on someone in a long time, either. The last person was six feet in the ground and scattered all over Morningside park.

It won't happen again. I was different, and Tex... was different.

"Sorry," I blurted out.

I knew hurting family went against everything we stood for. Giancarlo and Benito were the only constants that I had. Even playing with Tex couldn't come between us. My brother was annoying and knew how to get under my skin, but he was my brother. I'd do anything for him and Benito.

Gin turned and aimed a big dopey grin my way as if I hadn't cut him at all. He marched back to my side and ruffled my hair like he'd done so many times when we were kids.

"Got a little closer than usual. Better luck next time."

We might talk about killing each other and even inflict a few wounds, but deep down, nothing in this world could tear us apart. It was why we were one of the most formidable families in New York.

I grunted, slapping his bleeding hands away. "You're getting me dirty."

Gin laughed and let his hands drop. "You like blood."

I shook my head. "Not yours. Make sure you go get it checked and properly cleaned."

Gin waved me off. "They aren't that deep."

Our gazes locked as I contemplated taking him to the hospital myself. My brother was more likely to do the bare minimum wound care and would end up suffering for it later.

"Shouldn't you go check on the cop?" Gin asked, knowing how to distract me.

I bit the inside of my cheek. "After we go to the clinic."

Gin shook his head. "You know how I feel about those places. The smell of bleach and death in the air." A visible shudder wrecked his tall, muscular frame. "Not going."

"I'll call the doc, and she will meet us at your place."

Gin looked ready to argue with me, but I wasn't letting him. I might be the youngest of the three of us, but I was far more responsible than Gin.

"Where are you two headed?" Benito's voice cut through the club's music.

Gin winked at me, and I shut my mouth as he answered for the both of us. "Cut myself, headed home."

"You're going to let a doctor look at it," Benito said, leaving no room for Giancarlo to argue.

"Doctor this, doctor that. I'll be fine," Gin said.

"Enzo, make sure this idiot gets checked over and patched up."

I nodded, glad Benito didn't ask how it happened. He turned on his heels and headed toward his office.

"You know you owe me, right?" Gin said, knocking our shoulders together.

"I'm not doing your job for you."

It wasn't possible anyway. Where I felt odd and uncomfortable around crowds, Giancarlo thrived. He became the center of attention and drew people from all walks of life to him.

"Wouldn't think of it. You're more likely to creep everyone out."

"Then what?" I asked as we walked out the backdoor. His black 1978 Monte Carlo was parked right outside the door. "Benito told you to stop parking here."

Gin sighed and attempted to get behind the wheel. I snatched the keys away, and we had another silent standoff.

"I'm only letting you drive my baby because you're careful, but one scratch and *you* will have bleeding hands."

I nodded, knowing how serious my brother was about his car. He'd been working on it since we were teens. It had come a long way from scrap metal to a functioning car with fresh paint.

"And what Benito doesn't know won't hurt him."

I started the car and opened my mouth but shut it at Gin's next words.

"Unless you want to tell him you're fucking the cop he told you to keep watch over."

"One time," I grunted.

"Yeah, for now," Gin joked.

I couldn't find it in me to disagree, not when I'd been thinking about it on repeat. Seeing Tex tonight had only made me hungrier for him.

Getting Gin home was the easy part; his townhouse was still the same. I made a mental note to come back and clean. There was a layer of dust on his bookshelves and lampshades. The walls were painted in dark greens with burnt orange as an accent color. My brother lacked the ability to design or put colors together. Which was why he hadn't changed the place after his last girlfriend left him.

"Stop looking around. You aren't cleaning shit."

"You aren't doing it," I said. My fingers twitched at my side, the need to organize the place gnawing at my psyche.

"No, thank you, I know where everything is. You come in here, and I won't even know where the hell my underwear is." He pointed at me. "Don't touch my shit, Enzo. We've had this talk. Boundaries."

My shoulders dropped as I forced my gaze to focus on him. "Fine, but you need to get someone in here."

He shrugged. "I'll think about it."

The doorbell rang before I could point out every single thing that needed to be cleaned and why. I opened the door, and Melony stood on the other side. Her rich brown skin shimmered with painted-on glitter. Heavy pink and purple eyeshadow framed her big brown eyes. She smiled, and even her lips were covered in glitter.

"Can I come in, Mr. Vitale?"

"No, go away," Gin shouted.

Melony rolled her eyes. "Don't be a baby."

I stepped aside, avoiding glitter like the plague it was, and let her in. She made her way up the three stairs and into the living room, where Gin was resting on the green sofa.

"What did you do this time?" She took her jacket off, and a bright tutu and glitter mesh shirt greeted us.

"Man, doc, did we interrupt a party?" Gin asked instead of answering her. He looked tense sitting on the couch. His shoulders practically touched his ears.

She nodded without hesitation. She'd been around us long enough she was relaxed and treated us like we were any other client.

"You did. My niece's glitter ballerina ball." Melony unwrapped Gin's hands while still talking. "She was very excited, and it was going great till I got a text pulling me away."

Melony kept Gin distracted. I knew me standing there was only going to make him even more nervous. It didn't matter that Melony was only checking over a wound. Gian-carlo didn't do well with doctors.

"She turned fifteen today. You should send me back with a good gift," Melony suggested.

Slowly my brother's shoulders relaxed as she kept talk-ing. I cleared my throat, and our eyes met briefly.

"I'll leave you to it."

Melony waved me off and continued to talk about the ridiculous theme of her niece's birthday party. I stepped out of the townhouse and sucked in a deep breath. Now that I was no longer distracted by Gin my mind instantly raced to Tex. I ground my molars and pulled my phone out.

Fifteen minutes later, my car was dropped off. I was distracted the entire drive. Even through traffic, all I could think about was Tex and the way he'd laughed and hugged the woman at the club. He'd seen me, and I'd felt a spark the moment our eyes met but he'd turned away from me.

Remembering only made me angrier. I slammed the car into park in the parking lot of Tex's apartment. I hadn't planned on coming back, at least not this soon.

I was out of the car and at his front door in seconds. Gin's words came crashing through my mind before I could break the lock. *Boundaries.* Did it still count if I'd already broken in? I was tempted to call Gin and ask him the rules on boundaries if one had already been crossed or if I'd already done it. My head hurt. Instead of entering, I leaned against the wall next to it.

Minutes turned to hours, and it was well past two in the morning when I heard Tex's smooth voice. He was saying goodbye to the girl in the taxi. She waved at him, laughing as he stumbled toward the building. He didn't notice me right away, but the moment he was close enough and I could smell the beer on him, he jumped.

"Fuck!"

I caught Tex before he could fall back. He blinked rapidly at me. "What the fuck are you doing here, asshole? Here to go through my shit again? Once wasn't enough?"

My head tilted. I took in the anger in Tex's eyes and the way his mouth dipped in a heavy frown. *He is upset.*

"You're angry with me?"

"No, I love it when a guy who fucked me left me at a hotel alone comes back around randomly to clean my place and go through my shit. It's the goddamn best feeling ever."

"Then why are you frowning?" I asked.

"You...You can't be fucking for real." Tex shouldered me out of the way. He was still unsteady on his feet as he cursed under his breath, trying to get the key in the lock. "Motherfucking cocksucker," he continued to mumble under his breath.

I moved closer, my body nearly touching his. He went still as I reached around him and took the keys. I slid it into the lock and turned it with ease. Tex leaned back toward me as if seeking me out before he shook his head and snatched the keys away.

"Thanks, now fuck off."

He opened the door and stumbled inside. The fluffy orange cat greeted us at the door, and Tex scooped him up.

"Hey, Penelope. Ready for bed?"

I stepped in behind him and shut the door.

"You don't understand English?" Tex asked.

"I do."

He placed the cat back down. Penelope wove between my legs, but I stayed watching Tex as he headed for the kitchen.

"Where the fuck are my glasses?"

I opened the cabinet closest to the small white fridge. It

made sense to have them close to where he stored his drinks. I handed it to him, and it slipped through his fingers and crashed to the laminate flooring. Glass scattered everywhere.

"Fuck my life." He bent down to clean it, but I stopped him.

"Sit down. I will get it."

"I don't need you here. I can handle this." Tex wavered, and I glared at him.

"Sit." I pressed my fingers between his impressive pecs. I dreamt of fondling them too many times. Tex continued to stand there, and I got closer lowering my voice. "Sit, Tex, or I will make you, and we both know it will hurt." My head tilted along with the corner of my mouth. "Maybe you *want* me to hurt you again."

Tex's Adam's apple bobbed, and his pupils dilated, eating at the gorgeous blue of his iris.

"No?" Tex said, licking his lips.

"Then sit down." I directed him to the small living room.

He plopped down on the couch as I turned around. I made sure Penelope was locked away in his bedroom before fixing a cup of water.

"Drink this and take this."

"Not a drug to knock me out, is it?"

I smirked. "I want you awake for anything I do to you. Your reactions are too good to miss out on. It's ibuprofen."

I placed the pill in one hand and the cup in the other. Turning away from Tex, I focused on cleaning up the mess on the floor.

Nine
TEX

THERE WAS A STRANGE MAN IN MY APARTMENT.

No, scratch that. There was a strange man in my apartment who had fucked me better than I'd ever been fucked before and who was also a murderous bastard. Oh, and he was delicately picking up pieces of glass off my floor. He dampened a paper towel and went back to work as I stared at him.

What the hell is he doing here?

I drank down more of the water to wash the taste of beer and irritation out of my mouth. As the coolness slid over my tongue and washed down my throat, I couldn't tear my eyes away. Enzo finished up with the glass pieces and grabbed my mop next, giving the floor a good shine.

"What the fuck?" I muttered.

"There," Enzo said, more to himself than to me, as he

replaced my mop. His gaze flickered to me. "Now it's your turn."

I frowned. "My turn to what?"

Enzo walked over and stood beside my couch. "Drink the rest of your water, and come on."

"Why?" I asked.

I swear I saw his eyelid twitch. "If you ask me one more question, I'm going to haul you over my shoulder and move you myself."

My eyes narrowed. "I'd like to see you try that shit."

Wordlessly, Enzo plucked the glass out of my hand and yanked me to my feet. I stood there, staring at him wide-eyed, stunned that he had that much strength. I'd witnessed it myself, but it still shocked me. Normally, I wasn't an easy man to move, but Enzo did it without a second thought.

He braced himself, crouched, and I went up onto his shoulder as if I weighed nothing. The shock wore off as he carried me through my apartment.

"Put me down!" I snapped.

A quick, hard swat landed on my ass, and I blinked. Had he just slapped my butt? I wanted to protest, but my drunk brain wasn't equipped to handle this. We stopped off in my bathroom, and he dropped me onto the closed lid of my toilet.

"Clothes off." He pointed to the hamper in the corner. "Put them in there. And brush your teeth."

I gawked at Enzo. "There is something seriously wrong with you," I said. "Why aren't you taking the hint to leave?"

"There was a hint to leave?" he asked.

Unlike before, when he really seemed confused by my anger, this question was filled with smart ass-ness. I had told him directly to fuck off, yet he was still here. He turned his back to me and leaned over into the tub, turning it on and adjusting the temperature. My eyes ran over his backside. At some point, he'd taken off his jacket and put it somewhere, but I had no idea when. Was I that drunk? Or staring at other things a little too hard?

"Clothes," he repeated, a slight growl in his voice.

I wanted to tell him exactly where he could shove his demands. The beer had only made me bolder, and I felt some kind of way about him right now. Whether I wanted to fuck him or kick his ass, that was the question.

Enzo's hands were on me so quickly my head was spinning. He yanked off my clothes, tossing them into the hamper. I shoved out a hand in protest, but he simply knocked it away. When he shoved me back and ripped off my boxers, I found my voice again.

"Hey! I know how to shower by myself," I huffed. "Can you get out?"

Enzo looked down at me. "I can, but I don't think I should. You're drunk enough to slip and crack your head open on the faucet. Blood would splatter, creating a bigger mess. Based on your height and weight, there are multiple ways your fall could land you either in the hospital or the morgue."

"Jesus," I muttered. "That's so violent."

He shrugged. "Yes, but it happens."

His eyes moved from my face to my body. I watched as they did a slow tour of me, roaming over every inch of exposed flesh. He reached out, and I winced but stayed silent as he dragged two fingers over an old, jagged scar on my stomach.

"What happened?"

I glanced away, a cold glass of water suddenly thrown over me. "Nothing," I said, shoving him away and sitting up. "Get out so I can shower."

"I can do a better job."

"Out!" I snapped. "Go home already. Why are you even here?"

Enzo didn't answer me. Instead, his lips pressed into a straight line, and he watched as I struggled to stand up. I forced myself to keep moving. Damn, Chelsea had really drunk me under the table, and she was still perfectly fine. The woman was a demon. I stepped into the shower and groaned as the first spray of warm water caressed my skin.

I glanced at the curtain before I gave in to my curiosity and peeked through the slit. Enzo had taken a seat on the toilet lid I'd just been perched on. *He's really not going anywhere, is he?* What was his deal? I hadn't seen the man in days, and now he was refusing to leave. My stomach clenched as I realized in horror that I was comforted by that fact. I *liked* that he was ignoring me, that he wasn't going away.

Sighing, I snatched up the bar of soap and started getting to work as I tried not to think of why I was losing my damn mind. I was way too drunk to over-analyze myself like this and I didn't want to run into any uncomfortable truths. I focused on getting washed up. When I stepped from the tub, Enzo had a towel waiting, draped over his lap. He was staring at his phone, and my eyes swept over it quickly.

I could use that. Maybe I can get it from him.

I brushed away the wet, icky feeling that ran down my spine from that thought and stepped forward. When I reached for the towel, Enzo stood up and wrapped it around my body instead. He ran the cloth over me, collecting up droplets of water as his breath feathered over my flesh. My cock ached, and somehow, I forgot how to breathe.

"You're going to hyperventilate," he informed me. "Breathe."

I let out a big breath of air and the corner of his mouth ticked up, doing fucked up things to my insides. Enzo turned me toward the sink after he made sure the towel was tucked into place tightly and passed me my toothbrush. He swiped toothpaste on it and patted my ass.

"Brush."

"You're bossy," I noted. I shoved the toothbrush into my mouth. "And -nnonying."

"Mmm-hmm," he said, not paying me a lick of attention. He just stared.

I tried to ignore him, but it was impossible not to squirm under his spectacled gaze. Heat rushed through me, and I cursed the alcohol in my system. That was the *only* reason I would ever be into him. *Yeah, that's it. I'm just drunk and horny. Anyone would want to fuck a man that looked like that. But I know the real him. No way I want anything to do with that.*

I washed my mouth and face, and when I straightened up, he was still staring. "Why are you here?" I asked. "You haven't answered that yet."

"I don't know yet."

I opened my mouth and shut it again. Great, I was being stalked by a weirdo who happened to be part of a dangerous crime family. That wouldn't end badly at all. I trudged past him and walked to my bedroom. As I stepped inside, Penelope shot out. He hated being confined. I walked to my dresser and snagged a pair of clean boxers, shimmying as I dragged them up my hips. I turned, and my heart almost fell out of my ass. My back slammed into the dresser. Enzo was right there, silently hovering.

"Fuck!" I snapped. "Will you go home already? You're killing my buzz."

Enzo reached out and touched my scar again, mapping

it with his fingers. It was like he was obsessed with the thing. Just like the tattoo, I knew he wouldn't let it go until I explained what it was. I gritted my teeth.

"Old injury," I muttered. "Got into it with my old man one day, and he knocked me on my ass a few times. No big deal."

"Your father the—" Enzo's gaze met mine, and he blinked a few times. "Nevermind."

"What were you going to say?" I pushed.

"Doesn't matter," he said as he reached out and held the side of my neck. "Who was the girl? She yours?"

I got whiplash from the sudden change in topics and gawked at him. "Who?"

"The girl. Brown skin, big eyes, short little dress. The one at Blu," he said impatiently as I continued to stare. "You were all over her." His grip tightened on my throat. "Who was she?"

My stomach did a little flip as danger bells rang in my head. Was he jealous? Already? After the hotel, I'd thought it was a one-time thing, one night of intense, chaotic pleasure before we'd go back to our separate life paths and clash in the future. But here he was, standing in my bedroom, the pressure of his hand on my neck grounding me.

"A friend," I said finally.

"Her name?"

A shiver passed over me. No way in hell was I going to tell Enzo anything about Chelsea. The look in his eyes screamed a warning. She'd end up at the bottom of a river somewhere.

"Why?" I asked him.

"I just want to know."

I sealed my lips. There was no way I could tell him that I knew exactly who he was, so that was never going to happen. He'd figure out that I was investigating him. And that would be a death sentence.

"Doesn't matter," I said. "Like I said, she's a friend. Besides, she's so gay I wouldn't even turn her head."

Enzo stepped forward, erasing any semblance of space between us. My body overheated, and I tried to take a step back. However, I was still forced against the dresser. Enzo's body pressed against mine and my heart decided to speed up like it was a runaway train aimed at disaster.

His lips brushed against mine, and I moaned, unable to stop myself. I reached out and gripped his shirt, holding him against me in case he suddenly decided to change his mind and disappear. My cock throbbed as I pushed up against him, grinding against his body as his tongue drove into my mouth.

Enzo grabbed my arms and shoved me toward the bed. I fell in. The weight of his body covered mine as he dry-humped against my ass. He ripped the towel away and grunted as he rubbed up against me. For the second time in a night, I was able to watch his carefully tailored facade fall away.

But I didn't just want to be rubbed against. Instead, I shifted my weight and tossed him off of my back. Enzo landed on the bed, and I climbed on top of him, my body screaming to feel him again. Yes, he was a crazy, dangerous stalker, but my brain completely forgot about that when he was so hot and hard underneath me.

"Clothes," I demanded.

Enzo reached down, grasping the hem of his shirt. He pulled it over his head and tossed it aside before he gestured for me to get off. I moved swiftly, diving toward my nightstand and rooting around until I found what I was looking for. Lube and condoms in hand, I moved back over to see him trying to fold his clothes and knocked them off the bed.

He growled. "Hey."

"You're in my house now. Leave them on the floor if you want to fuck me."

Enzo glanced at the mess on the floor and then back to me. His gaze wandered a second time, and I saw him struggle before he attacked me. Enzo's mouth found mine, his tongue sliding into my mouth. I met it, tangling with him as I moaned and rocked forward, only air kissing my hot cock. It wasn't enough.

I shoved a hand into his chest and climbed back on top of Enzo. Popping the cap of the lube, I poured a generous amount over our cocks and slid a hand around them. Enzo's head tilted back, a swear on his lips as his gaze flickered up to the ceiling.

Panting, I laid on top of him and realized too late how intimate the position was. It wasn't getting bent over and railed from the back. It was being face to face with a man as I stroked both of our cocks together. His gaze fell on me, and Enzo's hand reached out. Slowly, he cupped my cheek, and a shock of panic shot through me.

I shoved away from him, my cock dripping and my heart pounding.

"Get out," I said, my voice turning shaky. "Get the fuck out!"

Enzo stared at me. "Did I do something wrong?"

"Get out!" I snapped again. "Out!"

His stare lingered, but he must have seen something because he climbed out of my bed and yanked on his clothes. Enzo wrenched open my bedroom door, and I heard his heavy footsteps as he moved through my apartment. The front door slammed, and I tore after him, quickly throwing the locks before I pressed my forehead against the cool metal.

Fuck. What was I thinking? What is wrong with me!

I didn't give a damn about getting his phone or trying to get any information on him tonight. What I'd done was screw up, and now my brain was revolting. I'd let Enzo into my body one time and I was this screwed up?

No, it's more than that. It was the way he touched me. The way he looked at me. Why couldn't I have just bent over and let him take me from behind again?

I slammed a fist into the door. "Idiot. Fucking moron, get it together!" I berated myself.

The sound of shoes shuffling away caught my ear, and I shoved my eye against the peephole. Enzo stopped and turned back to stare at my door. My heart squeezed as my hand gripped the doorknob. *What is that expression on his face?* I couldn't quite figure it out. The insane part of me almost ripped the door open to go ask. Instead, I shoved myself away and stormed to my bathroom.

I had to get the smell of him off me and erase the feeling of being so close to the man I was destined to put behind bars.

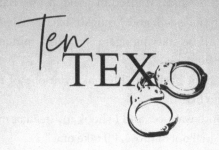

Ten
TEX

I STOOD ON THE CREAKING FRONT PORCH AND HESITATED. I'D made the trip and still didn't want to cross the threshold to the house I once called home. Sleepy Hollow came by its name, honestly. It was slow, quiet, and had completely bored teenage me out of my mind when we moved out here. I stared up at the baby blue, two-story house and felt a looming dread pool in my stomach.

"Are you going to stand out there all day or come in?"

"Oh, leave him alone, Henry," my mother chastised as she stepped to the screen door and smiled. "Hi, honey."

I smiled despite myself. "Hey, Mom."

She lit up and opened the door. Before I could say another word, she was in my arms. I hugged her back tightly and placed a kiss on the top of her head. I easily towered over her now, making me want to look after her even more. I had always been a mama's boy, even if our relationship could be...difficult.

"It's so good to see you! Why didn't you call?" she asked, tucking a brown strand of hair behind her ear. "I would have had lunch ready for you."

I waved a hand. "It's not an issue, Mom. I ate before I came." Her smile fell, and I quickly backpedaled. "But you know me. I'll be starving again in twenty minutes," I said, patting my stomach.

She lit right back up. "I'll make you one of those huge grinders you like."

My mouth watered, and I shook my head at myself. "I've missed the hell out of those. I'll take one."

I followed her into the house and closed the screen door behind me at the last second, making sure it didn't bang shut the way my father hated. Shuffling after her, I stepped into the living room, and nothing had changed. My father sat in his chair, a stack of books beside him but his gun out in front of him on the tray. He had taken it apart and was cleaning it when he glanced up at me.

"Tex."

"Dad," I said back, mimicking his deadpan voice. "What are you doing?"

"What's it look like I'm doing?" he grunted.

He put the gun down and picked up his pack of cigarettes. I could already hear my mother groaning about the smell. He slid one out and stuffed it into his mouth before lighting it, and his gaze finally fell on me again.

"What do you need?"

I stiffened. "Can't I just want to come and visit my family?"

He blew out a cloud of smoke. "No."

He's as lovely as always. I reached over and snagged one

of his cigarettes. He looked like he wanted to smack my hand the way he used to when I was a child. Instead he simply grunted, let me take a smoke, and lit it. Nicotine rushed through my body. I was able to breathe and push down the urge to shove him out of that chair and pummel him until he stopped being such a dick.

You know he'd kick your ass. He might be older now, but that man is strong.

That thought made me feel small beneath his gaze. As it always did. I blew out a cloud of smoke, glanced over my shoulder to make sure my mother was out of earshot and stared at the old man.

"I need some of your old case files on the Vitales. The chief has me working on them, and I figured you might have some things other people don't. Notes, recordings, anything."

He looked me up and down. "Leave it alone."

"I can't do that."

"Yes, you can," he said. "I doubt the chief has you working on anything like that. Do I need to call and ask?"

Suddenly I was transported back to being a kid, sitting in front of my father while he glared down at me and threatened to call my principal. My shoulders tried to slump, but I shoved them back and held my head up. I wasn't a child anymore. His words didn't have nearly the effect on me that they used to. Or at least I tried not to let them.

"This will help me make detective."

"No," he grunted. "It's going to get you killed." He shoved a finger in my direction. "If you know what's good for you, you'll drop this case and leave it the fuck alone."

He reached for his cane and tried to pull himself up. I moved on instinct, standing up and running over to help him to his feet. What I got was a cane shoved into my stomach.

"Did I ask for your help?"

You never do, asshole.

"No," I muttered.

"Then get the hell off me," he said as he tried again and rose slowly, a flash of pain showing on his face before it was gone. "Anything else?" he asked.

"I still need those files."

"Are you hard of hearing, boy?"

I gritted my teeth and ignored the urge to tell him to fuck off. "Nope," I answered. "Just determined. You used to tell me I lacked ambition and wouldn't get anywhere in life. Now I'm trying, and you're shutting me down."

He glared at me. "Look at my leg," he snapped as he tugged up his pant leg and showed me the dark, knotted mass of flesh that remained even after all the surgeries. "This is what happens when you mess around going after mobsters. And I was the lucky one, unlike my partner, who's six feet deep and rotting in a pine box," he snapped. "So when I say no, I mean no. Find a different way to make detective. I'm not helping you."

My face grew hot as my jaw tightened. "Why do I ever expect you will?" I snapped back. "You didn't help back then, and you don't help now. Let's be honest; the only thing you care about is yourself."

"You have five seconds to get out of my presence before I knock you on your ass."

We stared each other down, but I was the first one to cave. I turned on my heels, cursing myself out as I walked away like a little punk. I moved to the door, and my mother cut off my retreat.

"Oh, don't leave, Tex," she said softly. "I know your

father's cranky, but that's just because of his leg," she said, trying to reassure me. She reached out and rubbed my back. "Won't you stay for dinner? Maybe spend the night for once."

My heart clenched, and shame settled on my shoulders. I felt bad not staying around for her, but I couldn't stand being around *him*. *On top of everything else, he's robbing me of my mother.* The thought made the heat rise in my chest again. I glanced toward the living room.

"Sorry, Mom, but I'm working a lot lately," I said, which wasn't a complete lie. "I can't stay the night. Maybe we can grab something to eat one day."

Her smile faltered, but she pulled it back into place. "Ah, okay," she said, lifting her head and shaking off the sadness I saw in her eyes.

"Kate!" my dad bellowed, swallowed by a litany of swears.

"I better help him. He's probably ready for his nap," she dusted her hands off on her apron and pointed a finger at me. "Do not leave until I finish your sandwich."

I smiled at her. "Okay, Mom."

She jogged to the living room and cooed to calm my father's irritated tirade. I could hear them traveling up to the second floor and shook my head. The old man was too stubborn to downsize and get a house with one story, so, of course, it was mom's responsibility to help him out.

The sound of their footsteps faded as they went to the bedroom. I took the opportunity to jog down the basement stairs and walked to his office. The door was locked, but a quick walk over to the shelves and a dig around in the jars and I found the key. He always thought it was such a clever spot.

I slid the key inside the lock and let myself into his office.

There were stacks of files in boxes, but the most important ones were in the filing cabinet. Out of the two of us, he was the organized one and as much as I hated that shit when I was younger, right now I was grateful for it. I opened a drawer, flipped through the files and found the one I was looking for.

Vitale.

I snagged my phone and laid out the papers one by one. Carefully, I took pictures of each one, trying to keep them in the proper order. Front and back, I recorded every bit of information that I could.

"Tex?"

My heart raced as my mother called me. "Coming!" Shit, not enough time.

I quickly gathered everything up and stuffed some files into the back of my jeans, tugging my shirt over them. I shut the drawer and locked the door to the office. When I emerged to the main floor, my mom was frowning.

"What are you doing down there? You know how your father gets about the basement."

"Yeah, I was looking for some of my old stuff."

She looked me up and down. "Yeah, well, there's still a ton down there. Are you going to go through it anytime soon?"

"Soon," I promised as I followed her back into the kitchen. "I need to get going, Mom."

"Are you sure? Just stay for a little while."

"I really need to get to work."

She sighed. "You never stick around. I wish you wouldn't take off so quickly."

I wish you would protect me from him more. Or at least stand up for me. The words set heavy on my tongue, but I couldn't bring myself to say them. She was a good mother, and I knew she'd done the best she could, but when it came to my father she cowered. And part of me hated her for it.

"Don't forget your food," she said. She wrapped up the sandwich and then opened the fridge. "I made some chicken the other day too. And veggies. Here, take all of these."

I let her load my arms up with containers, effectively building a wall between my hurt and her shame. If all we focused on was food, the weather, the job, and every other trivial matter in between, then we would never have to talk about the chasm of pain that grew between us and threatened to swallow us whole.

"You sure you don't want to come out tonight?" Rourke asked.

I stared through my windshield at the place in front of me. How long had I been waiting? There was a slight cramp in my legs, and my stomach growled. I reached for the sandwich my mom had made and took a huge bite out of it.

"Nah," I mumbled. "I want to sit at home, relax, and do nothing."

"Fine," Rourke said. "Make sure you stay out of trouble."

"When do you ever know me to be in trouble?"

Rourke grunted, reminding me of the disappointed sounds my father made at me, and my stomach clenched. Suddenly, my appetite was gone. I stuffed the sandwich back into its container and slammed the lid closed.

"Alright, well, don't be late for work tomorrow," he said.

"I won't."

We hung up, and I went back to staring at Enzo's place. He lived in an apartment building that was a lot more lowkey than I expected. I'd thankfully found the place through my father's files; surprisingly, there was an address for all of them. He'd done a ton of work before packing it in, and I was glad I'd listened to my impulses and sought the files out.

The front door opened, and Enzo stepped out on his stoop. A man joined him. I looked through the papers I'd printed out, my mouth tugging into a frown.

"Giancarlo. The brother." I tapped the paper and glanced up at them. "Where are you two going?"

They walked down the steps together and disappeared into what I recognized as Enzo's car. Sliding down in my seat, I watched as Enzo took off down the road. When he was out of sight, I sat for a few minutes longer, but I couldn't wait forever. It was now or never.

I slid out of the car and pulled my jacket around me. The cool, fall air was biting at my skin as I waited around the stoop. Another minute ticked by before a mom walked out of the building chastising a little blond boy behind her. I smiled at them and slipped into the building. According to the file, Enzo's apartment was on the top floor. The man had an obsession with heights.

The elevator carried me up to the top, and I stepped out as I searched for his number. Clearly, the apartments were bigger on this floor because there were only two doors. Number 745 was his. I pulled out my lock-picking kit and set to work. As the tumblers moved and time ticked by, sweat collected on my brow. The sound of the door unlocking made me want to jump up and punch the air. I gripped the knob and let myself inside.

"Woah."

The place immediately had a homier feel than the hotel room I'd been taken to. Inside there were family photos on the walls, and something smelled delicious in the kitchen. I made my way there and peeked at the crockpot that was bubbling away. *What's he making?* I was tempted to take off the top and inspect it, but I forced myself to leave it alone. I moved past the kitchen.

Down the hallway was a bathroom and a guest room, or at least I guessed that's what it was. The room was bare except for a bed, dresser, and television set, but there was nothing personal there. I took a set of wrought iron stairs up to the second floor and found a bedroom. Attached to it was an office.

"Bingo."

I let myself into his office and rifled through his papers. What I was looking at looked legit. Building projects, an architecture firm, a development start-up. All legitimate businesses to hide the shady shit that they did. But it wasn't going to get me anything.

I walked to the computer and booted it up. A box asked for a password. Immediately, I dialed Chelsea.

"Yo," she said. "You in?"

"Yeah." I sat down and pulled out the USB she'd given me. "What do I do again?"

"Easy. Plug in the USB and restart the computer. Enter the BIOS by pressing F2 or the delete key. Under Boot options, set removable devices with boot sequence priority over the hard drive. Save the settings and reboot the computer."

I blinked at the computer. "What the fuck did you just say to me?"

She cackled. "Okay, hang with me. I'll walk you through it."

I did as she said, moving step by step. When the

computer came back on, the password was disabled. I logged on and browsed through his files.

"Don't worry about looking. You won't know what to do. Just clone the hard drive."

"How long is this going to take?" I asked.

"Depends on the size of the hard drive. The bigger it is, the longer it'll take."

My stomach twisted into a knot. Great. I was sitting in Enzo's apartment and had no idea when I was going to be able to get out of there. I leaned back in the computer chair and looked around.

"So, who is this guy anyway?"

"A bad man," I answered.

"Yeah? Well, why did you look at him like that when we were at Blu?"

"Like what?" I asked.

"Like you wanted to put his whole dick in your mouth and swallow."

Groaning, I pushed myself to my feet. "Shut up."

"Don't try to get out of the conversation. Answer the question, Texas. If he's so bad, why did you look at him like you *wanted* him to come down and talk to you? Like you wanted to be chased," she said, dragging the word out.

My jaw clicked. "The only thing I want to do is put him behind bars."

I walked out of the office and made my way down the hall. There was a picture of three boys. I wondered if they were the Vitale brothers.

"And once he's locked away, he won't be my problem."

She whistled. "Ah, I get it. He's the bad boy. You're the good guy. It's a match made in hell, but lust made in heaven," she sighed wistfully. "It's the perfect setup, really."

"You've been watching too many romance movies again."

"There's absolutely no such thing. I'm getting another call. Do you still need me?"

I shook my head. "Nah. I know how to do the rest."

"Good luck with your bad boy."

"Fuck off."

I hung up to the sound of her laughter. Walking through the rest of his place, I searched every nook and cranny. Enzo had a lot of books. They were stacked on shelves, lying on tables, and placed haphazardly in corners where he'd clearly run out of space. There was a new bookcase sitting on the floor, half put together. I ran my fingers over the clean, dark wood and continued to walk around.

Enzo's place was... cozy. Big, but comfortable. I could see myself curling up on a couch here or sitting at the kitchen table with a cup of coffee. I froze as the thought went through my mind. *What the fuck am I thinking? I don't belong here.*

Right, this was the home of the man that I was getting ready to send to prison for a very, very long time. I turned on my heels, ignoring the stupid fantasies that raged and returned to the office. The progress bar was still slowly filling.

I had no choice but to leave again and explore more. From what I could see, I learned things about Enzo; he preferred Jazz and was interested in instruments. There was no tv in his bedroom like there was in mine, but there were more books. In the closet was a range of expensive suits, but in his dresser were comfortable clothes that were soft to the touch.

I looked under his bed and spotted a shoe box. I dragged it out. Popping off the top, I glanced inside. There were pictures inside. Some of them were normal photos of pets, family, and birthdays long gone by. But as I dug through the box, I froze.

There was Enzo with a man who looked somewhat like me. Same dark hair and bright eyes that were gray instead of blue, but he was smiling so hard at the camera. Enzo looked stoic, but there was something in his eyes that looked like joy.

I continued to shuffle through the photos one by one. They turned from cute and sweet to sexy and wild. I quickly moved past those until the photos fell from my hands.

There, the last photo in the group, was the man from before. His face was bloody, one eye swollen shut as blood dripped from his mouth. There was a pleading look on his face and Enzo's hand was in frame, holding his chin gently. I would know that ring on his finger anywhere.

My stomach lurched as the truth dawned on me. Bile rose in the back of my throat. I scrambled up and raced for the bathroom. My knees slammed against cold tile, and I tossed the toilet seat up just in time to spew my dinner into it. It came up in chunks, gagging me and making my eyes water.

Enzo had killed his lover.

I spit until the last remnants of sickness were gone before I dragged myself to my feet. Once the toilet was flushed, I shuffled over to the sink and turned on the water. I drank directly from the faucet, water running over my mouth and rinsing out the rancid taste that clung to my tongue. I snatched up the bottle of mouthwash, swishing it around to dispel the grossness that coated my mouth.

Enzo Vitale killed his lover.

I knew it as much as I knew the sky was blue, and I paid too much in fucking taxes. Determination coursed through my veins. I stormed back to the bedroom and spread the photos out until I found the happy ones. I snapped pictures of them all and shoved the phone back into my pocket.

I was going to find out who that man was and confirm what I already knew. A small, niggling part of my brain screamed it wasn't true. That I would find the guy alive and well in the city. But the realistic part of me *knew*.

Carefully, I placed everything back in its original spot as best I could before I shoved the shoe box underneath the bed again. I stalked to the office to check the progress. Eighty-seven percent copied. Thirteen more to go.

"Oh shit, this thing is heavy!"

My heart stopped. I stared at the office door as I heard the voices speaking below. Slowly, I walked over and peeked through the crack in it.

"Why do you need another bookcase? You haven't even put that one together," a man complained, his Italian accent clear.

"I'm putting it together tonight," Enzo answered. "So I wanted another to work on when I'm done."

"Goddamn, you're weird," the man countered. "My idea of a good night is fucking and drinks, and yours is building a bookcase." He paused. "Is it because you're distracting yourself from a certain cop?"

There was silence. "I don't want to talk about that."

"Have you been keeping an eye on him at least?"

"Of course," Enzo said. "He went to that girl's house tonight, and they tend to stay together for several hours. I'll go by his place tonight and make sure he's there."

My body broke out in a cold sweat. Enzo knew I was a cop. Had he been watching me from the start? My heart dropped into my stomach, and I gripped it through my shirt. Shit. He knew who I was all along.

"Fine," the man answered. "Just make sure you're doing

what Benito says, or he'll be on both our asses." He grunted. "I'm getting out of here. You take care of that last cop?"

"Yeah, Ramada," he answered. "Found him on our casino boat and took care of him."

I felt like I was going to pass out. Ramada? It couldn't be the one from my precinct, right? I felt like the Earth was shifting beneath me. Enzo being a bad guy wasn't news, but it was still shocking to *hear* them talk about ending human life so casually.

"Good job," the man said. "Get some rest, okay? Night, Enzo."

"Night, Gin."

The front door closed, and my throat squeezed. I shuffled back to the computer and found the copy was at ninety-five percent. It would have to be good enough. I yanked it out and restarted the computer. It was quiet when I approached the stairs, and I waited.

Carefully, I walked down. Enzo was nowhere in sight as my heart pounded in my chest. *Maybe he stepped out with his brother?* I had to find some way to get downstairs and out of the building without them seeing me. Slowly, I walked to the door only to stop like a deer in headlights when it started to open.

"Enzo, I forgot my goddamn keys," Gin bellowed.

Something hard slammed into me, and I flew back into the kitchen. I crashed to the floor, and Enzo stood there, his eyes wild as he stared down at me. He shoved a finger against his lips, shook his head, and walked away.

"You left them by the front door," he said. "Try this table."

My heart sped up so fast I couldn't breathe. Did Enzo just protect me? His brother hadn't seen me, is that what he was after? The brothers talked, the keys jingled when they were found, and I couldn't stop feeling the urge to puke again.

"Okay, okay, I'm going," Gin said. "Stop pushing!"

"I'm ready to be alone," Enzo growled.

The door shut, and I pulled myself to my feet before I stuffed the USB drive into my shoe. I straightened up as Enzo rounded into the kitchen and slammed me against the counter.

"What the fuck are you doing in my house? How did you even find this place?" he demanded.

I swallowed thickly, but no words came. What the hell was I going to tell him that would get me out of his place in one piece with the evidence I needed? I looked into his eyes and drew on my years of being a lying, manipulative junkie.

"I missed you."

Eleven
Enzo

MY BLOOD RUSHED, AND PINPRICKS DANCED ALONG MY forearms and to my fingers wrapped around Tex's throat.

I missed you.

His words wrapped around me like a snake does to its prey, squeezing me until I felt as if I couldn't suck in air.

Why was he here? I knew the answer to that, and yet I refused to acknowledge it. Pain blossomed behind my eyes as a headache built. My fingers tightened around his throat out of reflex, and his eyes widened. Instantly my body responded, but I stayed still, refusing to give in to the constant pull between us.

My head tilted as my brows lifted. "What?"

Tex audibly swallowed his Adam's apple, caressing my palm. "I missed you."

It was too much going on for me to decipher what he

truly meant. Was he lying? Did he miss me, or was there something else?

Tex attempted to get up and I slammed him back against the cabinet, daring him with my eyes to try again.

He went still. "What? So it's okay for you to break into my place, but I can't do the same?"

"No."

Tex's brows dipped. "That's bullshit."

He didn't try and move or force my hand off his neck. It was a good call. I wasn't sure what I'd be liable to do if he had.

"I make the rules." I pressed my fingers against his flesh before loosening my hold once more. "Am I clear?"

Tex's breathing was erratic and the closer I leaned toward him the better he smelled. I got lost for a moment in his blue eyes. I'd been right to compare them to glass because Tex was going to cut me.

"I never agreed to that," Tex squeezed out.

"I don't recall asking."

We grew closer with every word that spilled between us. I doubted Tex even noticed he'd pushed himself away from the counter and was gravitating toward me. It was like we were magnets unable to fight the pull. The world had made us oil and fire, a combination that should never be mixed.

"Enzo."

My name on his lips was like a freshly sharpened knife sliding through flesh. Why? I'd made sure not to get attached to anyone. One night with Tex, and I was hooked. *Benito is going to be pissed off.*

The thought of my brother was like ice-cold water in the face and I pulled back before our bodies fully touched.

"You shouldn't have come," I said.

"Thanks for missing me too." Tex pouted.

Had I missed him? I knew he took up every thought in my head. Tex was a constant even in my dreams. I woke up wanting to touch him. Gin had called it; my obsession was dangerous.

I said nothing as I patted him down and took his phone and keys.

"Hey."

"Don't," I ground out.

I tossed everything on the marble countertops. The keys slid into the sink, and I didn't bother picking them up. I was too focused on Tex.

I took another step back as I tried to think of what to do. Asking him what he'd heard weighed heavy on my tongue, but the answer might result in me having to kill him. I pressed my lips together, refusing to ask the questions I needed to.

Tex fidgeted under my stare. "So that was your brother. I can kind of see the resemblance." His gaze flickered over to the keys and phone before landing on me once more.

Don't try it.

"We have different mothers." I pinched the bridge of my nose as something close to irritation and confusion banged in my head.

Giancarlo had been seconds away from seeing Tex. If my brother had caught sight of him? I doubted I could have kept him from killing Tex. He would have known Tex had broken into my place, which meant we were compromised. There was only one course of action; kill the threat. *Family first.*

"I can just go. You said you wanted to be al—"

My hand shot out and wrapped around Tex's throat once more and I tightened it.

"Or I can stay for a bit."

My hand instinctively relaxed, and the tightness in my stomach eased. He'd stay. Tex wouldn't end up causing a disaster, and my hand wouldn't be forced. I met his big blue eyes and there was fear there but unlike before there was no arousal accompanying it.

I pulled my hand back and stepped away from him.

"Go sit down," I ordered, pointing to the living room.

Tex moved around me, each step cautious.

"Don't do anything stupid, Tex."

I moved over to the fridge and pulled out the pitcher of water. I poured both of us a glass and carried it into the living room just as Tex sat down. His back was ramrod straight, and his gaze kept moving toward the exit. I sighed as I sat the glasses on the coasters resting on the coffee table.

"Water."

Text stared at it, and I sat down next to him. There was space left between us. "I told you already I prefer you to be aware."

He nodded and reached for the glass. We sat there in silence, the tension rising with every second. My fingers tapped along the glass, and my toes wiggled in my socks. Everything felt off, and my world was upside down. Each breath felt like it was grating against my throat and I had the dangerous urge to scratch at the flesh on my neck. Maybe then the weird sensation every time I breathed would stop.

"You have a lot of books," Tex said, popping the bubble around me.

He was probably talking at regular volume, but it sounded like he held a megaphone to my ears to speak. I flinched back and recovered quickly, straightening once more. The hum of all the appliances was getting louder, buzzing in my ears, and I held my glass tighter. The coolness did nothing to help with the heat attempting to bake me alive.

"Enzo?" Tex's face appeared before me, and I blinked slowly, but It was all too much. My mouth stayed shut as I stared at him, mentally screaming at him to shut up and sit down.

I needed everything to be turned off.

He reached for me, and I kept still, although it was the last thing I wanted. Tex's hand stopped just short of touching me and dropped. He looked around and picked up the bag of tools.

"Uh, want to put the shelves together?" he asked.

Why isn't he running? Now would be the perfect time while I was trapped in my head. I reached out for the tool bag, making sure not to touch him.

"I'll start on this one," Tex said.

I nodded. It was the most I could do as I sat back in front of the bookcase I'd been working on earlier. Reading over the steps and following them soothed me. The noise around me quieted down and to my relief, Tex said nothing else. It was as if he was a piece of furniture in my apartment, and I didn't have to give him a second thought.

Time ticked by, and I lost myself in my movements. The fire in my brain eased, and the room came back into focus. The bookshelf was done, and I was already halfway through filling it up with books.

I glanced over at Tex. He stared at the books in his hand.

"That's wrong." I pointed at the books he was haphazardly putting on the shelf.

Tex sighed. "Don't tell me you want them alphabetical?"

"No." I moved to him and noticed how closely he was observing me. "Each author and the series by which one I enjoyed the most."

He slowly blinked at me. "Wait, you've actually read all of these books?"

I nodded, grabbed the ones he had put on the shelf already, and moved them down to the bottom.

"Even the romance books?" His brows nearly kissed his hairline.

"Is that so hard to believe?"

He nodded. "You seem more like the historical fiction kind of guy."

"I have a few."

Tex made a face. "You know you come off nerdy and not at all dangerous, especially when you're talking about books."

I passed over a stack of books organized already. Our fingers brushed against each other, and tingles traveled down my arm and to my cock. "But you know that isn't true."

Tex stiffened as I placed the books in his waiting arms. Our eyes met, and I was no closer to making the decision I knew I needed to make. My stomach twisted in knots, making it uncomfortable to move around.

"I... um... Enzo—"

I shook my head. "Finish." I forced my feet to move and went to complete the other bookshelf.

We worked in silence. Now that I was more aware, I kept feeling Tex's eyes on me. I waited for him to do or say something, but he continued putting the books on the shelf. Another second passed before I was done with the silence between us.

I gave into the draw and moved while Tex was reading the back of a book. I twisted Tex around and shoved him down. "Fuck." He lost balance, and I grabbed his hand to steady him.

I said the first thing that came to mind. Tex had acted out. It was my job to remind him he should have stayed in his place. "Do I need to remind you who makes the rules?"

Tex's mouth opened and closed like a fish out of water, and I couldn't contain the smirk on my face. I flicked open the button on my pants and lowered the zipper. Tex's eyes followed every single movement. Instead of fighting me, he leaned closer.

Even now, when he should be running for the hills, he was at my mercy, reacting to everything I did to him. My cock twitched as need swirled in my lower abdomen.

Tex's impressive chest was rising rapidly with his breaths. His tongue poked out and swiped over his tempting mouth. "Y-yes."

I freed my cock. I didn't have to say anything as Tex opened his mouth and swallowed me whole. A moan caught at the back of my throat as pleasure plowed through me like a bulldozer.

My fingers in his hair, I cupped the back of his head and pushed my cock down deeper as ecstasy coursed through me. My toes curled and a throaty moan resonated around us. It took me far too long to realize it had come from me. I couldn't take my eyes off him. The way his lips stretched around my length or the way his gorgeous blue eyes watered.

I rocked forward, chasing the pleasure as it built higher and higher. Tex's moans around my cock sent vibrations right to my balls, making them tingle.

I pressed my thumb on the corner of his mouth and worked a finger next to my cock making Tex's mouth stretch wider. He stared up at me with an intoxicated look in his eyes.

My climax took me by surprise. I groaned, "Mine." Fell from my lips in a whisper.

Tex moaned loudly, his eyes fluttering closed as I filled his mouth with cum. I didn't have to instruct him to swallow. Tex's throat worked as he swallowed every drop before opening his eyes.

His hot tongue ran over my softening cock, sending little shocks dancing along my flesh as he cleaned me off. "You're tempting me to do it again."

Tex's lips quirked up in a devilish smirk. I wanted nothing more than to slam him down and take him apart. I thought he was my type, but Tex was more than that. He didn't just meet the requirements physically but in every aspect.

I wasn't the only dangerous one here.

He put my cock away, and I let him stand up. I didn't want to kill him. This time when I cupped Tex's face, I didn't allow him to pull away. I hardly ever kissed, but it had been the only thing taking up residence in my mind after our last encounter.

Our lips pressed together and a slow warmth erupted from our mouths and blanketed my entire body. I pulled him closer and swiped my tongue over the seam of his lips. I wanted a taste. No, I needed it like I needed air.

Tex opened up for me, and I dove in without a drop of hesitation. I tasted myself on his tongue, but past that, it was all Tex. I drew him closer as our tongues tangled together. He attempted to dominate mine, but I bit his tongue. Tex moaned as he gave in.

Why can't this be us? My eyes shut for only a brief second. I didn't want to stop kissing him. I didn't want to let him go just yet. A part of me screamed that Tex was mine. If I locked him away right now, he wouldn't be able to hurt the family and then I wouldn't be forced to end his life. I could play with him whenever I pleased, and I knew Tex would like it. He responded to me so beautifully.

My lungs burned with the need for air, and my head started to spin. I reluctantly pulled back. Tex sucked in a breath, his pupils blown and a hint of blush on his cheeks.

I let my emotions run rampant for another fleeting second before I shoved them all down in a box. I reached up and grabbed a fistful of his shirt, and yanked him back down on the ground. His knees clashed with the floor once more, and he grunted.

The outline of his dick was tempting, and I lifted my foot and pushed it down over his clothed cock. Tex's eyes widened as he licked his kiss-swollen lips.

"Tex…" I leaned forward and nipped his ear while applying more pressure on his cock. A whimper blessed my ears, and I basked in the moment. "Come upstairs or get out." My nails scraped over his scalp as I tightened my hold. "You leave…" I couldn't bring myself to say it, but we both knew what would eventually have to happen. "If you do, don't do anything stupid." *Please.*

I released him and took a step away from him. I stared at Tex for another second before I headed toward the stairs.

Please don't make me kill you.

Twelve

TEX

Was I pathetically lonely? Or did I have a death wish?

I pondered which was the correct answer as I stared at Enzo's front door. Leaving was the only intelligent decision, and yet my feet were planted on the floor. I could still taste him on my tongue, a delicious mix of salt and danger that made me want to go back for seconds.

The evidence is in my shoe. I need to get out of here and check it out.

Upstairs, I heard the sound of music starting up, and I frowned. Water ran, and I could imagine him slipping out of his clothes and stepping into a steaming shower. The look on his face when he left had been conflicted and...

Am I imagining shit, or was he upset?

Something had definitely come over him before. All I could think was to distract him with the project of the book-shelves, but something had happened. For that short moment, he wasn't a man who had murdered a cop that I knew. He was lost and unsure.

It's not like Ramada wasn't a crooked cop anyway.

Everyone knew about him and what he had his fingers in. When it came to lining his pockets, he was the best at it. *Am I justifying Enzo killing a man?*

It was slippery ground to walk on.

I walked over to the bottom of the stairs and glanced up. My stomach tightened and something laced through me. I felt the cold shiver of fear. I didn't want to leave Enzo alone, but I felt just as afraid to go to him. What if I never recovered? What if whatever twisted obsession I had became full-blown psychosis?

My foot lifted, and the moment it landed on the stair, I was speed walking. Against all my instincts that screamed go back, I opened the shower door and watched as water rolled down his skin. He gazed at me, and something in me melted.

Shit. Do I have daddy issues?

Chelsea was right; I was the good guy. He was the bad boy. And I was falling for it hook, line, and sinker. I kicked off my shoes, knocking them to the side before his hand curled around my shirt. Enzo yanked me into the stall, my back slammed against the wall, and his lips devoured mine.

I forgot how to breathe. My sense of reason was long gone, replaced with a burning need that tore through me. Enzo's tongue swiped against the seam of my lips. I opened for him, panting as my tongue slid against his. Enzo's hands gripped my shirt, tugging at it as a growl tumbled from his lips. That sound was enough to make my cock jump and desperately ache to be touched.

At that exact moment, Enzo's hand wrapped around my length, making my knees turn to jelly. I was easily bigger than him, but he had a way of making me crumble like I was nothing more than his toy. Every inch of me burst into flames as he tugged at my clothes, desperate and anxious.

"Enzo," I groaned as his mouth moved to my throat. Sharp teeth sank into my neck, and I swore as his fingers dug into my flesh at the same time. "Fuck."

Trying to strip Enzo of his control was always fun, but it was like he had none now. He tossed my clothes off, throwing them to the side before he grabbed my wrist and spun me around. My chest kissed the wall, my hips were yanked back, and I forgot how to breathe. A finger slipped into my hole, making my eyes widen as a whimper fell from my lips.

"Enzo, what's wrong with you?" I asked. My stomach clenched, and I realized the truth. I was worried about him. "Are you losing your mind or some— Shit!"

He didn't say a word. Every move Enzo made was deliberate and rough, like he wanted to tear me apart. Something wet slipped between my cheeks. I glanced over my shoulder. Enzo held a bottle of something, squeezing it between my cheeks with a determined look on his face. I peered closer and saw aloe vera. *He's so serious.*

"You're freaking me out a little."

Enzo rubbed his cock against my hole and grunted as he slammed inside of me. I saw stars. My knees tried to buckle, but he wrapped his arm around my waist and kept me in place as he began to rock inside of me. His breath feathered against my ear.

"You're mine," he growled.

Flutters erupted throughout my body. He'd said that when we were downstairs, that I was his. An anxious ball of energy twisted through me. I'd thought it was a spur-of-the-moment, *my cock belongs in your mouth, mine.* But glancing back at him, seeing that dark look in his eyes, I wasn't so sure. Was he really trying to claim me?

No, no way in hell. This is the last time I'm doing this.

It was easy enough to say that, but with Enzo pounding inside of me and his deep, growling groans echoing in my ears, it was hard to believe it. No one had ever felt so good. It was like his cock was made for me, perfectly equipped to push me over the edge and keep me crawling back for more.

"Fuck, I can't take this," Enzo groaned.

I reached between my thighs and stroked my cock. "Then cum inside of me," I said, immediately wanting to slap myself. *But I want it.* "Fill me up, Enzo."

He pushed inside of me deeper, rubbing against my prostate. My eyes rolled up. It felt like Enzo's hands were everywhere all at once. Nails scraped down my back, fingers tugged at my pierced nipples, teeth dragged over my shoulder. Enzo was on another planet, his face taking on a dusty shade of pink as he reveled in using my ass.

I shivered as I gazed at him. Feeling him inside of me without a barrier between us was so much more intoxicating. The more he thrust, the more my head became foggy. Some stupid part of me thought about experiencing this all the time. Having someone who couldn't keep their hands off of me, someone who would be obsessed with me until the end of time.

It's too good to be true.

My stomach dropped, and I felt the panic starting to rise. I needed to escape. But I was too far gone, and so was Enzo. He turned my head when I tried to look away, holding my gaze as his lips parted. It was like he wanted to say something. However, he sealed his lips, grabbed my wrist and fucked me like he was never going to see me again.

I came to the sound of flesh slapping against flesh,

spraying his wall with a stream of cum as I yelled his name. Enzo rested his forehead against my shoulder. Even when he was done, we stayed together, panting and holding onto each other while water rained down on our bodies.

It was as if neither one of us wanted to move. Enzo wrapped his arms around me, and I knew the second we stepped apart the illusion would shatter and the real world would come crashing back in.

———

"Here."

Enzo offered me a towel as I sat on the edge of his bed. I took it, pushing it through my hair to dry off the strands. My gaze moved up to watch Enzo as he walked around his bedroom. He wasn't in a hurry to get dressed, that much was clear. I watched an errant bead of water travel down the curve of his ass, and I sucked in a breath.

Fuck. He looks so good it should be illegal.

When he looked at me, I glanced away. *I need to get the hell out of here.* When I looked back, Enzo was still staring at me.

"I should go," I said.

Enzo nodded.

Neither of us moved.

The man was going to turn me into a crazy person. Every chance he got, he made me question everything I knew about him, the cold, hard facts in his files. I could almost see him as a different man. Someone with a dangerous edge, sure. But not the murderous psychopath he was.

I can't take him staring at me anymore.

"What was that? Earlier?" I asked. "You kind of just... froze."

"Downstairs?" Enzo asked.

"Yeah."

He shrugged. "It's nothing important. Sometimes I just get..." He trailed off, his eyes narrowing as he stared at the floor and then back at me as if he was only just remembering I was there. "It's not important," he finished. He paused for a while. "Are you staying?"

I blinked at Enzo. *Did he just invite me to stay the night?* I didn't know what to say to that. In another life, I would have happily stayed in his bed, hoping for another round or two. As I gazed at Enzo, though, I knew I had to get out of there.

Standing up, I folded the towel without thinking and placed it on his bed. "I should really get going. I have work."

Work that you know about. You know I'm a cop. Hell, maybe you even know I'm investigating you.

The words hung between us in the air, unspoken. A blanket of tension covered us both. Enzo's expression flickered for a brief second, and I saw a look of... was that disappointment? Disdain? Anger? The world shifted beneath my feet, and the immediate urge to make the situation right flared.

He killed his lover. And he killed a cop. Probably more than one in his lifetime. Think straight, Tex. There is nothing between us.

Right. The only way for Enzo Vitale to help me was for him to wind up behind bars and for me to finally make detective. *That* was my dream. My only reason for existing was to prove that I could do what my father did, but so much better. To show him and everyone else that I was no longer the screw-up they all knew I used to be.

Clothes flew into my face. I grabbed at them, and Enzo

nodded to the clothes he'd tossed at me. Mine were still soaking wet and lying in a balled-up heap in the shower. I had no choice but to slip into his black sweats and the soft, blue t-shirt. He gave me a jacket as well, and I slipped it on as he stood there, staring at me.

"Enzo—"

"You can see yourself out," he said, his tone clipped. When I turned away, he called my name. I glanced back at him. "Make sure you don't show up here again."

Red hot anger flashed through me. I kept my mouth shut, nodded, and exited his room before I said something that would get me killed. I snagged my shoes, shoving my feet inside. Something poked me in the sole. I removed my sneaker and glanced inside. *USB port.* Somehow, I had forgotten all about it.

Bile rose in my throat, mixing with the anger. There was no telling what I was going to find on that thing. I made a beeline for the door, resolving myself to find out the truth.

No matter how much it hurt.

Thirteen
TEX

THE STEADY RUMBLING OF PENELOPE'S PURRING WAS USUALLY the most soothing thing in the world. Tonight it simply grated on my nerves, putting me even more on edge as I sat on my bed going through my father's files. Penelope's tail swished, knocking into a folder and scattering paper across the comforter.

"Okay, that's it. I love you, but you have to go." I scooped him up, and he laid his massive paws on my shoulder, kneading me through the jacket I still wore. "How about a treat and some music?"

I carried Penelope to the kitchen and took out a can of wet food. He wound around my ankles, meowing at me so loudly it made me laugh. I sat his bowl down and turned on the TV. Soft, quiet music played as I turned off the lights, leaving only the soft glow of the nightlights I'd installed in case Penelope ever got afraid of the dark.

Yeah, that was stupid as hell. My friends pointed that out to me plenty of times, assuring me he could see in the dark, but it still made me feel better to know the lights were there for him.

I gave him a few long, firm pets, and his purring grew. Smiling, I batted his tail back and forth until I knew I couldn't procrastinate anymore. I stood up and sighed.

"Okay, no going back. I need to go through those files. Be good, Pen."

He ignored me as he pigged out on his food. That rapidly growing ache was back in my chest. I rubbed at it, trying to erase the oncoming bout of loneliness that used to lead to another bender. Penelope was amazing; he kept me alive. But sometimes it felt like I was still missing something.

I don't have time to ponder my depressing ass life.

I settled back in on the bed and returned to searching the files. There was a lot more information than I thought. Small things; hangouts, known associates, history. Most of it was probably useless, but I was praying for a needle in a haystack.

My phone buzzed, and I snatched it up.

"Yo," Chelsea said, her voice heavy. "Good to know you're not dead. I might have checked your security cameras when you got home."

"Why am I not surprised?"

"Are you okay?"

"No," I said truthfully. "A line of coke never sounded so good in my life."

"Don't do it," she said softly. "I know it's hard when things go upside down, but you know where it'll send you. Besides, you don't want to lose your job and have to start all over. Should I come over?"

I smiled at Chelsea's concern. We were old friends for a

reason. She was one of the few people who knew all my dirty little secrets, and I knew hers. Whenever I was about to slip up, Chelsea was the first person I called to keep me sober.

"Tex?"

"I don't know. Maybe you could—" My fingers slipped over the papers on my bed, and I paused. I sifted through them until I uncovered a familiar face. "Woah."

"Woah what?" she asked. "Tex?"

"Nothing," I said quickly. I searched the page. *Brycen Grennan.* Enzo's former lover. My stomach twisted into a tight knot. If I kept going at this rate, I would develop an ulcer. Then I really would be just like my father. "I think I'm okay for tonight," I told Chelsea. "I need to sleep if I'm going to figure this out tomorrow."

"Figure out what?"

"Who the fuck I'm dealing with."

I KNOCKED ON THE DOOR AGAIN, PEELING GREEN PAINT sticking to my knuckles. Rubbing my fist against my jeans, I froze when the door cracked open half an inch. An eye looked me up and down, and the smell of cigarette smoke wafted into my face.

"What?" a woman asked.

"Are you Abigail?"

"And who are you?"

I took out my badge. "Officer Caster. I wanted to ask you a few questions about your brother, Brycen Grennan."

"Why? I've already answered every damn question I can think of. Unless you found him, what's the point?"

I put on my best official-sounding voice tinged with

authority and sympathy. "It'll only take a few minutes. Please, ma'am."

She sighed and shut the door. The sound of a chain sliding off echoed in the empty hallway before she stood before me. Abigail looked like Brycen. They had the same hair and eyes. Dark circles were beneath her eyes, and a cigarette dangled from her fingers.

"Come in."

I followed her into the apartment. We sat down, and she tapped her cigarette against a heavy glass ashtray.

"I would offer you coffee, but I don't want this to turn into a whole visit," she said shortly. "Ask your questions and go."

"Right," I leaned back in the creaky, metal chair. "I was hoping you could tell me about Brycen. About what happened to him."

"You don't know?" she asked.

"I would like to hear it from someone who went through it."

That and I didn't exactly know. I'd done my research the night before and was able to find a few facts from the internet. However, I couldn't waltz into the station and go researching things. Everything was monitored. If I was caught looking up stuff I had no business sticking my nose into, I would be fired and could even be looking at charges. No, it was better to do this on my own.

"Brycen is... was... my younger brother," she said shortly. "He was doing great in life until he hooked up with that animal."

"Animal?"

"Enzo Vitale," she spat. "The whole family is filled with criminal thugs." She laughed dryly. "I used to be afraid to talk about them, but I don't care anymore. My brother might have been a lot of things, but he was good to me. To our family. Even if he drove us all insane."

I frowned. "What do you mean?"

"Brycen liked to run off. He was wild, you know? Partying, drinking, falling into bed with the wrong kind of men. I always warned him it was going to get him killed..." She trailed off, a tear rolling down her cheek before she wiped it away with her arm.

"And it did."

"Well, he's presumed dead at this point," she muttered. "According to the cops, he's simply a missing person, but I know the truth. My brother is dead, and Enzo killed him."

A shiver down my spine. "Why do you think that?"

"He used to send flowers here after it happened. There was never any card or anything, but I knew they were from him. Sometimes I would see him across the street, staring at the apartment. Or he would call and hang up without saying anything. He creeps me out," she said. She took a long, slow drag off of her cigarette. "I don't know what Brycen got mixed up in, but whatever it is got him killed."

"I'm sorry," I said quietly.

She shrugged. "What does sorry do? Men like the Vitales, they don't care about anyone but themselves. Killing people is part of what they do. I just wish my asshole brother had listened to me when I said that to him," she sniffled hard, her breathing a stutter. "Is that all?"

I reached across the table and laid a hand on hers. "Could I look at his room?"

Abigail laughed. "What more could you want from me?" she snapped. "You come in here dredging up history that's over two years old, and now you want to search his room? Well, guess what? There's nothing in it. I donated what I could, sold the rest, and anything that's left is in storage.

Now," she yanked her hand away from mine as her chair scraped against the linoleum floor, "get out of my house. I'm done. Unless you're telling me that the son of a bitch and his family are either in jail or dead, do not come back here."

I nodded. "Thank you for your time."

Abigail escorted me to the door without another word. As soon as the door closed, I glanced over my shoulder at it. I could feel her eyes on me through the peephole, so I kept walking.

I waited until I was back in my car before calling Chelsea. She picked up, her voice cautiously optimistic as she greeted me with her usual "yo."

"I need you to do your thing," I said. "Abigail Grennan. She has a storage unit somewhere, and I want to check it out. Can you find it for me?"

"Faster than you think," she said. "We should meet up for dinner."

"Not hungry," I muttered, ignoring the growling in my stomach. "I need some time to think."

"Tex, you don't sound good," she said, her voice strained. "Please, let's meet up for dinner, and we can talk about whatever's going on. Maybe I can help you figure it out."

I loved Chelsea, but I wanted to be on my own for now. My mind couldn't sift through the details if I had to talk to someone and put on a brave face, pretending I wasn't scrambled and lost. And so far, I was very lost.

Brycen Grennan was presumed missing, but his sister thought he was dead. Was he? Or was he simply gone? Abigail said he liked to run away, to disappear. Two years was a long time to wander, but I would, too, if I had a mobster on my ass. Especially if it was after that photo was taken where Brycen looked as if he'd been beaten up pretty badly. Maybe he was smart enough to go and stay gone.

"Tex. I'm worried about you," Chelsea said. "Whatever this is, you should drop it and move on."

"Have you reviewed the hard drive yet?"

"No," she muttered. "I'm trying, but a lot of it is in code. He was smart enough to encrypt damn near everything or have someone else do it."

"How long do you think it'll take you to get through it?"

"I'm not sure if I should."

I paused and gripped the steering wheel. "What?"

"You're getting obsessed," she said evenly. "I don't want to be part of the reason you spiral."

I pinched the bridge of my nose. "Just do it, Chelsea. Or give it back, and I'll find someone who can do their fucking job."

"Fine. Jerk."

She hung up, and I stared at the screen. Great. On top of feeling sick, I felt like an asshole too. I thumped my head against the steering wheel. *I'll apologize to her later.* I was so close to figuring out what was going on, but I needed more. Learning about Brycen was a pet project. I had no idea if I could pin it on Enzo. Or if it would be enough. I had to keep digging.

I was so close to making detective I could taste it. One big case, and I would be there. I rolled my shoulders, trying to ease the tension that made them tight. But it stayed there like a stone making my chest constrict and my skin feel tight.

I could be on the verge of getting everything I wanted. So, why did it feel so empty?

Fourteen
Enzo

THE SMELL OF CIGARETTES WEIGHED HEAVILY IN THE AIR AS I stood by the dock. Even the salty smell of the ocean couldn't force it away. My eyelids fluttered closed. I needed a second to get myself together. I was doing that a lot lately, trying to grab onto the control I prided myself on. But the moment I relaxed, the bluest eyes appeared before me framed by thick black lashes on a clean-shaven face. A sharp jawline that was perfect for nibbling on and soft pink lips that tilted up in a daring smile.

"Open the crate," Benito said.

My eyes flashed open at Benito's voice, and I forced it all down. If my brother noticed how out of it I was, history would repeat itself. I couldn't go through that again.

Three of our men jammed crowbars under the thick wood lid and cracked it open. The cover thunked down on the ground next to the box as the contents were revealed. Or lack of.

"Fuck," Gin groaned. Our eyes locked for a second before we both looked at Benito. He stood over the empty crate that was supposed to be holding the shipment of guns. Ones that we'd already sold.

"Open all the fucking boxes," Benito said through clenched teeth.

Gin and I picked up a crowbar and headed for the other crates. All the men were out there popping open the boxes. One by one, they were showing up empty. There was only straw.

Gin headed toward me. "What the hell do you think happened?"

I shook my head. Maybe if my mind wasn't scattered and my thoughts constantly bouncing back to a certain cop, I would have an answer.

The sound of a gun being fired echoed around us. We didn't have to rush to know what had happened. I straightened my back and walked over to my brother as one of the men lay on the ground, rocking back and forth as he held his bleeding knee.

"You were in charge of the shipment. I cannot fathom how two hundred assault rifles and unmarked handguns go missing." Benito stood over him, his gun steady as it was aimed at Benjamin's face.

"I don't know," Benjamin squeezed out.

He'd been with us for a while, nearly two years, and he had to know Benito's least favorite words were "I don't know." As if to remind him of that fact, Benito fired the next bullet into his other leg.

Benjamin let out an undignified scream that far surpassed the bang of the gun. He cursed as he clutched both bleeding legs. Blood splattered all over the ground and a few crates nearby. The sight was normal, and everyone stood there watching him as he tried to slow down his bleeding.

The angrier my brother got, the thicker his Italian accent got. "You expect me to believe that shit? Where are my guns?" Benito asked.

He looked at the others standing around, and they each avoided his gaze. *Not good.* My hands twitched. I'd be having fun later tonight. I could picture it now, the blood and screams of the truth finally coming to light. It usually filled me with a cold excitement that would last hours but it felt like nothing more than a fizzle at the base of my spine.

"So no one here knows?" Benito asked.

No one spoke up and Gin Rolled his shoulders back, looking just as angry. It took quite a bit to secure the guns and even more work to make sure they were delivered uninterrupted.

"Boss, I'm telling the—" Benito pulled the trigger, inevitably silencing Benjamin for life. His body slumped back against the ground. His legs fell at awkward angles as the bleeding slowed on its own. No one dared move.

"Anyone want to come up and talk, or is this going to be our night?" Benito asked calmly. His gaze swept over our men. There were a few who looked as if they were ready to bolt at the first chance they got.

"Try it and it will be the last step you take," Gin threatened.

A fuck up is a warehouse being found, but this was deliberate. The amount of money we'd just lost was a heavy blow. First, the warehouse with the drugs, and now this.

"Who was under Benjamin?" Gin asked.

Two men stepped forward. "We were."

Benito put his gun away. "The rest of you clean this shit up. You two, let's have a chat."

They nodded and followed my brother. I caught Benito's gaze and knew to follow behind them. Gin stayed to oversee the cleanup. We wove through countless shipping crates, some belonging to other families. The two in front of me glanced around nervously.

"I wouldn't try it," I said as the one on the right's steps faltered. He glanced over his shoulder, and his eyes widened as if he noticed me for the first time. He audibly swallowed.

"Boss, we only did what Benjamin said. We don't—"

"Good, then this will be a quick chat, and you can go home to your wives," Benito said.

It was a lie. He wasn't letting them out; they'd never see tomorrow's sun. They'd fucked up, and they knew it.

"Really, boss. I've given my whole life to the Vitale family. The organization is all I have."

I tuned out the guy's pleas; it was falling on deaf ears. Benito gave his all to the family and what we'd built, but he didn't tolerate anyone trying to fuck over our family.

The guy on the right twisted his body slightly and if I hadn't been watching since the moment we walked away from the docks, I wouldn't have noticed. As his buddy pleaded their case, he made a run for it.

"Don't kill him," Benito said.

I sighed as I chased after him, the cool New York air crashing against my face. My lungs burned with the frigid air sawing in and out of them as I gave chase.

He turned around with his gun in hand. He was making this harder for himself. I dove to the side just as he squeezed off two shots.

"I don't know anything," he shouted.

Then why are you running? I didn't ask out loud; I'd get to question him later. I waited until I heard him running again before chasing after him. I climbed on top of one of the shipping crates, the ice-cold metal burning my hands as I crawled over the top.

My gaze swept over the area, and I spotted him, his head poking out around a corner, waiting for me to come around. His gun was trained on the spot I would have appeared if I was still on the ground.

I took in a steady breath, raised my gun, and fired off my shot. The bullet cut through the air and landed in his arm. His gun dropped to the ground and clattered. I got up and jumped off the top, crouching as I landed.

I ignored the small ache in my knees. I was getting too old for this shit.

"Fuck, fuck, fuck." He was bent over, holding his arm.

I sauntered over to him, my gun still raised. He lifted his head, and our eyes met before I brought the butt of my gun down against his temple. He slumped over, and three more of our men turned the corner.

"Tie him up and get him to the warehouse."

"Yes, boss." They moved in unison.

I found Benito standing next to his car. "Tell me I don't have to get the entire shipping yard scrubbed."

I shook my head. "Single bullet wound."

He nodded. "Find out everything. Someone is fucking us over."

Gin jogged over to us, a light sheen of sweat coating his skin. "The guy usually on duty around here said he was dismissed multiple times in the past week. By our guys."

Benito swore. "Loyalty mean shit nowadays?"

"We will get this under control, Benito," Gin said.

It was rare Benito ever lost his composure for more than a split second. He took in a measured breath. "I know." He met each of our gazes before getting behind the wheel of his car.

"I just hope it's not a fiasco like two years ago," Gin said.

My stomach turned and I nodded in agreement. He placed his hand on my shoulder.

"We need to get out of here. We've caused enough of a fucking scene. They've derailed the police as much as possible."

The mention of police brought up Tex's face in my mind. Gin whistled.

"Enzo," he said in a warning tone.

"I know."

He stared at me before nodding. I turned on my heels and headed for my car. Before I pulled off, I checked to see where Tex was. I had a single tail on him now.

Tex was working but he was far across town and a relieved sigh slipped free. I needed to get things under control. *Soon.*

I DUG THE SCALPEL UNDER THE NAIL AND MOVED IT BACK AND forth slowly as muffled screams echoed around me. The fingernail came off, strings of blood and flesh sticking to the back of it. It was a decently clean take off. Beads of crimson bubbled up to the surface before running over and dripping onto the floor, joining the growing puddle.

The stench of urine perfumed the air, and I scrunched my nose in disgust. I glanced up at the man at my table. His green eyes were wide and red as he stared back at me, pleading without words.

"I've only gotten halfway through this hand, and you're

already calling it quits?" Disappointment drenched over my words.

He shook and nodded his head. "Still don't know anything."

I smiled. "Then I'll continue."

The other man was strapped to the ceiling. His eyes were dazed as he stared down at me. I could switch between the two going back and forth. The icy tendrils slowed me down, reminding me I didn't have to rush. Answers were what I was after. Once I got them, I was free to do as I pleased.

I removed all of his fingernails from one hand and then the next. I messed up on the pinky as he started to shake on the table. Removing the wet cloth from his mouth, he spluttered and coughed.

"Who are you working with?"

He shook his head. "No one. I swear."

I nodded and moved over to the one hanging from the ceiling. Blood dripped from the bullet wound in his arm. But with it elevated it had slowed tremendously.

My hand collided with his face, but the dazed look stayed in his eyes. I opened the cabinet we kept on hand and picked up the chainsaw at the bottom. It wasn't my favorite, but it worked.

"Wh-what are you doing?" the one on the table stuttered.

I didn't bother answering him as I pressed my finger against the throttle and pulled the cord to start it. The engine kicked to life, and the vibration rattled me down to my toes. If the guy on the table said anything more, I couldn't hear him over the chainsaw.

Stepping forward, I held it up. As if I'd dumped ice water

on him, the man suspended from the ceiling shook. The chains hanging from the ceiling rattled.

"What the fuck!" he shouted for help as he struggled, swinging around.

My fingers went numb the longer I held the chainsaw. I let him swing, but he lost control. His body started to move in a circle. Blood from his wound fell on my white shirt, making a crimson spot appear.

I focused on it for a second, drowning them both out and sinking into the bliss of chaos. Where some felt out of control, I felt normal. It was how I imagine everyone felt every single day, their brains not on fire and steadily trying to destroy them.

A slow smile curved my lips as I stepped forward and held the chainsaw out. He couldn't stop his body's momentum as he swung into the chainsaw. He got stuck, and the screams intensified as the chainsaw started cutting through flesh.

With him hanging, I couldn't get enough pressure to cut through the bone. I pulled the chainsaw free, blinking away the spots of red in my vision. I had to wipe my eyes and glasses clean. Blood gushed out of the wound and I could make out the muscles and bone I hadn't been able to get through.

His body swung back and forth limply. and I didn't need to look up to know life was flickering out of his eyes. I moved over to his friend, letting the chainsaw die down so I could talk to him.

"He was meeting some cop," the one on the table screamed. He shook his head, refusing to look at the other guy. "Please, we didn't know this would happen."

"What did you think would happen?"

"The guy was only supposed to take a crate or two." His

eyes bugged out as I pulled the string on the chainsaw. "Wait. Wait!"

The engine hadn't started, and I stopped letting it recoil back. I cocked a brow.

"I don't have a name." He licked his cracked lips before coughing. "I swear. Please."

"Who was it?"

He shook his head. "No idea. Only saw him once, and he wore a mask."

"In other words, you're no longer useful."

"Wait, I could point him out." He was grabbing at straws.

My head was shaking before he even suggested it. "Impossible to get every cop in New York to line up for you to pick out who you think it might be."

I'd have to dig into all of Benjamin's past work and see where and when money started to go missing, along with products. The chainsaw started up once more, drowning out the shouts and curses.

This is paradise.

Once it was all said and done, I stepped out of the room, cleaning the blood from my glasses as I slipped them on. Blood covered me from head to toe. I didn't need to see my reflection to know what I looked like. A smile stretched my lips as I stood there in the mess of my making. It was the only time everything wasn't overwhelming. No amount of noise, smell, or touch could deprive me of the calmness that coursed through me.

"Enzo," Benito called out.

I didn't jump, the reaction long ago beaten out of me. I turned to look at my brother. He normally never stuck around when I had to torture. A cigarette hung between his index and middle finger. The cherry glowed red before a tendril of smoke curled in the air.

I was so high off the moment of normalcy I hadn't even noticed the smell. Benito pushed off the wall, his weighted gaze rooting me to the spot as he stepped forward. He took another drag as he stopped right in front of me. He was far taller than me, but my brother had never ruled it over me, at least not since we were children. I tilted my head back slightly.

"You still have that picture?"

My stomach clenched, knowing exactly which one he was referring to. I fought to continue meeting his gaze head-on. The normalcy was slipping away before I was ready for it to.

"Yes."

Benito nodded and moved to walk past me. He placed a heavy hand on my shoulder and squeezed. "You know why I made you keep it, don't you?"

"So I wouldn't repeat my mistake."

Benito's hold tightened. "Are you?" I turned to look at my oldest brother. His gaze was unwavering. "Are you repeating your mistakes, Enzo?"

My heart rate slowed as my fingertips went cold. My instant answer should be no. However, Tex's face flashed before me and how I'd let him walk out of my place. I hadn't even checked him over.

"Enzo." Benito's voice dropped an octave. "Non mentirmi, fratello."

My tongue felt heavy in my mouth, and the blood that covered me felt tight. I wanted to wash it all off. The longer I stood there with it on me, the more it felt as if I was in a closet-sized room that was shrinking by the second.

If I told him the truth, Tex would meet the same fate. Or he'd be taken from me, and that thought made breathing hard.

"Focus." Rapid-fire Italian came from Benito.

To me, it sounded like garbled-up words with static being played over it. I opened my mouth to ask what, but that didn't work either. My chest began to burn, and I stood there frozen, unable to talk.

"Breathe, fratello." Benito pressed our foreheads together. "You're my brother, and we will always have each other."

"Familia is everything."

Benito pulled back, and some dry blood clung to his light brown skin. He wasn't bothered by it, but my eyes wouldn't leave the spot until he cleaned it off. He wiped his hand over it, and the pieces fluttered to the ground.

"Do I need to get involved?"

I shook my head. "I won't repeat the mistake."

Benito's shoulders relaxed. "Good." He patted my shoulder before walking toward the exit. He stopped before he stepped out. "Find out who's betraying us."

I would. I just hoped it had nothing to do with Tex.

Fifteen
Enzo

FOUR DAYS, AND I WAS STILL NO CLOSER TO KNOWING WHAT I should do with Tex. I wanted Tex under me at all times, but my wants weren't exactly reality. I knew that more than anyone.

I blew out a puff of air as I leaned against a light pole across the street of the fourth bar Tex had been to. In the time we'd been apart, he hadn't visited Blu once or shown up at my place. I know I told him to never come back but a part of me hoped he wouldn't listen.

The night was nearly over, and the early morning was creeping up. It was two forty-five, and the last bar was already emptying. I kept my gaze fixed across the street, waiting for a certain cop to exit. Four o'clock struck, and my stomach twisted. The bouncer who'd been lounging outside went in. Before I knew what I was doing, I was halfway across the street.

"Wait," I said.

He stopped and glanced my way. "Sorry, we're closed. Go drink at home."

"Emerson, come here," someone inside shouted.

"I'm not here to drink. I'm here to pick up my..." *My what? Toy?* My chest tightened, but the person inside called the bouncer again.

"I have to go. Maybe you missed whoever you're looking for." He attempted to close the door.

I cut the distance between us in two easy strides. With my hand on the door and foot on the ledge, I stopped it from closing.

"I highly doubt that."

He blew out a breath. "It's been a good night. Don't fuck it up. Get out." He stood taller and puffed out his chest.

If he thought he was intimidating me, that was hardly the case. If anything, it was annoying me. The more time he wasted stood between Tex and me.

"Emerson, I've been calling you. We have some guy passed out in the men's bathroom again," a woman said. She turned, and her green eyes widened.

"We're closed. Sorry, come back tonight." She popped a hand on her hip and looked at Emerson.

"I've been trying—"

"The man in the bathroom. I'm here to get him."

Both of them turned to look my way. The burly bouncer's gruff eyebrows dipped. "How would you know it's who you're looking for?"

"Did he text you or something?" the woman asked.

No. I wish he had.

"Black hair, blue eyes, chiseled jaw. His license number zero one two four four six three one."

She shrugged. "Fucking good enough for me. Come get

him." She turned on her heels but stopped just as the bouncer let me in. "His tab." She eyed me from head to toe. I didn't have to be a mind reader to know she'd picked out the designer clothes. I bypassed my gun and pulled out a roll of money. "This should more than cover it. "

Her eyes widened only for a second before she took it. "Yeah, third door down that hall." She pointed and I was already halfway across the small bar. Only two others were cleaning up. They glanced my way but paid me little attention, no doubt rushing to get out of there and back home.

I pushed the door open. Soft snores accompanied the hum of the lights above. The floor was black and covered in unknown substances as I headed toward the last stall. The door wasn't locked as I pushed it open with my toe. There on the floor next to the toilet was Tex. His head hung between his arms, his back pressed against the wall.

The stench of alcohol had nothing to do with being in a bar and everything to do with Tex. The closer I got the stronger the smell wafted off of him. I didn't want to touch anything here.

I kicked Tex's foot. One of his legs slid down, jerking him awake.

"Uh, fuck off." His words slurred as he leaned over. I caught him before he crashed to the floor.

The muscle in my jaw ticked with how hard I was holding it. "Get up, Tex."

He groaned and attempted to wrestle free. "No."

Now he wants to be difficult? I snatched up a handful of black hair and jerked his head back against the wall. "I wasn't asking."

Tex's eyelids fluttered as if he was having a hard time opening them. He groaned as he slowly blinked. I was met with watery blue eyes that captured my soul the moment they focused on me.

His mouth turned down in a frown. "The fuck?" Tex's gaze hardened the longer he looked up at me. I preferred the desire and fear in his eyes more, but I could work with anger.

"Why are you here?"

"Let's go."

Tex knocked my hand away, and his strands slipped through my fingers. He righted himself the best he could but was still leaning heavily to the right. A single breeze would knock him over.

A knock on the door interrupted us. "Hey, I want to go home. Hurry it up."

Tex pushed himself up off the floor, every movement shaky at best.

"Hey, did you hear me?" A guy stuck his head into the stall.

I stood in front of Tex. "Get out."

He took a step back. "Look, I just want to go home."

"And you will, but if you keep coming back here, you won't."

He audibly swallowed before turning back around.

"Wow, you're just an all-around gangster, huh?" Tex asked, laughing.

It sounded off as I turned back to face him. He was standing up, but he hadn't moved off the wall.

"You knew that when you met me."

His blue eyes focused on me. "Just like you knew who I was."

It wasn't a question, but I nodded all the same. His head fell forward, and his hair hid his eyes away from me.

"Tex..."

"Don't you mean officer Caster?" He shook his head and lifted it once more. "You shouldn't be here." His eyes seemed to water as his teeth dug into his bottom lip.

I moved toward him and pulled it free. He was slow to react, raising his hand to knock mine away but this time I stayed unmoving. "I'm here."

"You shouldn't be. We're enemies."

When it came to public opinion or even Benito's opinion, yes, we were. What did it say about me that I still wanted him? "Do you want me?"

Tex's mouth opened, but he clamped it shut and shook his head. My chest felt as if a blade had pierced through me.

"I shouldn't, but you make my fucking head hurt."

Doesn't he know he does the same to me? I pulled him toward me and draped his arm over my shoulder.

"You're filthy."

"Yeah, well, now I'm getting you dirty." Tex leaned heavily against me as we moved out of the bathroom. I kept him upright to my car a block away. The walk seemed to have sobered him up slightly as he looked around once I had him seated in the car.

"Where are you taking me?"

I closed the door and rounded the car. Slipping behind the wheel, I still didn't have an answer for him.

"Penelope has food?"

Tex nodded, his head bobbing before he grabbed it with both hands and groaned. "Bought those automatic feeders after my first overnight shift."

I nodded and pulled off, merging into traffic. Even at nearly five in the morning, New York was bumper to bumper. I caught Tex shivering in the passenger seat and turned the heat on as we rode in silence.

Before I knew it, we were pulling up to my apartment.

Tex had dozed off on the drive, and I was reluctant to wake him. Lines creased the corner of his eyes as he groaned in his sleep.

I parked in my reserved spot and turned the car off. We sat there for another minute before I woke him.

"Tex."

He jumped, his eyes bugging out as he looked around. He slowly settled down once our eyes met.

"Come on."

Tex didn't argue as I helped him to my floor and into my place. He took a step toward the stairs, and I grabbed him before he could walk any further.

"What?"

"Clothes off," I demanded.

Tex sighed as he yanked his shirt off and shoved his pants and boxer down his legs.

"Socks as well," I said, pointing to them.

"Fuck, you're so anal." He crashed against the wall as he attempted to balance on one leg. He finally pulled them off and tossed them onto the pile.

"Do you need help showering?"

"No!"

"Go get cleaned up."

Tex flipped me off but headed for the steps. I watched transfixed as his firm ass flexed with each step. That stupid tattoo was even pleasing to look at.

I shook my head and went about cleaning up before joining him upstairs. I showered in the guest bedroom, giving Tex some space, although all I wanted to do was go in there and chain him to my bed and tell him he was stuck with me now.

As appealing as that was, it wouldn't be easy making a cop's son disappear. There would be too many questions.

I headed for my bedroom and found Tex sitting on my bed with nothing but a towel around his waist. His upper body was on full display as he sat there staring at his hands.

"I tossed your clothes."

"What the fuck for?" Tex growled.

"You were sitting on that disgusting floor."

"That's what washers and dryers are for."

I shook my head, walking further into the room. "No amount of disinfecting could have gotten them clean enough to my liking."

"What the hell do you do when you spill blood on your clothes?" Tex's shoulders tensed as if he'd just realized what he'd asked.

The tension in the room thickened to a choking level, and I forced myself to continue to the closet. "I get rid of them."

"What?" Tex turned on the bed as I stepped out with a black pair of sweats for him and my blue pajama bottoms. I tossed him the pants as I slipped mine on.

"Keeping them is like asking to be caught. There is a lot of evidence in DNA. Even if I were to clean them, would it be enough?"

Tex's mouth hung open as he stared at me. "Are you seriously telling me this?"

I shrugged. "Put some pants on." My gaze traveled from top to bottom of Tex. Heat swirled in the pit of my stomach, and my cock hardened. *Even now, I want him.*

"Or what?" Tex shot back.

My head tilted slightly to the right as I tried to understand if Tex was testing me on purpose or if he was trying to elicit some kind of reaction from me.

"I will fuck you until you can't walk away from me ever again."

His eyes widened, his mouth opening and closing. I turned and headed downstairs, grabbing a glass of water. I handed it over the moment I walked back into the bedroom. Tex was dressed in sweats hanging low on his hips. "I'll sleep on the couch," Tex suggested.

"And cover it with your body oils?" My face scrunched up with disgust.

"My what?" Tex's mouth tilted up in a smile. "But you sit on it."

"It's for lounging, not sleeping." I waved my hand, unwilling to start the same old argument I had with Giancarlo whenever he stayed over. "You will sleep here next to me."

"That's...." Tex looked away from me. "Dangerous."

I hummed as I pulled the comforter back. "And that turns you on?"

Tex's head whipped around to stare at me. "It doesn—"

"Don't lie, Tex." I fixed him with a stare dragging my gaze down his body. A visible shiver wrecked his muscular frame. I smirked at him. "Don't you have better self-control?"

"No," Tex answered right away.

I knew the answer, but I hadn't expected Tex to say it aloud. His eyes dimmed as he looked down.

"Never have," he added.

I'd been looking into Tex. There were a few incidents when he was a teen hanging out with the wrong crowd, but he'd never gotten in trouble. Expelled three times but nothing past that. I'd wanted to know everything about him but that ran the risk of my obsession growing.

Not that it isn't already running rampant.

"Get in bed, Tex," I ordered.

He licked his lips, looking at me and then at the other

side of the bed. His eyes were bloodshot, and no doubt he was exhausted. The sun was already breaking the horizon, but thanks to the blackout shades, the room stayed lit by artificial light only.

"What happened to Brycen Grennan?"

All the air in the room was sucked up, and I was left breathless as I stared at Tex. His lips were moving, but not a word reached my ears.

I was dragged back into the past.

"I'm sorry," Brycen cried.

"Bullshit," Benito shouted.

His eyes met mine, and I drew back my fists once more. His gray eyes pleaded for me to give him mercy. My heart was firmly lodged in my throat, and my stomach was at the bottom of my feet.

"I messed up." Brycen's eyes bore into mine.

What could I say? He hadn't just messed up. He'd attempted to take my family away.

"Messed up is being called into the police and telling them a few things. Reporting it to Enzo right away would have worked in your favor. But that's not what you did, was it?" Benito paced, his fists hung at his side.

My brother was always careful what he showed people outside our family, but his pain was visible. Tears slid down Brycen's cheek, clearing a few spots of blood. I couldn't find it in me to enjoy this. Inflicting pain on others was a moment of peace for me, and Brycen was robbing me of it along with my heart.

"Hey!" A sharp slap to the side of my face dragged me out of my memory. I blinked and met blue eyes as the gray ones faded to the farthest part of my memory.

"Shit, there you are," Tex said, letting out a breath. His thumb stroked along my cheek and over my beard.

It was a comfort that not many would give me. My

brothers were the only ones to ever do so. Even Brycen had been weary at times. Whenever I checked out, he stayed far away.

Tex, on the other hand, always moved closer. I reached out for him and pulled him down to the bed. He grunted as I rolled on top of him and smashed him against the mattress with my body.

"Hey, what the hell, Enzo?" He slapped his hand down against my side, but I didn't move.

I pushed my face against his neck and breathed him in. It was calming in the way it quieted the noises around me and grounded me to the spot. Tex wiggled under me.

"Stay like this," I said.

"Only if you talk."

Was that a fair trade? Before my mind could make up the answer, my mouth was moving. "Brycen was someone important to me."

Tex stiffened under me, but I kept going. He asked for the story; I'd give it. There was no phone or recording device on him. It was just the two of us in bed, alone.

"We met at a charity event; his date had left him behind. But that entire night, we kept finding ourselves talking. He was wild, cheerful, and—" *Everything I am not.*

I could feel Tex's heartbeat. I closed my eyes, basking in it for a second before I continued.

"One thing led to another, and I took him back to the hotel."

"The same one you took me to?" Tex asked.

"Yes."

Tex stiffened under me. I got the sense I might have said something wrong. I tilted my head back, but he refused to look at me.

"Okay, you guys fucked, and then what?" His words were blunt and sharp at the same time.

"He stayed around. Taking up residence in the hotel suite. It soon turned into more. Brycen was what I wanted, and he was happy to hand himself over to me."

Maybe that should have been a sign.

"We were together for a few months before I realized something was different about him. He always needed money and what I gave him was never enough. Things would go missing at the hotel, and when I asked him about it, he said his sister needed help."

I took in a breath. "She did. She was in the hospital at the time, so I gave him enough money to pay the bills so he wouldn't be stressed out anymore."

Tex's dark eyebrows scrunched together. "She's swimming in medical debt."

Should I be surprised that he'd done his homework? Tex was wild unlike Brycen, there was intelligence in his blue eyes. There were similarities but so many differences. Maybe that's why.....

"He wasn't giving her any of the money. But I overlooked it all." My stomach twisted as shame reared its ugly head.

Tex reached up and touched my shoulder. I normally hated being touched so much, especially when I was forced to go through my own emotions but Tex's hand was like a warm blanket.

"After a few months of being together, he started disappearing at random times. I didn't think much of it. I only visited the hotel once or twice a week." Looking back on it, there were a lot of signs I should have noticed. "However, I slowed down on how much I was giving him. He was going to overdose if he kept it up. Brycen had sworn to me he was going to get help and slow down. But that never happened. Instead, he started meeting up with the cops."

Tex stiffened under me one more. This time, I attempted to comfort him in the same way he'd done me. I had no idea if I was doing it right.

"He sold intel on my family, but with me keeping him at the hotel, he didn't have nearly enough info to keep up with his drug habits. We nearly had New York locked down. All of sudden cops were busting businesses down, storming in on shipments. Things were going bad and fast." I pressed my face against his neck and took in another deep breath. "We were in constant shootouts with the NYPD and other families." We'd lost so much and couldn't find out where it was coming from.

History is trying to repeat itself, but it isn't Tex. I knew down to my soul that he wasn't the reason for any of the shit happening. He wasn't Brycen.

"I wasn't the only Vitale he was seeing."

"The fuck?" Tex shouted.

I cocked a brow at his visible anger. *Is he mad at me?*

"So not only was he a rat, he was a cheating piece of shit too?"

Laughter tumbled free, and I hid my face as I tried to gather myself. When was the last time I laughed with someone besides my brothers?

"Yes, but to be fair, we'd never said that we were together. I'd assumed him staying meant he was fine with being mine."

"How did you find out it was him?" Tex asked.

Anger rolled through me, remembering all the blood and the pain. "He shot my brother."

"What?" Tex attempted to sit up, but I forced him back down.

I never wanted to see Benito drained of color or sweating in pain another day in my life.

"Is he... is he alive?" Tex asked.

"You saw the picture." I didn't have to ask him. It was written all over his face. "My brother gave it to me to remind me what happens when I no longer put family first." It hadn't been a reminder just for me but the both of us.

"That's fucked up, but also..." Tex shrugged. "I don't want to say nice, but it's clear you guys have each other's back."

I nodded.

Tex fidgeted, and I could tell he had a pressing question. I waited for him to finally voice it.

"Did you love him?"

I pulled back and looked Tex in the eyes. My brows dipped as I thought about the question.

"Never mind." He shook his head and avoided my gaze.

I placed all my weight on one hand, used the other to grip his chin, and turned his head so that he was facing me. "I can't say that I did. Brycen met many of my needs. He was someone I wanted and even cherished at times."

Tex stiffened under me again.

"But I could never tell him I loved him."

Tex searched my face. He must have been found whatever he was looking for because he relaxed under me.

"You didn't want to do it," Tex asked.

"Kill Brycen?"

Tex's face blanched as he stared up at me. His head jerked up and down.

"There is a lot in life we don't want to do, but we have to."

Tex bit down his bottom lip, abusing the flesh. I pulled it free and swiped my thumb over it, wanting nothing more than to give in and taste him.

I moved a little, staring into his eyes. "My turn."

"Your turn?"

"What are you going to do?" I asked. "Now that you know."

Tex squeezed his eyes shut, and I knew it was too much to ask of him right now. I moved forward and brushed our lips against one another before rolling off him. "Get some sleep. You have today off, so sleep as much as you can."

"How..." Tex groaned. "Never mind." He moved and got under the cover next to me.

I grabbed the remote and turned the lights off before hitting another button that closed the curtains. The room was blanketed in darkness. A few seconds ticked by as I stared up at the ceiling. I knew Tex wasn't asleep yet. His breathing hadn't evened out.

My stomach clenched. *If he leaves this time, will I stop him?*

Tex surprised me, moving closer until we were nearly touching. His heat called to me. It was like a moth to a flame. I knew this was bad, yet I didn't want to pull away. He laid his head on my chest, and I instinctively wrapped my arms around him. He stiffened for a second before relaxing. Silence built between us, neither one of us falling asleep or moving.

Tex's soothing voice broke the quiet. "Will I end up like Brycen?"

My arms tightened around him. *I hope not.*

Sixteen
TEX

I stared at Enzo as he slept beside me. At first, I'd been wrapped in his arms, trapped, but not hating it. It took a while, but I was finally able to break free. Now, I couldn't stop gazing at him, thinking about the night before.

My head pounded lightly, and it was enough to get me to slip out of his bed. I padded downstairs to the kitchen, found the coffee maker, and turned it on. The smell of it brewing was enough to make me shake off some of the sleep that tried to cling to me. I pulled out a mug from the neatly arranged cabinet and set it on the counter, staring off into space.

Brycen Grennan was on my mind again. This time, however, I felt different about it than before. He'd cheated on Enzo with his own brother. And he'd used him. *That doesn't mean it's okay to murder him.* My stomach clenched.

No, it wasn't okay, but I could understand his rage if

those things happened the way he said they did. Their world wasn't like mine. I'd been cheated on before, and the most I did was egg a guy's house and car. In the Vitales' eyes, that had to be a much more serious offense. And it wasn't as if he *wanted* to kill Brycen...

Excuses, excuses, excuses.

I groaned and ran my fingers through my hair. There I was again, justifying a man who killed. It didn't matter if he didn't want to do it or if Brycen had cheated. Morally, I knew right from wrong and what Enzo had done was very wrong. Yet I couldn't stop seeing things from his side. *What the hell's the matter with me?*

"Are you okay?"

I jumped at the sound of his voice. The mug tumbled off the counter, and I caught it before it could crash into the ground. Sighing, I straightened up. Enzo snagged the mug from me and set it on the counter.

"Why are you so jumpy?" he asked.

"No reason," I muttered, lying through my teeth. "Why are you awake?"

Enzo shrugged. "I like to get up early. Always have." He procured a mug for himself before those dark eyes fixed me with a stare. "Are you okay?" he asked again.

Does he actually care about me? The only people who seemed to give a damn were Chelsea and Rourke. Everyone else asked, but you could tell their minds were already somewhere else once the question was asked. As if they were waiting for the obligatory "I'm fine" before they could respond to you in kind. Not Enzo. He stared at me, waiting, really wanting to know if I was all right.

"Yeah," I said finally. "Better than last night."

He nodded, seemingly satisfied I was telling the truth. "Does that mean you're okay with what we talked about?"

"About you killing someone?" I asked.

The tension came back, filling the space between us. Enzo nodded. "Yeah."

I laughed dryly. "I'm a cop, you know? Knowing that you've killed someone, I'm supposed to turn you in. Do something about it."

"But you're conflicted."

"I am."

Enzo reached out, his palm grazing against my cheek as he caressed me. There was a moment of worry and sadness in his eyes that instinctually made me move closer to him. Everything in me screamed to comfort him. Shit, I was slowly getting tangled up in him for more than the amazing dick and thrill of danger. I was starting to care.

Enzo's lips brushed against mine. "I can't convince you to quit your job?" he asked.

I laughed, and his lips pulled into a smile against mine. "No, you can't. I like my job."

"Do you?" he pressed.

I nodded. "I mean, for the most part. Or I will when I make detective."

"Is that why you were looking for me at Blu?"

I opened my mouth and shut it again. I had no idea how much to tell Enzo or leave out. He nodded without me having to answer.

"Why don't you give up your lifestyle?" I asked. "It seems like you don't care for it."

Enzo frowned. "There is no getting out. My family is everything to me."

Why did that hit me in the chest? Something close to jealousy gnawed at me, but I shoved it down. When I glanced away, Enzo grabbed my chin and directed my face back to him.

"What?"

"Nothing," I answered. "Your family is important to you. I get that."

It just feels like there's always something more important than me out there. To everyone I know.

"Talk to me," Enzo demanded.

"I want some coffee and breakfast," I said, sidestepping the conversation as I pulled out of his grasp. "In that order."

Enzo grabbed my wrist and spun me around. My back brushed up against the counter as he glared at me. Would I ever get tired of that irritated look on his face? My cock jumped to attention, and I told it to go the hell away. I had to stop fucking Enzo, or I was going to lose my mind.

"Please, tell me what you were just thinking. I don't understand." His eyebrows knit together, and he frowned. "I want to understand."

I opened my mouth to fire off some smart-ass retort. One look into his eyes, and I couldn't do it. Slowly, I'd begun noticing things about Enzo. He was a crazy, dangerous man, but there was more to him than that.

"I was thinking how people always put others before me. How... I was kind of jealous that your family would be more important than me if we were ever more than we are now. Which is nothing, but—"

"You think we're nothing?"

I blinked at him. "Besides some hot sex? I don't know."

Enzo dragged me toward him. "Didn't you hear when I said you were mine?"

A shiver ran up my spine. "Y-yeah," I muttered. "But that's just something people say when they're screwing."

"I don't just say things."

My body heated up. I had no response to that other than to stare at Enzo and the anger that crossed his features. He laid his hand on my throat and squeezed, pulling me closer until our lips met.

"I'm not letting you go, Tex," he whispered.

"What if I wanted to leave right now?" I asked, my lips against his, dying to feel him kiss me more.

"I've given you plenty of chances. I won't hand out anymore."

There was a resolve in his voice that I didn't want to test. At least the sane side of me didn't. The horny brain side of me almost wanted him to hold me down and never let me escape. *Then I will know he really cares about me.*

Goddamn, I need therapy.

Enzo pulled away and poured coffee in our cups. He pulled out creamer and sugar. Together, we made our drinks the way we liked. I glanced over to see how he liked his and found him watching me at the same time. I quickly focused on my own drink.

"My family is important to me," Enzo said. "But so are you. Why else would I spend so much time making sure you're safe?"

I stared at Enzo, my stomach flip-flopping all over the place. He knew exactly what to say to trip me up. I focused on my coffee again. The first sip drew a moan from my lips. It was like liquid gold coursing down my throat and awakening my senses.

My phone buzzed on the countertop, drawing me back to reality. I snatched it up when I saw Rourke's name on the screen.

"Don't answer that," Enzo said.

I gazed up, and his eyebrow was lifted. I frowned. "I have to. It's my partner. He's probably wondering where the hell I am."

"I thought you didn't have to work today?"

Nodding, I stared at the screen. "I don't, but Rourke and I usually catch up on our days off. Coffee and a walk through the park to talk about life, work, and everything else."

"You like him," Enzo said tightly.

"He's a good friend."

"Just a friend?" He shot back.

I blinked at him and smiled. "Yes, a friend. Chelsea is also a friend. All of my friends are exactly what I say they are. Don't get that look in your eyes."

"What look?"

I rolled my eyes. "That look that says you want to do something illegal to anyone you think is too close to me."

Not that I hate that it's his first instinct. Something might be wrong with me, but that's fucking hot. I would never in a million years tell Enzo that, though. He would take it as a reason to do something insane.

My phone stopped ringing, and I finally focused on it again. "Shit. I need to call him back."

Enzo grabbed my phone, shoved it into the hem of his pants, and picked up his mug. He sipped at it, walking away before he tugged open a drawer and began digging.

"There are a few good food places around here. We can either go or order something for delivery."

I groaned. "Give me back my phone."

"What do you want to eat?" he asked, picking out a stack of takeout menus. "We slept kind of late, so breakfast or lunch is an option."

I raised a brow at him. "You're going to keep pretending you don't hear me, aren't you?"

Enzo glanced at me and smiled. "What do you like to eat the most?"

Fuck. He's so cute.

Never thought I would use the word cute to describe a man like Enzo. Shit, I was doing all kinds of things I never thought I would do. As I took a sip of my coffee, I realized I wasn't drinking and didn't have the urge to do so. The thought of grabbing some blow and doing a few lines was gone as well. As Enzo poured over the menus, all I could do was think about how calm I was with him. When I wasn't pissed off.

How am I supposed to do my job when I'm all mixed up?

"If you don't pick something, I'll pick for you," Enzo said.

"Fine." I grabbed a menu and flipped through it. Rourke could wait. For now. "I'm craving Greek food."

Enzo took out my phone and held it out toward me. "Password."

"I don't want you digging around in my phone."

"Mine is upstairs. I'm only using it to call in food for us," he said patiently.

I stared at him, unsure of how much I wanted to give him. Slowly, I entered my password where he couldn't see it. When he took it back, Enzo dialed the number to the restaurant and pressed my phone to his ear.

What did it say that I could trust him more than other, more upstanding people I knew?

Seventeen
Enzo

I WANT TO KEEP HIM.

The words were on repeat in my head like a catchy jingle from a commercial as I pictured coming home to Tex. Seeing him every night in my bed. Every morning as he moaned around a mouthful of coffee.

"What now?" Tex asked.

We cleaned up the kitchen after eating. I normally checked in on what he was doing before getting back to work. I was no closer to finding out who was double-crossing us. There were multiple cops and feds on our payroll. As far as I could tell, none of them had an influx of money coming in. Still, if they were bold enough to fuck my family out of money, then they had to be smart enough to cover their tracks.

I couldn't exactly ask Tex to help or get him involved. It

was best if he stayed clear of it all. At least then Benito wouldn't have me eliminate him.

"What do you normally do on your days off?"

"Lately?" Tex looked nervously at me. "Not much."

"You've been investigating me on your days off, haven't you?"

"What do you do?" Tex asked, avoiding the question.

We sat there in silence, neither one of us willing to answer. I stood up. "We can watch a movie or read."

"Movie first," Tex said.

He was up and headed to the living room, only to stop short. "Ummm, where is a tv in this place?"

"You didn't have time to check out all the rooms?" I asked as I turned right and headed down the hall. The laundry room had a door next to the dryer that looked like a cabinet, but it was a passageway to another room.

"I did," Tex said, hot on my heels.

I opened the doors and stepped through into a secret room.

"Holy shit." Tex moved past me and plopped down on the soft double recliner. "You have your own movie theater. Damn, money really does buy happiness."

I hit a button on one of the walls, and the computer that controlled what we watched appeared. "What did you want to see?"

"Horror? Or something actiony?"

I looked through my collection, trying to pick the perfect movie. Tex materialized behind me. Before I knew it, he was scooting me over.

"Oh, a Bond movie is always good."

Were they?

"Please tell me you've seen them," Tex said.

"No." I hadn't been into movies as a kid and wasn't into

them as an adult. There were a few good documentaries I enjoyed. It was the only reason I'd allowed Giancarlo to talk me into the movie room in the first place.

"That's it. We're watching all of them." Tex shoved me to a seat, and we plopped down.

"You know what would be perfect?" He licked his lips as if he was still hungry. "Popcorn."

I stood up and pulled out the popcorn machine from the back closet.

"This place has everything," Tex said wistfully. His phone rang, breaking the moment, and I was tempted to snatch it back away from him. Tex checked the screen and shoved the phone back into his pocket.

"Hurry up. Your mind is about to be blown."

I doubted it, but I couldn't help but be pulled into Tex's excitement. Settling in next to him, I watched as the movie started. My gaze skirted to him, looking at the excitement that lit up his face as he shoved a handful of popcorn into his mouth.

"Stop staring at me and pay attention," Tex said, elbowing me.

I turned my attention back to the screen and forced myself to pay attention. As the movie went on, I stole little glances at the man beside me. *I can't believe I'm doing this.*

The ending credits rolled on the screen. By the third movie, I had fewer questions.

"It's getting late," Tex said but made no move to leave.

Turning off the screen, I stood up. "Come on, we should check on Penelope."

Tex nodded. He sat there for another second before he got up and grabbed the containers that had held our popcorn.

"You don't want to vacuum the place before we go?" Tex asked.

Most people would have rushed me along, telling me I could clean it later. "Yes."

Tex nodded. "Is there special cleaning equipment in here?"

"The cabinet next to the closet door."

Tex went over to it and pulled out the cleaning supplies. He handed me the vacuum as he used the lint roller on the recliners, even those we hadn't used.

"Stop watching me. I know you saw my place while it was a mess, but I know how to clean."

"Why are you cleaning now?"

Tex's black brows dipped, and his nose scrunched up. "Because I can tell it was bothering you. During the last movie, you kept looking to the floor where some popcorn had fallen."

I had, but I hadn't thought he noticed.

"There, all done," Tex said.

He put the stuff away but in the wrong spot. I went behind him and fixed it.

"Noted, everything has a spot. You know it's impossible to memorize them all. Get a label maker or something."

"I don't mind going behind you and fixing it."

Cleaning was the one thing I had completely under my control. There was no extra thought that went into it.

Once everything was cleaned up, we headed to the parking garage. Tex was silent the entire time, his shoulders slumped. I expected him to continue talking during the drive, but he was quiet until we pulled up to his apartment complex.

"Well, I guess I wi—" Tex hopped out of the car. "Where are you going?"

"Inside," I said, pointing to his door.

Tex opened his mouth, but I placed a finger over his lips. "Don't waste your time. I'm not going anywhere."

A heavy sigh left Tex as he gave in. Keys in hand, he jammed into the lock in seconds. He put in a code on the wall, and I eyed it.

"New security?"

"Someone broke into my place," Tex said, giving me a pointed look.

I hummed as if it hadn't been me. I found Penelope weaving between my legs, meowing for attention.

"How did you come up with the name Penelope?" I picked the beautiful orange cat up, scratching behind his ears as he purred in my arms.

Tex moved closer and began to pet Penelope. My chest tightened, and I tried to grasp onto what made me feel that way. It was tangled up in the webs of emotions that I constantly tried to untangle.

"It's a boring story." He tapped his finger on the cat's nose. "Isn't that right, Pen?"

A soft smile graced Tex's face, and I was instantly hit with the desire to chain him up. I wanted him to smile at me like that, only me.

"Why are you staring at Pen like that?" Tex took the cat from my arms, and I couldn't help but glare at the orange fur ball. "Enzo, you hurt my cat, and I swear there is no jail cell that will keep me from killing you myself."

The corner of my mouth quivered as I attempted to keep from laughing. "So, there is a line you're willing to cross."

Tex shook his head. "Hurting a man's fur baby is asking for it."

I lifted my hand and placed the other over my heart. "I swear I will never hurt a single hair on Penelope's head."

Tex shook his head as he placed the cat down. He slowly rose, and his blue eyes focused on me. "Do we need to go over a list of people you aren't allowed to hurt?"

"Will you try to leave me if I hurt any of the people on said list?"

"Yes," Tex shot back. He crossed his arms and let out a groan. "This is insane."

"You can give me the list once we get home."

Tex's arms dropped to his side. "What? I am home."

I was already shaking my head before he could finish his sentence. "We are here to get a few of your things. We can even take Pen."

"You don't have anything for him at your place," Tex argued.

I walked past him toward his bedroom.

Tex was right behind me. "Are you even allowed to have pets at your place?"

I went through his closet, picking out what could go and what I'd replace.

"Are you listening to me, Enzo?" Tex asked.

"I own the building."

"Fucking rich asshole. Of course, you do."

Tex attempted to grab things out of my hand. I pushed him down to the bed and gave him a stern look.

"I didn't say I was staying with you."

I grabbed a bag and began neatly filling it with clothes. "I don't recall asking."

Tex's mouth opened and closed. I stepped over to him and pushed his chin up to close his mouth.

"Grab whatever you absolutely need."

Tex looked ready to argue with me and I placed a finger over his lips.

"Again, I wasn't asking. Either do it, or I will."

He glared at me, and I was seconds away from tying him up and tossing him in the trunk of the car. He must have seen it in my face because Tex got up and started grabbing things while muttering curses under his breath.

We left his place and headed back to mine within two hours. Plenty of time for what I had being delivered.

Penelope meowed the entire ride on the elevator.

"I know, Pen, we're getting kidnapped, but don't you worry. Enzo has a nice-looking couch for you to scratch up."

My back stiffened just as the elevator doors slid open. Tex practically skipped out of the elevator and headed for my door.

"Remember you said—" Tex stopped in his tracks. "What the hell is all this stuff?"

A mountain of boxes were stacked on both sides of the door. A few had the brand names on display. The moment Tex read them, he turned to me.

"You bought him a cat tree?"

I shook my head. "I bought him four cat trees. Two can go upstairs, one in the living room and the other is mounted on the walls."

Tex's jaw dropped as he continued to stare at me. I squinted, trying to decipher if it was a good or bad thing. *Is he upset or possibly annoyed?*

"What about the rest of the boxes?" Tex asked.

I opened the door, and he walked in with Penelope in his cage. He sat him down and helped bring in the boxes.

"I read that cats enjoy small places to nap. I don't want boxes littered around the place, so I got a few alcoves for Pen to sleep in. To avoid him ruining my furniture, I got six scratching posts."

Tex whistled. "That's a little overkill, don't you think?

Pen is one cat unless you're thinking about getting your own."

I shook my head. "It has never crossed my mind."

He stopped moving and I was forced to work the large box around him.

"What... what about when, you know."

My head tilted as I tried to come up with the answer. "I don't know."

Tex groaned. "Whatever this is." He pointed between us. "Is... I don't know, done."

I ate up the distance between us in four easy strides. My hand circled his neck as I pulled him close. "I thought I made myself clear; I am no longer giving you chances to leave me."

Tex's eyebrows dipped. "And when you go to jail?" He cleared his throat and stood up taller. "I'm a cop. You're the bad guy."

I stared into his eyes. "You weren't very good in school."

He blinked at me. "What, why would you say that?"

I let him go no matter how much I wanted to march him upstairs and ruin him until he couldn't think of anything but being under me.

"You're shit at listening." I grabbed another box and handed it to him. "I'm never letting you go, Tex Caster."

"Okay, got the last piece up. What are you making?" Tex asked.

He peeked over my shoulder as I stirred the food.

"Fuck, it smells good." He groaned in my ear.

My body heated instantly, my cock stiffening. His chest

was pressed against my back and I could make out the hard ridges of his body through the thin t-shirt.

"Step back," I said.

Cool air greeted my back, and I almost asked for him to come back. Black hair flopped over Tex's eyebrows as he moved to the side. His gaze was heavy on the side of my face, and I fought not to react.

"Why?"

"You distract me, and risotto is a delicate dish."

"I'm distracting you? How?"

I sighed. "You being so close makes me want to bend you over the counter and fuck you as I hold a knife to your throat."

Tex sucked in a sharp breath, and I glanced his way momentarily. His pupils were blown, and he looked more than ready for that to happen.

"I'm not against it, but I'm a little shocked you'd use your kitchen knives."

My mouth turned down in a frown. "I wouldn't. I have a knife on me at all times."

"That's... Fuck, that's hot."

"Go check on Penelope," I ordered.

"Fine, he's never been a lock-me-away cat. He hates that shit." Tex headed toward the downstairs bathroom, and I heard the tinkling of a bell shortly after.

"He's free and zooming around the place," Tex said.

I made a mental note to order more lint rollers and an air purifier. I kept an ear out, listening to Tex whisper to the cat and cheer him on to try his new scratching posts. It was strange to have someone in my personal space that wasn't family. Even then, I sometimes waited for them to leave with bated breath.

Tex and Penelope playing relaxed me further, and I found myself engrossed in the dish I was making.

I dried my hands and placed the plates on the table before heading to the living room. Tex tossed one of the silvervine balls up on the cat tree, and Penelope chased after it. I watched him for a moment longer.

"You being a creeper?" Tex asked.

"Dinner is ready."

He smiled and got up. "Good, I'm starving." He stopped short of entering the kitchen. "If you want me to move any of the setup, let me know. I wasn't sure if anything would feel out of place for you."

It was new, but I found I was more accepting of it. "I'll let you know." It took my brain a little longer to tell me if something wasn't right sometimes. Part of me enjoyed the fact that Tex was concerned about my comfort.

We both got washed up and sat at the table. Tex's face lit up as he took in the creamy shrimp risotto with mascarpone, a dish I'd perfected over the years.

"Can't believe you made this," Tex said.

"There are a few things police files won't teach you about me."

Tex paused with the spoon halfway to his mouth. His blue eyes flicked up to me and widened. "Did you just make a joke?"

I shrugged and spooned my food. "I can make them on occasion."

He reached across the table and touched my forehead. "Are you sure you aren't sick?"

I smacked his hand away. "Eat."

Tex laughed as he dug in. The most alluring moans came from Tex as he ate. I wanted to hear them all the time.

They were better than jazz. My cock stiffened, and I was forced to adjust as we sat there and ate.

Ringing broke the moment between us. Tex reached for his phone, and his smile dimmed slightly. He chewed on his bottom lip as he stared at the screen.

"Who is it?"

"My friend."

I peaked at the name Chelsea. "That's her third time calling today."

Much like the other times, Tex forwarded the call. His shoulders slumped the moment he put the phone away.

He was silent for a long bit, and I let him be. Something was bothering him, but I couldn't figure out what. I bet Giancarlo could. He was fantastic at reading people. Even Benito could understand other people. People's actions and words were nothing more than a constant jigsaw puzzle for me to put together. I never had all the pieces, and it left me confused and guessing.

"She's calling because the other day, I was kind of spirling." Tex shook his head. "Maybe a little longer than that."

I grabbed his plate, and he followed me over to the sink. He leaned against the counter, not looking at anything in particular. I kept my mouth shut, waiting for him to finally tell me what happened the night I picked him up off the dirty floor of the bar's bathroom.

Tex rubbed his arms as he spoke. "I've been wild my whole life." He let out a dry laugh. "That's an understatement. I was the kid other parents warned their children to stay away from. The ultimate fuck-up."

I handed the rinsed plate over and he grabbed it and placed it in the dishwasher.

"I got into everything, and I mean everything. Soon I found alcohol wasn't doing it, and I got into drugs."

My back stiffened. Brycen's face fluttered to the surface of my psyche for a second, but they were so different from each other. Brycen had never told me about his problem. Tex didn't need to. I hadn't asked for anything specific, but he was giving it to me all the same.

"Nothing on your record indicated that you were that bad. A few graffiti incidents but nothing more."

Tex laughed. "Why am I not surprised you looked into me?" He didn't sound upset. "My dad was a big-shot detective, and he pulled strings anytime I got caught."

"The same dad that left a mark on your body?" I barely contained my rage. My hand tightened around the glass cup. Before I knew it, pain erupted over my fingers.

"Shit, Enzo." Tex grabbed my hand, jerked it over to the other side, and turned on the water. "The fuck is your problem? Be careful."

The cuts were shallow, and I'd had worse. Tex yanked me around the kitchen anyway until I was forced to sit down. No one had ever cared if I got hurt besides my brothers.

Tex ran around the kitchen, grabbing paper towels. "Where is your first aid kit?"

"Top right cabinet." I was so stunned all I could do was answer him.

He grabbed the first aid box and was in front of me in seconds. I held out my hand for him, and he meticulously inspected it.

"It's not too deep," I said.

"Are you a fucking doctor?"

I blinked at Tex's anger and the worry rolling off him in waves.

"No, but—"

"Then shut it. I've taken a first aid course."

Warmth blossomed over my chest, and I found it hard to breathe as Tex checked over my hand. He picked out tiny pieces of glass. With every piece he pulled out, he stopped and stared up at me. I was too lost in the overwhelming possessiveness and want trying to consume me.

"Tex." My voice was soft even to my ears. What was he doing to me?

"Does it hurt?" Tex asked, his blue eyes scanning my face as if he'd find the answer.

It didn't hurt but something felt strange and it only intensified every time Tex was near me. I shook my head, my mouth too dry to speak.

"I'm almost finished." Tex went back to cleaning the wound before bandaging it. "All done."

The moment he dropped my hand, I gave in to the screaming voice in the back of my head. I grabbed Tex and crushed our mouths together in a heated kiss. Tex groaned, submitting to me.

I pulled back, my heart racing as the need to be inside of him dragged me further into the abyss of desire.

"And now?"

"And now what?" Tex asked breathlessly.

"Are you still spiraling?"

He stared at me for a long second that felt like an eternity. "Probably."

I audibly swallowed. He wrapped his arms around my neck, and his fingers wove through my chocolate brown strands.

"But I'm not craving drugs or even alcohol." He licked his lips as his eyelids lowered and his pupils dilated. "I found something far more intoxicating and just as deadly."

Eighteen
TEX

I didn't give a shit about what I was doing anymore. The outside world was messy and complicated. But in here? With Enzo? I knew where we stood. He was who he was, and I was who I was. We weren't pretending, although we *were* ignoring the inevitable. This would all fall apart eventually.

My mind quickly shoved that thought under the rug as Enzo's lips crashed against mine. He moaned, his tongue swiping at the seam of my lips as he shoved me into his bed. I don't even remember how we got up there; my brain was completely enamored with Enzo.

His hand shoved underneath my shirt, fingers grazing over my nipple. Enzo tugged one of my nipple piercings, and my back arched up from the bed as I chased his touch, wanting more. I opened my mouth, accepting him inside. Our tongues clashed, fighting each other, but I was no match for Enzo. And as much as I liked to fight, part of me didn't want to be a match for him right now.

In Enzo's arms, I could fall apart and know that he would take the lead. He'd tell me where to go, how to move, and how to hold my position until all I had to do was rely on him. The thought of having someone to rely on sent butter-flies through my stomach. He was there, even when I didn't want or expect him to be.

I'm getting way too attached.

Staying with Enzo hadn't been part of the plan, but I'd given in. Being at his place was better than another stint in rehab; at least here, I had great dick, delicious food, and Penelope. It was a break from reality, but one I desperately wanted to cling to.

"Where's your mind?" Enzo growled against my ear. "If you start daydreaming, I'm going to think I'm boring you and go harder," he said, punctuating his words with a bite to my shoulder.

"You... ah," I moaned, shaking my head to force myself to focus as my body tingled all over. "Are you threatening me?" I asked.

"You'll know when I'm threatening you."

"Noted," I muttered. Every red flag lit up from here to California and back. I promptly ignored them all. "So, do something that doesn't bore me."

Enzo tugged my nipple piercing, and I pressed my lips together. Somehow, a stupid, goddamn whimper still slipped free. The corner of his mouth ticked up. I shoved a hand against his chest, but he refused to let me push him off. Instead, he attacked my neck. His teeth sank into my skin, drawing a hiss and a moan from me. His hand slipped between us, working my zipper down until he cupped my balls and gave them a very firm squeeze.

"Fuck," I bit my bottom lip, lifting my hips and pressing against his palm.

"Stay."

Enzo climbed off of the bed, and I was left panting. I propped myself up on my elbows. "What are you doing?"

"Didn't I say stay?"

I plopped back down. "What the hell are you doing over there? Come back already."

"Do you miss me that much?"

I pulled a face. "More like my dick is going to explode if you don't touch me."

"All I heard is that you miss me."

I rolled my eyes. Enzo was different than I expected him to be from reading his file. There was a gentle, playful side that I never would have expected. If Enzo was any other man, he would be perfect for me.

He's still a Vitale.

A hand wrapped around my ankle, and I slid down the bed. Enzo was on me before I could even sit up. He had a determined look on his face as he stripped me out of my clothes and tossed them aside. I stared at them on the floor, in a heap, and raised a brow.

"You don't want to clean those up?"

Enzo gazed at them and then back to me. "You're more important right now."

I'd be lying if I said my heart didn't do several flip-flops. Enzo wasn't looking at me, too busy staring at my body, but I couldn't take my eyes off of him. Did he even realize what he'd just said?

"Ah," I cried out, snapped back to reality. "What are you doing?"

Enzo didn't answer me. Instead, he tugged on the nipple

clamps he'd attached to me. I lifted with it, but he shoved me right back down to the bed.

"What part of stay don't you understand? I see I'm going to need to punish you."

I swallowed thickly. "What the fuck are you talking about?"

Enzo went right back to ignoring me. He climbed off the bed, my eyes tracking every movement he made until he returned. Enzo carried over a towel and laid it down before he picked up a sizable flesh-colored dildo. He poured lube over it, stroking the cock with his hand as I stared up at him.

"Spread your legs."

I swallowed hard. "I don't even get a please?"

Enzo moved between my thighs and shoved them open for me. My heart sped up to an alarming rate. The head of the toy pressed against my hole before more lube ran over my flesh. I stared at Enzo, who was captivated by what he was doing. That little smile returned to his face, and I gave in. That look was so disarming.

My breath wooshed out of me as he pushed the toy inside inch by inch. I would expect him to fuck me himself, but instead, he focused on the toy. I felt myself opening, stretching. My hands gripped the sheets as Enzo watched me, and my skin felt like it was going to burst into flames. He worked the toy deeper, rubbing against my walls. What little composure I had fell away as soon as the dildo pressed against my prostate, and I saw stars.

"Enzo."

He laid on top of me, his lips brushing against mine. "Hmm?" he asked, biting and sucking my bottom lip.

"What are we doing?"

The words fell out of my mouth, and I wished I could stuff them down and make them disappear. Whatever this was, I didn't want to jinx it right now. The rest of the world was difficult as hell. Couldn't I pretend for a while longer?

Enzo didn't so much as blink at the question. "We're having sex," he answered. When I gave him an exasperated look, he kissed me again. "And whatever the hell we want to do. Why can't we figure it out later?"

The protest that perched on my tongue died as he kissed me again, shutting up all my rational thinking. My eyes fluttered closed. When they opened again, I noticed that Enzo was naked. He'd stripped quietly and efficiently. Now I was being treated to a hot-as-hell display of his body, his cock heavy between his thighs and dripping with pre-cum.

Enzo moved between my thighs. When the head of his cock pressed against my hole, my eyes widened. Slowly, realization dawned on me. Enzo didn't plan to play around with me, only using the dildo. He was going to try to stuff me full of his cock too.

My heart raced, but I didn't even think about trying to stop him. Enzo relinquished control of the dildo over to me.

"Don't stop," he told me.

I licked my lips. "Fuck. Okay."

Enzo smiled, and it was enough to make me want to put on a good show for him. I worked the toy inside of me, twisting it in and out as a groan slipped free. Normally, I only did this when I was alone. When I looked up, Enzo watched me intently. He stroked his cock while he did and spread lube all over, his eyes never leaving mine for more than a few seconds.

By the time he was back on top of me, I was practically climbing the walls with need. He nipped my jawline as he pushed against my already occupied hole. I sucked in a breath. My body erupted into flames as he drove in deeper.

My toes curled, my head spun, and I surrendered to how good I felt.

I could get used to this.

I stopped questioning right from wrong, Enzo's past, what he did, and what he was involved in. None of it mattered when I closed my eyes tight enough and focused on how damn good he felt when he was pressed against me.

"Enzo."

"Keep moaning my name, Tex," he said, his voice a breathy whisper. "The more you do it, the more I know you're mine."

I couldn't even think straight enough to protest. My hole stretched even more, the slight pain slowly evolving into pleasure as Enzo tugged on the nipple clamps. The bit of pressure intensified, and sparks danced over my skin while my head spun.

Enzo slid in deeper as I clenched around him. My hands shot up, gripping his back as my nails dug into his flesh. The look on his face was priceless. The mask he normally wore had fallen away, replaced with pleasure and freedom. He thrust deeper until he was buried completely.

"Fuck, I'm full," I groaned, rolling my hips as I marveled at how good it felt. "Only ever done this once—"

"By yourself?"

I blinked up at Enzo. For a minute, I'd forgotten I was speaking out loud. Enzo stayed still, staring at me, his eyebrows pinched.

I swallowed hard. "You don't want to know the answer to that."

Enzo slammed into me, his cock driving to my core. The last bits of my sanity unraveled. *Should have kept that thought to myself.* It was too late to go back now. Shit, even if I could, would I? Enzo was fucking me so beautifully that I didn't regret it.

He reached between us and pressed on my lower belly. "I can feel my cock moving inside of you," he panted. "I really am going to make you mine."

A shiver passed through me. "You're crazy."

"You have no idea."

I had a bit of one. Every jolt of Enzo's hips made the sound of skin against skin echo in his room. For some stupid reason, as he tugged on my nipple clamp and left kisses on my mouth, I felt emotions rise. In another life, I could be Enzo's. And he would do anything for me.

My back bowed as cum stained our bodies, and I cried out for the man I refused to let go of. I clenched down hard, trying to keep the toy in me as long as possible. Enzo swore. His kisses became sharper and more urgent as teeth scraped against my flesh, and I was transported to heaven.

Enzo's moaning against my mouth made me want to cling to him even harder. Warmth filled my hole, but it was muted behind latex. I almost wished I'd asked him to fuck me without it.

Enzo laid on top of me and buried his face into my neck. We both panted in the silence, but it wasn't uncomfortable. I was zoned out, and Enzo? Who knew what went through that man's head.

A sharp tug of my nipples threw me back into the present. "Hey," I growled. "Cut that out."

Enzo chuckled, the sound enough to make me want to hear it on an endless loop. "Let's talk about that comment you made," he said, sitting up. "Who was it that filled you up before?"

I saw that wicked glint in his eye. "I would never tell you in a million years," I whispered. "You're insane."

"And you keep coming back."

He was right about that. "Can't seem to help myself." I yawned, blinking to try to stay awake.

"Tex?"

"Yeah?" I mumbled, falling into the pleasant buzz that traveled through my body.

"Am I really helping you?"

I glanced at him. Slowly, I raised a hand and pushed my fingers through his hair. It was soft to the touch, thick, and smelled amazing. The more I stroked his hair, the more he clung to me, cuddling against my body like I was going to disappear.

"I'm not nose-deep in a pile of coke, so yes," I answered honestly because I knew the truth helped him. "I feel better here. Maybe it's because I know no matter how much I screw up, you and your family have done much worse." I tensed. "That's not what I—"

"No," he said, shaking his head. "It's the truth." Enzo's fingers ran over my skin. "Go to sleep."

"I need to clean up."

"No, you don't. Leave that to me."

Enzo finally pulled himself free of my arms. As he slid out of me, I held my breath. *Damn, I feel empty.* I wanted to tell Enzo to slide himself back in. At least until I fell asleep. Instead, I kept my mouth shut and watched him walk to the bathroom with the toy in his hand.

I was losing the fight against sleep. My phone buzzed, and I snagged it off the floor. Chelsea. Rourke. My father. The only person I responded to was Chelsea.

Tex: I'll call you tomorrow. Don't worry about me, I'm fine. And sober.

Chelsea: Asshole. Glad you're okay.

Tex: I'm sorry.

I laid my phone on the nightstand and sighed. Tomorrow was going to suck. I owed Chelsea an apology, I had to talk to Rourke, and my father probably realized I'd broken into his files. Massaging my temple, I gazed up when a dark shadow fell over me and jumped as Enzo stared down at me.

"You scared the shit out of me!"

"Sorry." Enzo held up a towel. "Be still and go to sleep. That phone can wait until tomorrow." He glanced at it. "Put it on silent."

Arguing with Enzo was pointless. I was quickly learning that. I shut off the sound and noted the look of approval on his face. Once he was done cleaning me up, he slipped into bed beside me. Enzo's arms circled my body before he sat up.

"Now what?" I asked.

The pressure on my nipples disappeared. Both of them throbbed. I reached up to touch them, but Enzo slapped my hand away gently. His fingers caressed me, and my body took that as a green light to get revved up again.

"What's the matter?" Enzo asked.

I rolled over to face him. "If you keep doing that, we'll be right back at it."

Enzo kept his eyes focused on mine as he resumed rubbing. A shudder ran up my spine. I opened my mouth to tell him we were doing it again but stopped short. The meow and scratching at the door made us turn in that direction. Enzo groaned.

"I'll let him in."

"Thanks," I laughed. "He's needy."

"Like you."

I blinked at Enzo's retreating back. I didn't think I was needy, but maybe I was kidding myself. My thoughts turned to Penelope as he ran inside the room and hopped up on Enzo's bed. He made himself at home, curled up on my chest, and promptly started falling asleep. Enzo glared at him.

"Leave my cat alone. You're gonna have to share me."

Enzo growled. "Never." He climbed into bed anyway and laid beside me. "So, why is he named Penelope?"

I grinned. "When I got him, the person I bought him from was sure he was a girl, and I was a huge fan of *Criminal Minds*. Penelope was an easy choice. I found out she was actually a boy when I took him in to get fixed and never changed the name. He doesn't seem to mind." I yawned, relaxing all over again as I pet Penelope. "He loves me anyway."

Enzo was so quiet I thought he'd fallen asleep. I glanced over, only to be met with his intense gaze. He left a kiss on my lips.

"What was that for?" I asked.

He shrugged. "I felt like it. Now go to bed."

Enzo tossed the blanket over Penelope and me before sliding under it himself. He gave Penelope one last glance, sighed, and cuddled up against me. I snickered under my breath. Who knew a man like Enzo Vitale would be jealous of a little old cat?

Nineteen
TEX

ROURKE WAVED A HAND. I JOGGED OVER TO HIM, PULLING Enzo's long, gray jacket around me more tightly. He'd insisted I take it instead of the worn hoodie I usually wore when I was off duty. The man was a pain in the ass, but I couldn't deny his jacket was warmer and smelled like him. Maybe that was the real reason he wanted me to wear it, so I would be surrounded by his scent, unable to think about anything but him, his cock, and the way he'd made me scream his name this morning.

"Where the hell have you been?" Rourke asked.

"I needed some time off. Sergeant wanted me to take a break after the shooting with Carl anyway, so I took it."

He frowned. "She knows about you going after the Vitales."

I stiffened. "What?"

"Why do you think I've been calling you?" He grumbled. "The chief put together a task force to handle the violence escalating around the Vitales. Once Sarge figured out it was you who accessed her files and started going after them, she decided you would be the best choice for the team instead of firing your ass. Probably because the chief was impressed."

Speechless, I followed him into the coffee shop. "Why hasn't she called to scream at me?"

"I told her I would handle it," he said. "Two coffees. One black, one with sugar and vanilla creamer." He glanced at me. "You hungry?"

I shook my head, still dwelling on the bombshell he'd just dropped on me. My sergeant knew exactly what I was up to, and now I was going to be part of a task force. The dream I'd been pursuing was within reach. So why did my stomach pitch so hard?

"Caster."

I blinked at Rourke. "No, I ate already."

Rourke raised a brow. "You? Usually, I have to make you eat before you pass out." He grabbed our coffees, paid, and passed one of the cups to me. We found a spot over in the corner, away from everyone else. "I know this is a lot to process, but like I said, I've been trying to contact you for days, and you never pick up. Where have you been?"

I drank from my coffee to avoid speaking. *Sleeping in a mobster's bed.* There was no way I could say that out loud. "I told you I needed some time off. And I've been looking into the Vitales."

"What have you found out?"

I shrugged. "Not a ton. What I have found doesn't matter. There's no evidence to support anything."

"Tell me anyway."

My fingers gripped the coffee cup tightly. Hot liquid splashed over my fingers and stung my flesh. Cursing, I sat the cup down. I reached for the napkins along with Rourke and started soaking up the hot mess.

"Like I said, it's nothing. I can't share it right now, anyway. My source is..." *Stolen? Is that a good word?*

"Fine," Rourke said with a sigh. "You need to give me something, Tex. I'm your partner. Shit, I'm your friend, man."

He was, and I hadn't been treating him like it. Rourke looked out for me. However, the thought of telling him about Enzo and Brycen made my chest tighten.

Enzo would kill me.

"When I have something to tell you, I will," I said. "I was going to check out a storage unit today that might have some answers."

"I'm going with you."

"No," I said quickly.

"Tex," he growled. "I'm going with you, and that's the end of that. Sarge wants me on your ass, and I plan to be right on it until she says otherwise. You're not the only one who has their career on the line." He pointed at me. "You fucked up, man. And now it falls on both of us."

I swallowed hard. Rourke's no-nonsense expression had taken over, and the gentle way he spoke before disappeared. He was always like that, calm and cool until you pissed him off. *To be fair, I did get him in trouble with Sarge.* I was lucky she hadn't decided to rat me out and have my ass fired. And that Rourke had my back enough to be on my team.

"Sorry," I muttered. "Yeah, of course, you can go with me."

Rourke nodded, his face relaxing. "Thanks. I'm not trying to be a hardass," he said slowly, "but my livelihood is on the line too."

"I know."

"We need to do this together. Remember what you're

after, Tex. Detective. It's what you've been bitching about since the day we met."

He wasn't wrong about that. I'd talked about being a detective for so long it was part of me. *I'm closer than I've ever been.* This task force was going to get me to my goal. Finally, I would show the world I wasn't the strung-out loser everyone thought I was.

Thoughts of Enzo distracted me. I could see the hurt on his face, the anger. Even if he didn't kill me, he would be devastated. *Or at least that's what I'm telling myself.* Everything we've been doing could be a lie. *And I'm falling for it.*

I couldn't imagine Enzo playing along for this long, though. If he wanted to kill me, he could. Enzo could make my body disappear in the blink of an eye and not think twice. Instead, he was taking care of Penelope and me, holding us close when there was no reason to. Could anyone really play a game as long as we'd been dancing around each other?

Picking up my half-empty cup of coffee, I tossed it in the trash. No matter what Enzo was doing, whether it was real or fake, I had a job to do. What we had couldn't last forever.

"Let's go check out that storage room," I said.

"Are you okay?"

"Yeah," I said, nodding my head until I could almost believe it myself. "I'm fine. Let's go."

"We can take my car." Rourke carried his coffee out. "Are you sure you don't need another drink?"

"No," I said, my stomach churning. I wasn't sure I could hold anything down if I tried. "I'm good."

Brycen's entire life was laid out in a series of boxes. *Is this what it's like in the end? Everything you are reduced to a cold, empty room?* The knot in my stomach hadn't subsided. I pushed through it, shuffling old mail before placing it to the side.

"What are we looking for?" Rourke asked.

"I have no idea," I muttered. "When I find it, I'll know."

"That's reassuring."

"Shut up and look."

"Yeah, yeah," he said.

We went back to scouring the boxes. Old clothes, shoes, even stuffed animals were in there. My brain wouldn't stop coming up with scenarios where Enzo had seen Brycen in a certain outfit, or he'd gone to a carnival with the man and won him a prize. The more I went through, the angrier I became. Not because Enzo had killed him, though. The feeling was... stranger, more twisty and desperate. And I realized I wasn't pissed; I was jealous.

Of a dead guy. Great. What the hell is Enzo Vitale doing to me?

A heavy notebook dropped out of one of the boxes, thudding against the concrete floor. I picked it up and flipped through it. As I read some of the text, I knew what it was a diary. Brycen's words enamored me, and I couldn't look away.

"Did you find something?"

"Not sure," I muttered, turning the page. "Just reading for now."

"Guess I'll keep looking then."

I nodded but stayed focused on the book.

...I think I'm in love with E. We went out of town today. E gave me whatever I wanted.

...I never thought I could be so happy.

...Am I doing the right thing?

...He knows. I know he knows, and I'm terrified. I wish I could tell Abi, but she wouldn't understand. I'm fucking scared.

My heart clenched. The more I read, the more the story twisted. Brycen wrote that he was scared of Enzo and Benito. He wanted to get away, but he couldn't. I flipped to another page. He had another slip-up. He was back on drugs worse than before, from what I could tell by looking at his slanted writing. I turned the page, my heart racing, only to be met with nothing.

I frowned at the sight of ripped-out edges where the pages should be. Someone had torn them out. My stomach clenched. *Did Enzo do this? Or Benito? Giancarlo? Why get rid of these pages and not the whole journal?*

Nausea rose in my throat. What if those missing pages concealed the truth about Enzo and what really happened with Brycen? I closed my eyes, trying not to think about it. Enzo had explained it all, and I'd been on his side. But what if he was lying?

"Caster? What's wrong? You look pale."

I stared at Rourke. "What?"

"Are you okay?"

No, I was far from okay. The story Brycen told was different from what Enzo had shared with me. Brycen was in love with him, he cared about him, and he never even mentioned Benito. Had I really let Enzo talk me into something that was an outright lie?

Why am I even surprised? He's a criminal. Of course, he lied to me.

I forced myself to focus on Rourke, whose face was pinched with concern. "I'm good. I should have eaten more this morning."

"Okay," Rourke said slowly. "What's that?" He nodded toward the book in my hand. "Anything interesting?"

I stared at the leatherbound book. "No, just an old diary. It doesn't have much in it." I tossed the book back into a box. "Anything over there?"

Rourke turned his back on me and started talking about one of the boxes. I used that brief moment to snatch up the journal and shove it into the waistband of my jeans. Rourke turned around as I was yanking down my shirt to cover up the book.

"I can't find anything here," he said. "There's some notes scribbled down I might be able to look into, but otherwise?" He shrugged. "This is a dud."

I sighed. "Let's call it." I closed the box in front of me and put it back on the ground where I'd found it. I stacked another on top. "I hope this is all back where it's supposed to be. We don't exactly have any right to be here."

Rourke frowned. "It should be fine." He shook his head. "You have me doing illegal shit, Caster."

"Last time, I swear." We let ourselves out. "What's next?"

"You coming to face Sarge and the chief. They'll give you orders on what to do, and we'll go from there. Don't worry. We'll toss these guys so far under the prison they'll rot there."

I let out a smile, but it felt awkward on my lips. "I know," I said. "I need to run a few more errands. Can we meet up tomorrow before work?"

"You got it. Go home and try relaxing," Rourke said as we slipped into his car. "Things are about to get crazy."

I believed him. When I got back to Enzo's apartment, I knew exactly what I was going to have to do. Even if it made my skin clammy.

I need to get out of his place.

Whether Enzo was lying or telling the truth wasn't the problem. I was now officially on the team against him. There was no way I could go on sleeping in his bed and pretending to be happy when I knew what was to come.

I had to leave Enzo alone once and for all.

Twenty
Enzo

A BAG WAS TOSSED DOWN THE STAIRS JOINING A PILE OF others. I didn't have to go through them to know they were full of Tex's clothes.

I took the stairs two at a time, racing against time. I stopped short of my bedroom to see Tex on his knees, trying to get Penelope to go in the cage.

"Come on, Pen. We have to hurry up."

"What are you doing?" The words came out of my mouth, but I felt detached from my own body as I stared down at Tex.

He went still, Pen trotting away from him and over to me. I was unable to bend down and pet him, afraid one wrong move, and everything would shatter before me.

"Enzo." Tex licked his lips as he faced me. His gaze dropped to the bags in my hands before they moved back to my face. There was a visible battle storming in his blue eyes.

Tex blinked, and the knot forming in my stomach tightened.

"Enzo, you knew this wasn't going to last."

"I didn't." My chest felt as if a knife was steadily piercing it.

"Come on. I'm a cop. I—"

"You are *mine!*"

Tex's mouth snapped shut as he stared at me. How could this happen? This morning we'd been wrapped in each other's arms, and now he was what? Planning on leaving me?

My heart rate picked up. I itched as if I was covered in ants. I knew it wasn't true, but it didn't stop me from involuntarily twitching as I fought the urge to scratch.

"Enzo, I can't be yours," Tex whispered as if he was afraid to admit it.

I snapped. In the next second, I charged at Tex. He saw me coming and slid on the floor around me. He was up, and I turned on my heels, chasing after him. Our feet thudded against the tile floor. Tex jumped down the stairs, and I was right behind him. I ignored the ache in my body; it was nothing compared to the need to get Tex.

He nearly made it to the door. His fingers brushed along the handle when I tackled him down.

"Fucking bastard." Tex drew his arm back, and his fist cut through the air before landing on my face.

My head whipped to the side, but I held onto him tighter. The taste of blood fueled me as I grabbed his wrists and slammed them to the floor.

"Enzo, get off!"

No, if I do, you will leave.

"Tex, you need to think about what you're doing."

His eyes widened. "You have got to be shitting me right

now." He jerked in my hold. "You're the one holding me down."

"Because you were going to leave."

"I have to!" Tex's blue eyes pleaded with me, but I ignored them.

I couldn't let him go. Not even if my brother asked me to. Tex had become something far more important.

"What happened?" I could fix it. "This morning was great. We had plans for dinner, only for me to come home to find you packing."

Tex looked away. For a short second, he stopped fighting against my hold. "I came to my senses. Can't live in fantasyland forever."

Is it so hard to be with me? Tex turned his head slowly back toward me, and our eyes met once more. I'm not sure what facial expression I wore. I felt too out of control to even think about it, but whatever Tex saw had him reaching out to me. I hadn't even realized I'd released his wrists.

I closed my eyes for a brief second and pressed my face against the palm of his hand. It was so grounding, and he wanted to take it all away.

"Enzo, this can't work."

Why the hell not? I jerked back and glared at Tex as I got up. I yanked him against me and pulled the handcuffs from his back pocket before I snapped them on his wrists.

"What the fuck?"

I said nothing as I yanked him behind me, dragging him to the guest room. Tex pulled and fought the entire way, but now he was truly stuck.

"I should have locked you up when I had the chance."

Tex audibly swallowed when I shoved him onto the queen-sized bed.

"Enzo, this is crazy. You can't—"

I had my blade out in seconds and sliced through his clothes. His mouth hung open as I tore every piece of fabric from his body and discarded it to the side.

"Maybe this is why Brycen was scared of you."

Time froze as Tex's words sank in.

"You said he was in love with you and cheated. Or did he even do it? Was it just a lie?"

I sat up, my hand shot out, and I covered Tex's mouth and squeezed his face, barely restraining the emotions that threatened to override me.

Killing Brycen had little to do with his cheating. It hurt, but in the end, I'd also seen how devastated Benito had been by it. Neither of us had known. Brycen had done much worse.

Words kept getting stuck, and it angered me even more. I stared at Tex's wide eyes.

"He loved no one." It certainly wasn't me. There was so much more, but my brain continued to misfire, and words jumbled up. Instead of talking, I'd show Tex he belonged to me.

Tex scooted up the bed as I ripped my clothes off. I grabbed his ankle and yanked him back down.

Grabbing his bound wrists, I pressed them to the bed as I reached over to the nightstand and grabbed the bottle of lube. I didn't look twice at the condoms. I wanted to claim Tex in every way possible. I needed him to know mind, body, and soul. He was mine and mine alone.

"Enzo, you can't be serious," Tex said breathlessly.

I moved between his legs and slathered my cock with lube. I rested the head of my cock against his entrance. *I want you so badly, and I know you want the same.*

"Tell me you don't want me." My blood was rushing so loudly I feared it would block out Tex's reply.

His mouth opened and closed and his eyes shimmered. "I... I." Tex closed his mouth, closed his eyes, and stole away the beautiful blue jewels.

My hand collided with the side of his face, and his eyes snapped open.

"Don't look away from me." I wanted to see the look in his eyes as he destroyed what we had.

Tex licked his lips, and a single tear broke free. "I can't." The words were nothing more than a strangled sound, but I understood them.

I plunged inside of him with no condom. The heat sucked me in and stole all of my reasoning. Our moans mixed as I fully seated myself inside of him. I rested my arms on either side of Tex's head and caged him. Leaning down, I lapped up the tear that had fallen and kissed both of his eyes.

"You're mine."

I pressed our foreheads together and pulled back before snapping my hips forward. The sound of our flesh clashing together was nothing compared to the moan that I drew from Tex.

Tex whimpered. "But—"

"No buts."

I took his mouth in a demanding kiss. I wanted to own every inch of him. I wanted it so ingrained that he knew who he belonged to down to the fiber of his being.

"Say it," I demanded.

I pulled back and rolled my hips just like I knew he liked it. Tex's legs lifted as his head tossed back. His mouth hung open as he let out breathy moans.

There would never be enough of him. I thought I could quench my interest in him, but all it did was open an unhealthy obsession. I couldn't fathom Tex, not near me, not mine. It was a reality I had no desire to be a part of.

My teeth sank into his skin repeatedly, decorating his chest with multiple bite marks. It wasn't nearly enough. I wanted to possess him thoroughly.

"Please let me cum," Tex begged.

"You cum by my cock, or you don't cum at all." I leaned forward, folding him practically in half. "I can keep fucking you until you do."

"Fuck," Tex shouted as I pounded into him.

His body attempted to suck me in and never let me go. If only Tex's mind was so honest. He wanted me just as much as I wanted him.

"Enzo, please." Tex's head tossed back and forth as he pulled against his restraints.

I slowed down, and Tex's eyes widened. "No."

I cocked a brow at him. A light sheen of sweat glistened over his body, a body I'd worshiped on multiple occasions since I opened my home to him.

"Don't you dare stop," Tex said.

Anger rolled through me, and I snapped my hips forward, jolting us. "I thought you wanted to leave me, and now you're begging me not to stop."

Tex whimpered. "You're not being fair."

I dropped his legs and leaned forward. I bit his ear. "Fuck being fair. If I have to take you apart in order to keep you, I will."

"I fucking hate you."

Tex wrapped his bound wrists around the back of my neck, pulling me close. He kissed me as if he couldn't breathe without me. I'd give him all the oxygen he needed as long as he stayed with me.

I laid open-mouth kisses from Tex's lips to his ear. "I'll

gladly take all of your hate." I continued to fuck Tex, ecstasy coursing through my veins with every thrust. "Just be mine." I felt as if I was pleading.

I pulled back and met Tex's eyes. A trickle of blood slid from the corner of his mouth. I groaned as I leaned forward and kissed him again.

Tex's mouth opened. The coppery tang of blood greeted me, but past that, it was all Tex. He was all I wanted. A cry tried to escape him but I swallowed it down, sealing our mouths together. His hole tightened around me, halting my movements and sending endless pleasure rocking through me. I groaned into the kiss as my climax crashed through me. I was robbed of my senses and tossed into chaos.

I was lost for a few heartbeats, drowning in bliss, before I dragged myself back and stared down at Tex. He'd passed out, cum decorating his torso and chest. His body was lax under me, and I was tempted to keep rocking myself inside of him regardless of the fact I'd cum already.

I cupped his face and pushed some of his black hair back. "I can't let you leave me," I whispered, kissing him softly. "You can hate me, but I lo—"

Ringing pierced the air, and I glanced over at our clothes on the floor. I reluctantly pulled out of Tex but stopped short to see my cum dripping from his hole.

I found my phone and answered it without thought.

"Hey. Where are you?" Giancarlo asked.

I stared at Tex on the bed. My heart was still trying to break out of my ribcage. My head was spinning, and I had no real grasp on reality.

"Earth to Enzo."

I blinked, realizing I hadn't answered Gin. "Home."

There was some commotion before blaring music came over the line, followed by silence.

"I'm out back. Are you okay?"

No. I couldn't bring myself to answer. I was stuck. It phys-ically felt like my mouth was glued shut.

"Enzo, make a sound if you need me to come over."

Seconds ticked by, and Giancarlo didn't rush me. I needed someone. Tex was passed out, and he was bound to make things worse. I closed my eyes and grunted.

"Already on my way."

I hadn't even noticed the sounds of the engine in the background.

"Do you need a clean-up?" Gin asked.

I shook my head and remembered he couldn't see me. Forcing myself to speak felt like glass scrapping over my tongue. "No." It was a simple word, yet it took me what felt like forever to say it.

"Okay, good."

Giancarlo stayed on the line with me the entire time. Talking about who knows what. My mind wandered, but no matter where it went, I always kept my gaze on Tex.

Even at this moment, he was all I obsessed over. Time ticked by, and I slowly moved from my spot and over to the guest bed. I grabbed the cover, but instead of yanking it over Tex's body, I tossed it to the ground.

"Enzo!" Gin shouted, his voice echoing in my home. "Well, aren't you a cutie?"

His voice got louder as he grew closer to the guest room. Gin opened the door with Pen in his arms. His gaze instantly dropped to Tex, and I moved toward him.

Gin put the cat down and raised his hands. "I'm not making a move on him. I'm just checking." Gin audibly swallowed. "He still alive?"

"Yes."

He nodded. "Want to come out?"

I shook my head, knowing it was ridiculous that I couldn't talk like I normally could. "I... I want him upstairs." Each word was a little easier than the one before.

Giancarlo didn't question me and grabbed the discarded blanket. He tossed it at me. "Cover your man. The last thing I need is you cutting off one of my fingers because I touched his skin."

I nodded my appreciation and rolled Tex up. He groaned but was still out cold. Gin and I carried him upstairs, Pen on our heels the entire way up. We laid Tex down on the bed, and I instantly started cleaning him up.

Gin left the room, and I was glad he was giving me the time I needed. I went about making sure I took care of Tex. Bruises were already forming on his hips, and bite marks on his chest and neck.

Once he was all cleaned up, I pulled the blanket up. Pen hopped on the bed next to his owner. I took Tex's wrists and uncuffed them. I kissed him, wishing I could wake him and say something, but I was more likely to take him again and again until all he could think and feel was me.

I headed downstairs once I was cleaned and dressed.

"Want to talk about why there is a cop passed out in your bed with your cum leaking out of his ass?" Gin asked.

My shoulders tightened, and I glared at my brother.

He shrugged. "I had a few sugar-coated options, but let's be real, Enzo. You're essere stupido."

"I know." I couldn't deny it, but there was no way around it.

"You know what you have to do."

I shook my head. "He's mine."

"Enzo—"

"Gin, lui è il mio tutto."

Giancarlo looked ready to strangle me, but even that wouldn't change what was happening. "Cazzate!"

It wasn't bullshit; Tex was something more. When I was with him, I nearly felt whole. I wasn't constantly trying to decipher everything around me. He made things easier. Of course, he made them just as complicated as well, but complicated was my life.

"He is nothing more than a fixation," Gin stressed.

I stepped toward my brother, meeting his gaze head-on. Gin groaned and tossed his arms up, bowing out of our silent battle of wills.

"Benito isn't going to like this," Gin said.

"What am I not going to like?" Benito asked, stepping through my door.

Twenty-one
TEX

THROBBING. IT WAS ALL I COULD FEEL AT FIRST. AND THEN A weight on my chest, the feeling of Enzo's soft sheets, and a blanket on top of me. I forced my eyes to open.

"Meow!"

Penelope yelled in my face. I groaned, rolling over until he hopped off of me. With the weight on my chest gone, I could breathe easier. *I'm back in Enzo's room.* My mind was jumbled until I remembered what Enzo had done.

The throbbing in my body intensified as I pictured every moment from earlier. I didn't even know how long *earlier* was, but I could still taste blood on Enzo's kisses and feel his cock claiming me again and again.

I climbed out of bed, stopping as soon as the floor squeaked. When Enzo didn't come rushing in, I kept moving. I rooted around in the drawer and found my clothes.

"We've got to get out of here, Pen," I muttered. "For real this time. I'm not staying."

My job was waiting; my career and future were on the line. If I stayed with Enzo, I would be throwing all of that in the trash. I walked to the bedroom door, my heart racing as I cracked it open.

"What the fuck are you thinking?"

"I know what I'm doing," Enzo replied.

"Do you? Didn't I remind you of what happens when you think you have shit under control?" The man snapped, slipping into rapid-fire Italian I couldn't understand. "Where is he?"

"Leave him alone," Enzo's voice deepened, nearly a growl. "If you touch him—"

"You'll what?"

"Will you two calm down?" That was a voice I recognized. Giancarlo. "Since when do I have to be the voice of fucking reason?"

Shit, is that other voice Benito Vitale?

A cold sweat arched down my back. Out of everyone in the family, he was the most dangerous. His file was thicker than anyone else's, and the things he'd done... I shivered. *Can't think about that. Gotta get out of here.*

It took everything in me to quiet my breathing. My feet padded down the cool stairs one by one. The shoes I'd been about to put on were by the front door. Could I even reach that? I kept Penelope clutched to my side. He was usually quiet when he was on me, and I prayed he stayed that way. I dipped into the guest room, grabbing my wallet from the pants I'd been wearing. *No keys.*

"You'll get rid of him," Benito growled.

"No."

Silence.

"Enzo, I'm not asking."

"And I'm not going to do it," Enzo said evenly. "He's mine."

More silence followed, so loud I could hear my heart pounding in my ears.

"I'll do it myself," Benito snapped.

My chest squeezed as I took a step back. The sound of Benito drawing closer made every hair on the back of my neck stand on end. Images of crime scenes and what he'd done played in my head one after the other. Severed limbs, empty eye-sockets, cold blue bodies. I imagined all of them being me, and fear trickled down my spine.

Come on, Caster. If you're going to go down, then do it swinging.

I steeled myself, waiting to be eye to eye with Benito. Instead, I heard a grunt, a thud and the sound of fighting.

"Fuck. Will you two knock it off?" Giancarlo asked. "Goddamn it!"

I slipped Penelope into his crate. When I glanced in the direction of the kitchen, I could hear them fighting, but I couldn't see them. That meant they couldn't see me either. Turning, I examined the area around me. The bag I needed, the one with my most important shit, was still at the bottom of the stairs. I snagged it, juggling everything as I fled Enzo's apartment.

I stopped outside of the opened door. I could still hear the sound of flesh colliding with flesh. *Is Enzo going to be okay?* He was a dick, but I didn't want him to get hurt.

"Get off of him, Enzo!" Giancarlo yelled.

I took that as a sign. Enzo was winning. Besides, they were brothers. He would be fine. If Benito found me, I wouldn't be.

The elevator dinged as the doors slid open. I checked on

Pen in the crate. He yelled at me, letting me know exactly how he felt about the situation.

"I'm sorry, bud, but I can't have you sliding around in the car." I crouched down, rifling through the bag. I'd tossed my keys on top of it, but they weren't there. "I guess we're walking. Wallet," I said, yanking it out. "We can get a taxi."

When I hit fresh air, I took in a slow, even breath. I glanced down at myself. Walking around with no shoes on, disheveled clothes, a cat carrier, and a plastic bag full of clothes, I looked crazy. *This is what my love of danger gets me. What the hell was I thinking?*

My phone wasn't even on me. I couldn't call Chelsea and have her pick me up or Rourke. I was stuck. And I couldn't go home.

Enzo knew where I lived and how to get in.

Glancing around, I made a decision. Rourke's place wasn't far. I had been there a few times to watch the game, talk shit about work, and drink too much beer. He'd give me a place to crash if I told him what was going on.

I just had to make it there. Half dressed, freezing, walking on the disgusting New York ground. All of the bad decisions I made as a teenager came flooding back to me. I thought I'd grown up, but apparently, I was wrong. I was still chasing the high, but this time the name of the drug was Enzo Vitale.

"WHAT?" ROURKE ASKED FOR THE THIRD TIME.

I rubbed the water out of my hair with a thick towel. Rourke had given me the couch and let me use his shower. Penelope was out roaming and pissed off. I couldn't even look at him without him yelling at me.

"Caster!"

I jumped. "Sorry." I plopped down on the couch. "I said I need a place to stay because of Enzo. He knows where I live. He already broke into my house. I can't go back there."

"And why the hell is he after you? Did you get caught or something?"

I glanced away. I wanted to stay silent while still protecting a man that I had no idea who he really was. However, I knew the rules. Partners were supposed to tell each other everything. If I kept lying to him, the case was going to bomb, and I would have no one to blame but myself.

"I've been living with him."

Rourke choked on his beer. "What?"

"You've gotta stop saying that," I groaned. "I went after him, things got complicated, and I moved in."

He frowned. "So, what? You've got a thing for a mobster?"

"No," I spat. "It was a small, stupid fling. That's it." My stomach clenched. "It was nothing."

"You slept with a suspect," Rourke said. "It's not nothing. Do you know what this could do to your career?"

"I'm not stupid," I said evenly. "And I don't need lectures that I would be hearing if I was at my father's house right now."

"Your father did his job," Rourke snapped. "He was a decorated officer. You're fucking a mobster. Did you ever think he was right to get on your ass?"

I stared at Rourke, and he stared right back. My jaw clenched so hard my teeth ached. Fuck my father. Why was Rourke kissing his ass so hard?

Maybe he's right. Everyone always says my dad is a hero. Am I the only one who resents him this much?

"Tex," Rourke sighed. "I'm not trying to be an asshole, but you've got to know this is fucked up, right?" He pushed his fingers through his hair. "If anyone ever found out..."

"Don't tell them," I said quickly.

"If you have feelings for him, you could compromise this whole thing." That frown was back. I was seeing it a lot more often lately. "I need to know if you're willing to do your job. Can you put him behind bars?"

"Yeah," I muttered.

"Could you pull the trigger on him?"

A scream echoed in my head, along with the desire to punch Rourke in the face. The violent thought was brief but strong. I sucked in a breath. *Where did that come from?*

Enzo. The answer was quick and clear. Ever since I'd met him, I started going backward. Yeah, I left the drugs alone, but I was back to being impulsive, short-tempered, and wild. Enzo had done this to me.

"Yeah," I answered, feeling waves of apprehension wash over me. "I could."

Rourke searched my face. I felt like at any moment he would call bullshit and yell at me for my stupidity. However, he nodded and passed me a beer after cracking it open.

I took it and gulped down half the bottle before pulling it away from my lips. Rourke stared at me. "Long day," I muttered.

"We have work tomorrow. It might be a good idea for you to turn in early."

"Do you think he'll find me here?"

"Yep, and soon," Rourke said. "These guys are not only smart, they have scores of people that will do whatever they tell them to do. I'm sure they know we're close. Finding my place won't be that hard."

"Then I need to go," I said, standing up. "I'll look into staying somewhere else."

"Sit down," Rourke cut in, waving a hand. "No matter where you go, you would be in danger. At least here, it's us against them. No one innocent will get hurt." He shook his head. "This is an even bigger reason to shut the Vitale's down and throw their asses in prison for a long time."

I nodded, but my mouth felt like it had been glued shut. Enzo would be behind bars, and I wouldn't be able to see him again. Was the last time we spent together really going to be angry sex and unspoken words?

My throat felt like sawdust was clogging it, and I swallowed down more beer to erase the feeling. I already knew that things between us wouldn't end well. So, why did it hurt so damn bad?

Penelope meowed, hopped on the couch, and rubbed against my arm. I scratched behind his ears and moved to stroking the length of his body fast and hard the way Enzo did it. He instantly began purring, the sound so loud it rivaled the noise of the TV.

"What are you going to do with that cat?"

"Pen?" I asked. "I need to get him a few supplies, but he'll be okay here."

As I spoke, Penelope trotted over to Rourke. My partner frowned, lifted his hand, and tried to pet Penelope. A growl echoed from Penelope's throat before he hissed at him. Penelope's back raised, his tail high as he reached out a paw and struck out at Rourke.

"Goddamn it," Rourke yelled, jumping from his seat as I joined him. "You need to take that thing somewhere else!" He looked at his bleeding hand. "Shit, that burns. I need to clean this. Find somewhere for him to stay until we finish this case."

"He didn't mean it," I said. "He's just stressed."

"Yeah, stressed," Rourke muttered. Turning on his heels, he walked down the hall. "I mean it. Find somewhere for him to stay. I'm allergic anyway."

I gazed down at Penelope. "Why'd you do that?" I muttered. "You're supposed to be a good boy."

He grumbled again, the sound bordering on a growl. Shaking my head, I deposited Penelope back into his crate, but this time he went willingly. I knew where I could take him. Chelsea loved Pen and wouldn't mind protecting him until the case was over.

The thought of Penelope not being by my side only made my shoulders slump more. Enzo was gone. Penelope was about to be sent away. All I had left was my dream staring me in the face if I solved this case.

Do I even want this anymore?

I stuffed that thought down hard and fast. Being a detective was everything I wanted. I couldn't allow anyone to get in my way.

Twenty-two
Enzo

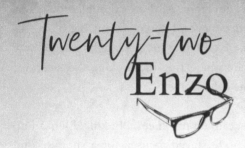

CHAOS WAS AN ENDLESS POOL THAT I WADED IN, UNABLE TO escape. Darkness closed in around me, and my limbs grew heavier with every movement. The pain didn't register, only the ache in the middle of my chest.

"Fuck, it smells like bleach in here." Gin's voice echoed through the constant fog that surrounded me.

I continued to scrub the grooves between the tiles. My fingers had gone pruny, and I barely resisted the urge to cut the pads of my fingers off.

"Enzo," Gin called.

I didn't look up from what I was doing. If I continued to clean and move, then reality stayed far away. I could hold the little control I had over myself.

A heavy hand landed on my shoulder, and I went stiff. My stomach rolled. The tiny voice in the back of my head screamed for it to be removed.

"You have to stop this. If you aren't out there looking for him, you're in here cleaning." Gin's hold tightened as he tried to pull me up. "Shit, Enzo, this isn't good. When was the last time you slept?"

Sleep? I couldn't anymore. All I ever thought about was Tex. When I closed my eyes, I could see his big blue eyes glaring back at me. I could hear his soft laughter or the way he moaned when he was eating my cooking. No sleep for me; it only made the ache worse.

"Enzo!"

I stopped and sat up on my knees. Blinking, I looked up at my brother. My gaze stayed focused for a short second before I noticed the stack of books on the kitchen table. Standing up, I moved toward them and removed them from one surface over to the living room. Books were scattered everywhere, half on the shelf and the others in varying piles.

Bile burned the back of my throat as I stared at the cluttered mess. *How have I forgotten to finish this?*

"Shit, Enzo. I've never seen the place like this. You have to get out of here."

"He might come back," I said. It was my answer every time after searching for him for three days straight. Tex hadn't been at his place or his family home. I'd even gotten information on his partner but nothing.

If it wasn't for Gin, I would have walked directly into the precinct.

Gin growled. "You have to get your head together. Benito is only going to let so much slide."

I don't care.

"You either come willingly, or we can do it like old times."

Gin cracked his knuckles, and I stared at his hands. They were just as bloody as mine.

I sighed and placed the books down. "Where are we going?" I had no desire to be tied up and tossed in the trunk. I wasn't sixteen anymore. That shit wasn't funny. Knowing Giancarlo, he'd drive around for a few extra hours just to make me suffer.

"Benito called for us."

The bruises on my body were a testament to how angry my brother was with me, but I'd given him the same share of bruises. There was no way he was okay with how I'd defended Tex.

"Come on, stop thinking so damn hard. You know how Benito is. This is business."

I nodded and headed for the door, but Gin stopped me.

"Shower and fresh clothes. Shit, if I didn't know you, I'd think you were in love, and now your heart's broken." Gin started laughing as if it was the most absurd notion. and Maybe at one time, it had been.

Now I wasn't so sure.

I went to the guest room and cleaned myself up. I hadn't been able to go to my room without staring at my bed in disdain. There was a reason I never allowed people into my space, and I'd opened it up to Tex. I missed him. I even missed the bell jingling around Pen's neck.

The drive to the club was nothing more than a blur. Everything was muted, and if I wasn't focused, everything sounded as if it came through a thick filter, making it soft and warped.

Even stepping into the club wasn't jarring. It was an annoyance but nothing I couldn't handle. We made our way to Benito's office, and each step felt like I was walking closer to a shark-infested tank. My brother wasn't one to let shit go. I knew he was still angry about Tex, but it wasn't something I was willing to roll over about either.

Gin opened the door, and we stepped through. Benito was sitting behind his desk, looking over paperwork. The moment we walked in, he looked up with no emotion displayed on his face as he gazed at me.

"Done chasing after the enemy?" Benito asked.

"No."

Giancarlo sighed as if another fight was about to break out.

"He didn't even stay. That shows you he never cared in the first place," Benito said.

Time seemed to freeze around me as I stormed over to my brother's desk and swiped my hands over it. Everything flew to the side as my hands crashed down hard on the wooden desk. "That isn't true."

Benito's gaze hardened, refusing to give an inch. It made him a great leader but a shit brother sometimes. "Enzo, we've been over this. The way you perceive things are different than others."

My fingers curled, and my knuckles scraped against the wood. Could I have been wrong? The time I'd spent with Tex had felt like so much more. I shook my head.

"Not this time."

"Enzo—"

I stood back up and met my brother's gaze head-on. "No. Tex is different."

"He is a threat to this family."

Benito wasn't wrong. Tex's job was a threat, but Tex himself... I wasn't sure.

"He stays off limits," I said.

Benito looked ready to argue, but Giancarlo walked over.

"That's it, I'm calling it. We are done fighting. We're

brothers." He leaned against the desk. "You both were hurt differently in the past."

Benito scoffed, but I knew the truth. My brother had fallen for Brycen; he just hadn't known that the man was playing us both.

"Enzo, is Tex different?"

I nodded without hesitation. "He is." I met both of my brothers' gazes.

Benito stared at me for a long while before he growled under his breath. "You're willing to risk everything we have for him?"

"Yes."

Benito's face showed nothing as we stared at each other. The tension thickened with every second that passed. It was easier to keep a hold of my emotions with Tex not being so close. That day at my place had been one of the few times I'd ever lost it on one of my brothers.

Benito's eyes said "I'm not." He didn't have to say it out loud. My stomach turned, and I prayed it never came down to me having to face my brother in a life-or-death situation, but for Tex? I would.

"We need to stay focused," Gin said.

"Did he get anything from your home?" Benito growled.

"No, I don't keep anything there."

The tension was so thick I was on edge. Normally, being around my brothers gave me a little bit of peace but right now, I had to watch every move and word that came from both of them. Tex's life depended on it.

"Benito," Gin said.

"Shut up!" Benito pulled out a cigarette and lit it with a match. "The cops are always a bother. I will handle it in time." He lifted his hand, cutting off any protest that sat heavily on my tongue. "Another one of our shipments was taken, and four of our guys are dead."

"Fuck," Giancarlo growled.

"How?" I asked. It wasn't adding up. The information we had on the guy clearly stated he was some cop, but he wasn't on our payroll. I'd checked multiple times.

"Get your head out of the clouds and do your job," Benito said. He stared at me. "I need my brother, not a traitor."

I resisted the urge to flinch and nodded. Telling him I would never betray him was pointless. Benito had already made up his mind; it was up to me to show him that I was behind the family. And that Tex didn't need to be killed. The latter was going to be a bit harder, but I'd do anything to prove it.

We continued to go over what we'd each found. I hadn't found shit in the past week; too busy looking for Tex. I couldn't tell Benito that, so I stayed silent. His unwavering gaze told me he already knew I hadn't been doing my job.

When our meeting was done, I turned and hightailed it out of there. The tension was even getting to me. I normally thrived under it, but I was feeling out of sorts.

Stepping out of the office, I faced the blaring club music. It was full like always, even on a Thursday night. I leaned over the ledge and stared down at the sea of people.

Familiar blue eyes framed by thick black lashes caught my attention. A square jaw and lips I dreamt about had me taking the stairs down two at a time. I was on the floor, rushing through the crowd of people. Sweaty bodies pressed against me slowing me down as I headed for him.

The closer I got, the further away he ran. I chased after Tex wanting nothing more than to catch him. This time, I wouldn't let him escape. The backdoor flung open, and a few seconds later, I ran out.

Instantly, I spotted the jacket he'd been wearing. My feet couldn't carry me fast enough to him. I wanted to call out his name, but my mouth stayed shut. I grabbed his shoulder and turned him around.

"Shit, what the fuck, dude?" A stranger with a heart-shaped face and brown eyes stared back at me. A mouth that wasn't Tex's turned down in a frown. He jerked out of my hold. "Man, the hell is your problem?"

I knew what I saw. There was no way I was hallucinating. I grabbed the stranger before he could go anywhere.

"Where did you get this jacket?"

"What business is it of yours?"

I stepped closer and looked down at him. Either he saw his death in my face, or his instincts kicked in. The stranger's body went stiff, and he broke eye contact.

"Some guy tossed it at me with some cash and said stay there."

"Where did he go?" The desperation in my voice rang in my ears. I just needed to see Tex. No, that wasn't true. I needed to hold him and keep him close.

"He ran across the street. I didn't see which—"

I pressed hard against the pressure point in his shoulder. The stranger's legs wobbled, and he let out a strangled cry. His hand reached up to wrap around my wrist, but I only applied more pressure.

"O-okay."

"You're wasting my time. Which way."

He released my wrist with trembling fingers and pointed to the left. I let him go and ran. Cold air sawed in and out of my lungs. The burn was nothing compared to the steadily growing ache. I came to a stop at the street light and looked each way.

My heart was pounding, and my lungs burned. I searched each way, but there was no Tex. I pushed my fingers through my hair and tugged. In the place of the tumbling emotions crashing through me, one took control. The one emotion I understood above all.

Anger.

"If I can't have you, then no one can."

Twenty-three
TEX

Fire burned my lungs as I turned another corner and then another. *Shit, shit, shit!* I hadn't meant to wander into Blu, but my feet had taken me there as if I was on autopilot. I'd tried everything to get Enzo out of my head, but he was always there. I'd convinced myself just one glimpse of him would be enough, and then I would disappear, but he'd seen me too.

Enzo's dark eyes on mine had made shivers run up and down my spine. One look, and I wanted nothing more than to climb into his bed and ride his cock until he smiled for me. At Blu, I was reminded that he never smiled all that much except for when he was with me.

My heart pounded as I leaned against an alley wall and sucked in a cigarette smoke-filled breath from someone nearby. The woman raised a brow at me, and I nodded. I'd probably scared the hell out of her. I closed my eyes and drew in another long, deep breath until my heart stopped racing out of my chest.

That's it. I can't go looking at him anymore.

My only job was to look into the Vitale family. No more little trips to stare at Enzo. No more driving by his place in the new beater car I'd picked up. And no more thinking about him as anything other than my enemy.

I pushed off of the wall, trudging down another set of alleys until I came out near my car. Sliding behind the wheel, I stared off into the distance. My life had been going so smoothly, but now it was a chaotic mess.

Not like it's anyone's fault but my own. I should have never gotten into bed with him.

The thought of never feeling his hands on my body or his mouth on mine was enough to send me into a full-blown depression. I opened my glove compartment and snatched the pack of cigarettes. Tapping one out, I shoved it into my mouth and lit up. I hadn't smoked in years, but I'd turned into a chimney overnight.

I started up the car and drove straight to Chelsea's. Penelope would be happy to see me, and I him. I needed some comfort.

"Yo," Chelsea said as she opened the door. "Come on in."

I stepped into her colorful apartment. "Where's Pen?"

"Probably somewhere around here, peeing on something. He's a revenge pisser," she said as she clicked her tongue. "Pen, Papa's here!" She turned to me, looking me up and down. "You smell like sweat and cigarettes. Where the hell have you been?"

"Out," I mumbled.

"Where out?"

I frowned. "Don't ask."

Chelsea groaned. "You went to go see Enzo again, didn't

you?" She followed me as I walked through her place in search of Penelope. "Tex, if you keep popping up at Blu, it sends the wrong message. How can either of you move on like that?"

I clenched my jaw so hard it hurt. She wasn't wrong, but I didn't want to hear it either. A flash of orange shot past me, and I went after Penelope. I scooped him up into my arms.

"Hey, baby," I cooed. "Why are you running away?"

Penelope yowled and shoved away from me. I put him down. As soon as he was on his feet, he ran away, disappearing into Chelsea's bedroom. I stared after him as my face fell. If I was depressed before, it was worse now.

"That cat holds a grudge," Chels muttered. "Just like his Papa."

"I do not." I sighed, wanting to chase Penelope down but knowing that wasn't the answer. "Got any food?"

"Shower first," she directed. "I can't take another three breaths full of you right now."

I lifted my shirt and sniffed. "Fair enough."

My shower was quick, mostly because whenever I spent time alone, I thought about Enzo. I quickly stepped out, drying my hair still as I walked back into the kitchen. Chelsea popped two plates on the table, teeming with overstuffed tacos.

"Where have you been staying?" she asked once we both sat down.

I bit into a taco and shrugged. "Around," I said. "Couch surfing mostly. If I stay in any one place too long..."

"Enzo will find you."

"Exactly," I said, trying not to show how I jolted when she said his name so casually. "So far, so good."

"You can't keep living like this." She frowned. "It can't be healthy for you."

I shrugged again. "The case is progressing. Sooner or later, he'll be behind bars, and I can live my life again."

"Even when he's locked up, you think this is going to stop? Tex, he's the kind of man who won't live this down. Once you send him away, he might kill you. Guys like him don't care."

"He's not that bad." The words slipped free before I could stop myself. *Why am I defending him?* I cleared my throat. "He wouldn't kill me."

"No?" She raised a brow. "Are you sure?"

I opened my mouth. Images of Enzo fucking me for dear life in his guest room came back to me. That look on his face had held something dangerous, something... powerful. As much as the crazy in him turned me on, I was now on the outside looking in. If that insanity was trained on me, Chelsea was right; no matter how much I didn't want to admit it, I could end up dead.

"Did you find anything on his hard drive?" I asked, trying to change the subject back to something cold and clinical. The investigation.

"Some stuff, nothing too important. He's very thorough, but it's nothing about his job, at least not on the surface. I'm sure he's encoded some stuff deeper, and I'll find it. He's smart." She nodded. "Give me a little more time? What are you going to do with the information once I find it? It's not like you can give it to your boss. You got it by breaking into his place."

"I know," I nodded, grateful that she'd stopped using his name. "It won't be admissible in court, but it might lead me to something that is. Everyone's counting on me now. I have to succeed."

Chelsea's frown worsened. "Seems like you're trying to make everyone else happy. But what about you?"

I blinked at Chelsea. "Being a detective will make me happy."

"Are you sure?"

"Jesus, Chels. Please get off my back."

She threw up her hands. "I'm just asking you to look at things, that's all." Penelope meowed, interrupting our argument and the tension that had started to grow. "Yeah, your Papa's here, being an ass."

I scooped Pen up into my arms, and he was over his hissy fit. "Don't listen to her. She's crazy."

Chelsea threw shredded lettuce at my face. "Shut up, or I'll kick you out."

"You hear that? She'll put us on the streets, Pen."

"Not him," she said. "Just you."

I scoffed. "What a dick."

Chelsea smiled, and I returned the expression. No matter how hard life was, I needed to remind myself that I gave a damn about her. It wasn't her fault my life was a cosmic shit show.

I SEARCHED UNDER THE MAT FOR THE KEY I KNEW WAS UNDER there somewhere. Rourke kept my uniform at his place, which was a good thing. I couldn't let my bosses know I was slumming it. They would think I couldn't handle my shit. I mean, I couldn't, but I had to pretend I could.

"Found you."

I snagged the key and shoved it into the door. Quietly, I shut it behind me. Rourke and I had to work together anyway, but if he was still asleep, I didn't want to wake him up. I made my way down the hall and paused as I heard a voice.

Guess he's already awake.

I balled up my fist, ready to knock on his door, but paused. Whoever he was talking to, I couldn't hear them. He was on the phone.

"No, tonight isn't good. I need to take care of shit." Silence. "Get off my ass!" Rourke snapped. "I know what the fuck I need to do. You do your goddamn job, and I'll do mine! Fucker."

I jumped at Rourke's yelling. Since when had he ever lost his temper like that? He'd been getting on my ass since we met, but that was just him. This? It was something different.

I thought better of knocking on Rourke's door. If he was having a bad morning, I wanted to stay on the other side of that shit. Turning on my heels, I went to the hall closet and retrieved my uniform.

"Caster?"

"Yeah, it's me," I called back. I pulled out my uniform, stepped back and found Rourke standing in the hallway. "What's up?"

"When did you get here?"

I shrugged. "Just now," I lied. "Need my uniform for work. You almost ready?"

He peered at me closely before he nodded. "I will be in ten."

"Me too. Let's pick up food on the way to the precinct. I can't be late again."

"Fine. Let's get moving."

I paused. "Are you okay, Rourke?"

He turned back toward me. "What do you mean?"

"I don't know. Lately, you seem a little off, that's all. I was wondering if you're okay."

His eyes narrowed. For a brief moment, I felt ice trickle

through my veins before the look on his face dissipated and the fear I felt went right along with it. *What the hell was that?*

"I'm good, kid," he said before nodding toward me. "Are you coming or not?"

"Yeah," I said, still trying to shake of unease that crept down my spine. "Yeah, I'm coming. Sarge wants us to go over the files before the chief gets in and needs to be caught up."

"Then let's do it," Rourke said, disappearing into his room.

"Yeah."

I stared after him for what felt like ages. *What's his problem? Is he acting like this because I'm staying here more often? Or because he knows I fucked Enzo?*

Rourke had never been all that short with me. Straightforward and a pain in my ass, sure. Short and snappy? No. Something was going on with him.

I stepped into the bathroom and closed the door. *Whatever's going on with him, it's not my business. But partners are supposed to tell each other everything.*

Both sides of me warred, trying to figure out the best way to deal with this. In the end, I put on my uniform and swallowed it all down. Rourke would talk to me eventually. The last thing he needed was me pushing him into a conversation he wasn't ready to have. The same way he respected my privacy, I needed to respect his.

"Ready?" Rourke asked when I walked into the living room, his bad mood gone.

"Yeah."

He nodded, looking me over before he smiled. "Sorry, I'm in such a shit mood. It'll pass."

"I'm sure it will. We've all been there."

"Exactly," he said, gathering his keys from the coffee table. "You get it."

"I do," I said, laughing awkwardly. "I need coffee."

"Me too!" He grinned. "I'd rather not snap at work and get fired."

Just like that, we brushed past the situation, but it sat in my gut like a stone. I sucked it up and prepared myself for the day ahead. The chief and Sergeant White were waiting for answers. I needed to give it to them.

Life was so much simpler a few weeks ago.

Twenty-four
Enzo

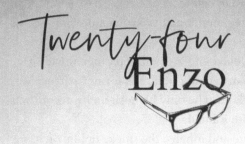

"Sir, I swear—"

Bang. The ringing of the gunshot cut off any other words he was going to say. Hot blood splashed across my face and over my hands. I stared down at my hand painted with crimson drops and felt nothing.

A whistle cut through the air, and I looked away from my hand to find Gin waltzing in. His gaze danced over to the body in the chair.

"You've been going through them faster and faster. We can't replace them with how fast you're disposing of our men." Gin kicked the chair, and the body hit the ground, adding more blood to the pool already decorating the floor. "Another traitor?"

I nodded. The shit went deep, but all they could give me was the same fucking name. Ramada. He was dead. I'd seen to it myself, and I didn't make sloppy mistakes.

Giancarlo pulled out a cigarette, and I took one from him. "Think his ghost is haunting us?"

"He's the last ghost I'd be worried about."

Gin laughed, but I couldn't join him. As of late, I laughed even less than before.

"So the cop they mentioned is Ramada or someone he worked with?"

I groaned. "I looked into his former partner already. He's the one who ratted Ramada out." His former partner was the straight-laced kind. The only blemish on his record was his partnership with Ramada.

I lit the cigarette and inhaled the smoke holding it as my mind wandered. It went right to Tex, fueling the anger in me and shoving any fatigue I might have felt down. I took the cigarette and pressed the lit end to my thumb to put it out. Releasing the smoke, I called for some of our men to come in and start cleaning up.

"Shit, Enzo," Gin growled as he stared down at my hand.

I barely registered the sting. "Don't worry about it. I have to follow up on another lead."

He grabbed my arm. "You need to sleep."

Why couldn't he see I needed to keep busy, or I'd end up doing something reckless? Like storming into the precinct and killing anyone who got in my way in search of Tex. I looked at my brother and his hold on my arm loosened enough for me to break free.

"Enzo, I get that you're angry—"

"You don't get anything." I stepped away from him. "I'm doing what needs to be done for the family."

I turned on my heels and headed out after washing my hands and face. We each had a job, and I needed to go back to focusing on mine. I'd let so much slip by as I focused on

Tex, but that wasn't the case anymore. Tex had made it clear we were enemies and nothing more.

I ground my teeth. Like every time I thought of Tex lately, I wanted to punch something or kill someone.

"Sir," one of the men held up my keys, and I took them.

My mind was an endless sea of turning thoughts. I was so distracted I hadn't noticed getting behind the wheel. Or even driving. I had no idea where I was going, but my mind was blank as buildings flew by. Before I knew it, I was pulling to a stop. I blinked and groaned at the sight of Tex's apartment.

Why the hell am I here?

I knew he wasn't there. I had a man on the place the entire time. I spotted him as he walked around the building and went inside. My stomach twisted, and my grip on the steering wheel tightened. Deep down, I knew I needed to let him go. This was Brycen all over again. Maybe my hands were too bloody to hold onto someone.

No, Tex is mine.

He could keep hiding, but eventually I was going to find Tex Caster. My phone rang, drawing my attention away from the building.

"Sir, there is something you might want to see."

"Send me the location. I'll be there shortly."

The message came through. I gave Tex's building one last cursory glance before pulling off and hitting the highway.

Ramada's place was in a well-off neighborhood. One too nice for a meager cop salary. He'd been single. The moment I stepped into his place, I could see why.

This place is disgusting. I avoided stepping on anything that would stick to my shoes.

"What did you find?" I asked.

I slipped gloves on, realizing I had neglected to clean as well as I should after killing the last guy. My skin crawled with the knowledge, but I forced the need to go clean up down. Instead, I followed behind one of my men to the computer.

Sitting down, I clicked on the mouse, and the screen lit up. He was right. I did want to see this. There were a few hidden files, some even password protected. If it was worth hiding, it was worth looking into.

"Has anyone come over here to check on him yet?" I asked.

Blake came around the corner and shook his head. "No, sir. He has no family, and he is only a few weeks behind on bills."

I nodded. "Leave nothing important behind."

Blake went off to handle it with the others, and I focused on what I needed to do. Computers were far simpler than humans. They didn't have complicated emotions or dreams that got in the way of them working.

The computer was slow, and I resisted the urge to move things around. It dinged as the software I'd installed on it was done. It combed through all the files available. My men were trashing the place even more, looking for who knew what.

If only it was so simple with a sign over it stating right here is what you need to figure out who was trying to take your family down. The computer chimed, and I went over the hidden files.

My family's name came up on multiple occasions and a few businesses we were involved in. Ramada was far more invested than we'd thought. I took a picture and sent it over to Benito. I continued to scour the files. A few more names popped up, but one I saw just as much as our name scratched at the back of my head.

Dillan Mathews. It wasn't my first time seeing his name or even hearing it. He was one of the few dealers working under our family. His track record was commendable. I checked over the books personally, and he hadn't attempted to skim any money off the top. Not to mention he wasn't involved with any of the gun shipments. What the hell did he have to do with any of this?

There were too many questions and not enough answers.

A low-end dealer's name came up a few times. "Blake. Carter." Both of them came over to me, ready for orders. "Find him." I passed over the picture of Dillan Mathews.

Something told me to look further into him. I rarely ignored my instincts except when it came to a certain cop.

"FIND HIM?"

Blake shook his head. "But we found out he was picked up a few months back."

I gestured for them to continue and Carter picked up where Blake had left off.

"Dillan was picked up on possession and distribution charges. The case was air tight. They had someone willing to testify."

"But?" My stomach tightened.

"The boss hadn't put in a word for him to be cleared, and it was never reported. But Dillan went free the next day," Blake said.

"Who was the witness?" I asked.

"Carl Rodgers, a meth addict. One of Dillan's regulars."

I scratched at my chin, the hair rubbing against my fingertips, reminding me I needed a trim. "What else?"

"He's been making his payments like usual, but it's never him anymore. His cousin said he hasn't seen Dillan in weeks but was told to keep sending money."

"The drugs?" My head was starting to hurt.

"Someone is selling them, but we couldn't get the answers out of the cousin."

"Couldn't?"

Carter cleared his throat. "He didn't have any answers."

I grabbed a drink and poured it as I sat down. I preferred doing the torture myself, but I couldn't be everywhere all the time. Carter and Blake were a few of our men that I knew were capable of getting answers when need be. I sipped my drink, the alcohol like liquid fire as it went down.

"Who was in charge of the bust?" I asked.

"Ramada and Chandler," Carter answered.

I was up in seconds and moved some scattered books around before I found the file Benito had handed over to me. There, clear as day, was the last name on the lists. Aaron Chandler was thirty-six and was fired. Unlike Ramada, he didn't get to keep the retirement package or even leave with pay. Everything they'd done together was placed on his shoulders. However, in the end, it was brushed under the rug, and he was able to go a free man.

Why hadn't I killed him yet? A devilish smile and tempting eyes came to mind, and I was instantly hit with anger. The glass broke in my hand, and I stared down as it cut into my flesh. Something other than anger swirled in my chest. I shoved it all away.

No more distractions.

Guess it was time I finished the list. "Ramada's partner

was James Till. How in the hell were they the ones to bust Dillan?"

Blake looked at my bleeding hand and moved to grab a towel. I took it and placed it on the table, ignoring it and focusing on what was before me. Answers.

"Till was out on paternity leave. Ramada and Chandler were temporary partners," Carter said.

No wonder I hadn't put them together. They were in the same precinct but from what I had gathered, they were never together. I chastised myself for missing something that I normally would never overlook. Glaring mistakes one after another, all because I'd allowed myself to be distracted.

"Sir," Blake said, pointing to my hand. "You should—"

"You two can leave."

Carter pulled Blake, and they turned and headed for the door. They stopped just shy of leaving. "You want us back on Caster?"

Hearing his name sent a violent reaction through my body. I clenched my fist, and the glass pieces bit further into my flesh.

Yes. "No, he's not important right now." The lie was like ash on my tongue, but if I kept saying it, I was bound to believe it even when I buried him.

Twenty-five
TEX

I raised a hand and hesitated before I knocked on the door. What was it about coming home that always made me pause? I sucked in a breath. Every alarm bell rang. *I should turn around and leave.* If my father wasn't threatening to go to my Sargeant about the missing files, I would have. There was no way to get around what I'd done.

My knuckles rapped against the screen door. I stood up a little straighter, staring ahead. One ounce of weakness, and he'd be on my ass even more. The door creaked open. I stared down at my mother. The older I got, the tinier she looked.

"Hey, honey." She smiled, but the look was forced. "What are you doing here?"

"Is Dad around?" *I already know he is. When does the old man leave?*

"Yes, he's in the living room." She opened the door and

let me in. "What's going on with you two? He won't tell me anything."

My lips pressed together. I didn't know what to say to her that wouldn't make her look at me with disappointment in her eyes.

"Nothing," I said shortly. "I'll go talk to Dad."

"Oh. Okay." She frowned. "You two play nice."

I suppressed the scoff that threatened to break free. Nice. There was never any nice when the two of us were left alone. One of us always ruined it. I walked into the living room, and he looked up, a sneer twisting his lips.

"What the fuck were you thinking?"

Ah, we're starting already.

I shoved my hands into my pockets. "I asked you—"

"I know what you asked me," he snapped. He grabbed his cane, pushing himself onto his feet to glare at me. He always did that when he wanted to be intimidating. Had he forgotten I'd grown up since then? "I told you to stay the hell away from the Vitales."

"Yeah, I know."

He sneered. "You don't know jack shit, or you wouldn't have ignored me and did whatever the hell you wanted to do."

I stared at him. Did he think I was still a child? Okay, stealing from him wasn't right, but did he have to talk to me like that?

Rolling my shoulders back, I clenched my jaw tightly until pain shot through it. Sharp pinpricks of pain focused my attention.

"I needed it for my investigation," I said. "There's a whole task force revolving around the Vitales, and that wouldn't have happened without it. I have people watching my back."

"That doesn't mean shit," he grumbled. "You want to be some kind of hot shot, that's what this is. Wanna play hero? All you're going to do is get yourself killed."

I scoffed. "Like you? From what I've heard, everyone says you were a hero, but the truth is you were just as bad as me. Charging in head first, getting yourself shot. How can you get on my ass when I'm your exact carbon copy?"

He stared at me. I glanced away, toying with my fingers. *Shouldn't have said that.* I hadn't meant to let it slip free, but the hypocrisy of what he was saying smacked me in the face like a ton of bricks. As the silence grew between us, I shifted from one foot to the other. He stayed silent until I looked up and met his angry gaze.

"What did you say to me?"

I willed myself not to take a step back. My father ran over me backward and forward when we were together, but I wasn't in the mood for that shit right now.

"I said I clearly got it from you," I said.

He took a step toward me, but I stayed still. When his eyes narrowed, all I could think about were all the times he'd torn me apart as a child. My father rarely ever put his hands on me, but his ability to rip me to shreds with a few well-placed words was truly a talent.

"You're nothing like me," he said slowly.

My stomach dropped, turning into a pit of anxiety as that look came over his face. *Turn around and leave. I can get the hell out of here right now and never have to hear another word out of his mouth.* I tried to make myself move, but it was like my feet were glued to the floor. Somehow, he still had a hold on me.

"When I was your age, I was following in my father's footsteps. Every man in this family has been a cop, then a detective, and moved up the ranks. You've been fucking around, Tex. Every chance you had straight out of high school, you blew. How many times did I find you strung out upstairs?"

"Stop," I said, my voice trembling despite how hard I tried to make it stop.

"Once I kicked you out, how many times did I find you in that shitty little apartment you used to live in so out of it you didn't know I was there?"

I still live there.

"How many times did I have to threaten you with going to prison before you finally cleaned up your act? Huh, Tex?"

My head snapped up, and I realized I'd been staring at the floor. It was a familiar thing to do, staring at the old, worn-out threads while he yelled at me.

"I don't want to talk about this," I said.

"Oh, I'm sure you don't," he snapped. "The only thing you've ever wanted to do is get high and be a lazy, ungrateful asshole. You act like you had such a bad life when you've been nothing but spoiled."

"Spoiled?" I stared at him as the shock settled in. "You call having to deal with your abuse everyday spoiled? How many times did you come home drunk off your ass after a shift just to scream at Mom and me?"

"That's not abuse. Grow up."

"Telling your son he's worthless and your wife she's useless is abuse," I snapped right back at him. "But you didn't give a damn. You were always the cop. The hero. If anyone knew how you treated us—"

"Enough."

"—they wouldn't have called you that shit. If they knew, they would have looked at you like another one of the criminals down at the station." I laughed. "Who am I kidding?

Your friends saw it, and they never said anything. All they would do is cover for you."

We stared at each other, neither one of us backing down. The weight on my chest hadn't lessened even after dumping some of the frustration that had lived in me since I was a child. The stone was still there, growing as he glared at me like I was just junkie trash on the street in his eyes. Like I wasn't his son.

Goddamn, I need a hit. A drink. Anything.

"Where are my fucking files?" he asked.

"Henry." My mother walked in carrying his lunch. She sat it on the little table he had chosen to eat at since I was a kid instead of spending time with his family. Once she was done, she turned, frowning at both of us. "Whatever is going on, stop it. Lunch is ready." She disappeared. "I'm bringing you a plate too, Tex. We'll eat together."

I wanted to tell her I didn't have an appetite, not anymore. Pulling the files from underneath my armpit, I shoved them at my father. He stared at them before he snatched them out of my hand.

"Is this all of them?" he muttered.

"Yeah."

"Every last one?"

I sealed my mouth shut. I'd already answered him once; I wasn't about to do it again. My father loved a well-trained dog, but I was sick and tired of playing. He looked up at me and raised a brow.

"I asked you a question, boy."

"And I already fucking answered it."

The words exploded out of me, coated in red-hot anger. My nails dug into the soft meat of my flesh. If my nails were any longer, they would have cut into my skin. Instead, I felt the sharp, stabbing pain and swallowed it, letting it seep into me and soothe my emotions.

"Don't you ever curse at me," he said evenly.

I rolled my neck. "Then don't do it to me."

"You need to learn respect again."

"Give me something to respect, and I will," I bit back.

"Fuck you," he spat.

"Fuck you too!"

The crack of the cane against my face was hard and fast. It felt like lightning kissing my skin. Wetness rolled down my cheek, but it wasn't tears. I reached up and touched it. Blood stained my fingers, deep, dark, and slick. Searing pain washed over me. I could hear screaming, but it was far away, like listening to the ocean in a seashell. As if it wasn't even real.

"What did you do! Henry, what the hell did you do?"

My mother's hands grabbed at me, urgent and hot. The smell of garlic from her fingertips made me recoil. It was just like when I was a kid, one of those rare drunken nights when my father's temper was too hot, and I paid the consequences.

"I didn't mean to do that," my father grunted. "The boy was mouthing off at me. It was a reflex."

The same kind of reflex I've heard you had with suspects? Or prisoners?

I'd heard whispers about my father, but I never wanted to believe they were true. Now, I was pretty damn sure they were. I'd been brushing shit off and pretending he wasn't as bad as I remembered.

I was right. He was worse.

"Get off," I said as my mom dabbed at my bleeding cheek with a towel. "Mom, stop! Fuck."

I picked myself up off the floor. Mom's doe eyes tugged at

my heartstrings, making me want to pull her to me and apologize. However, she was just as guilty as he was. History was repeating itself, and I was a scared kid getting blood wiped off of my face while she bribed me with treats and another hour of TV past my bedtime.

My chest squeezed so painfully that I could barely breathe. The images were too strong. The feeling of helplessness grew.

I can't be here.

I didn't look back at my father or mother as I turned on my heels and stormed out of the house. Her voice followed me, shaky and sorrow-filled. The old me would have stopped and gone to her because she was just as much a victim as I was. But I was over that bullshit. I was the one that should have been protected, and she was still defending him.

He didn't mean it. How many times had she whispered that to me while cradling me in her arms?

Shivers raked over my body. I opened my car door, sliding inside before I slammed it. I risked one glance back and caught sight of my mother hurrying down the stairs.

I've never peeled away so quickly in my life.

What was I thinking? I shouldn't have come back to this goddamn house.

My throat tightened, and my hands gripped the wheel so tightly it hurt. No matter what I did, my father was never going to give a damn. If I failed, he wouldn't blink an eye. If I succeeded? He would still remember all the times I failed.

I'd tried so hard to change things between us, to prove that I wasn't a pathetic screw-up. Now, I was sure that was how he would always see me.

A stoplight forced me to look into the rearview mirror. My cheek was still bleeding, as my face swelled.

Hospital, then a place to sleep tonight.

I wished I was going where Pen was. Never had I ever needed a warm, comforting hug more. My mind flashed to Enzo; the way he held me, talked to me, and kissed me. I felt the pricking of tears gathering behind my eyes and forced them down. My father's words echoed in my head.

Real men don't cry.

God, I needed something to numb the pain.

Twenty-six
TEX

I LOOKED AT THE BANDAGE ON MY CHEEK. SO FAR, IT WAS clean. No more bleeding through the white cloth. Thankfully, the cut hadn't been deep, but it still ached. I was on my fourth ibuprofen, and the pain was still there. Maybe it was all in my head, psychological throbbing instead of actual, physical pain.

"Caster, have you turned in your reports?"

Sargeant White peered at me, waiting expectantly. I heard what she said, but for some reason the words weren't sticking in my brain. She raised a brow.

"Um, yes, reports. Yes, Ma'am, I turned them in already," I said as I nodded to myself.

"Anything I need to be caught up on?"

"Not from my end," I said slowly. "We're still looking into things. Rourke went to grab something to eat, but he'll be back. I have a meeting after work with someone to look into some digital footprint stuff."

"An informant?"

I shook my head. "An independent contractor."

She looked me up and down. "Well, see what you can find. The chief is on my ass."

"I know." I glanced at his office and made eye contact. A shiver ran up my spine before I turned back to her. "He's been staring at me nonstop."

"His job is on the line. You'd be staring too." She patted me on the shoulder. "Come on, Tex. You can do it. This is what you always wanted, right?"

Right. A dream come true.

I watched her walk away as my phone started to ring. The button flashed, and I picked up the receiver, pressing it against my ear.

"This is Officer Tex Caster."

Silence greeted me. I looked at the number on the screen, but it was blocked. *Great, someone being an asshole.* My finger hovered over the end button as a thought came to me.

"Enzo?" I whispered.

The call disconnected. I pulled the phone away, staring at it. *Was that really him? Why would he be calling me?*

You're mine.

He'd said those words to me more than once. I belonged to him, and that he would never let me go. Maybe I'd been delusional to think that as the days and then two weeks rolled by, he had forgotten about me. I imagined the look in his eyes, the devastatingly dangerous gaze that rocked me to my core as he fucked me the last time we were together.

My body craved him. One last hit, and I would be okay. I

could dream about our time shut away from the world and pretend that it wasn't a passing fling for both of us. I just needed one more taste...

The phone rang again. I reached out and snatched it up. "Enzo, you can't keep calling me h—"

"Um, Texas? Are you okay?"

I groaned. "Yeah, yeah, I'm good." I wiped a hand down my face. "What's up, Chels?"

"Has Enzo been calling you?"

"No. I don't think so. Hey, my boss is staring me down. Do you have information?"

"Right, we'll talk about it later." I heard the sound of her fingers flying across the keys. "This hard drive is really interesting, but I didn't find anything about your case on it. He's really careful," she said, avoiding the E-word. "What I *did* find out, however, is that whoever is currently toying with the Vitales is more than likely a cop."

I froze. "What?"

"Yeah, I mean, it makes sense. They know all the ins and outs of how crime families work. They're meticulous, careful. Cops don't make a whole ton of money. This could be their side hustle." She started typing again. "Besides, what I've been able to find online supports that theory. There's talk about a new cop on all the usual places, and the rumor is he knows how to get you whatever you're looking for. Guns, drugs, girls. You name it; he's got it."

"Is there a name?"

"Bunch of screen names, but nothing real," she said.

"Shit. Can you keep digging?"

"Already on it. One more thing. I did some digging around about Brycen Grennar. According to my contacts, he definitely was into some heavy shit. Word was that he was sleeping with two Vitale brothers, and on top of that, he was working as an informant."

My stomach flipped. *Enzo was telling the truth?* I gripped the receiver a little harder.

"What else?"

"Get this. Because of Mr. Grennar, things went sideways with the Vitales. Giancarlo Vitale ended up being in prison for a little while, their business was thrown into chaos, and a friend of theirs or at least an associate was killed. They had to pay the family a huge sum of money to cover the cost of the funeral and to take care of his family because he was the provider. And that's when Brycen disappeared."

That's when Enzo had to kill him.

It made sense now why Benito had made him kill Brycen. Too much had gone into a spiral when he worked with the police. My throat felt tight. Enzo hadn't been lying. However, now that I knew the truth, fear ran up my spine.

If Brycen was killed because of so little, what would the Vitales do to me? I was more than an informant; I was a cop. I shuddered, thinking about it.

"Thanks, Chelsea."

"I'll update you as soon as I have more." She paused. "Be safe out there."

"Always."

I hung up the phone and stared at the computer screen. Everything was becoming more complicated by the day. Glancing up, I looked around the bullpen. *Is it someone here?* I'd overheard Enzo and Giancarlo talking about Ramada. Did he have something to do with this before he was killed?

My teeth sank into my bottom lip as I thought about my colleagues. Who could be working with the Vitales?

BLARING MUSIC AND THRASHING BODIES BUMPED INTO ME. ALL of it was nothing more than background noise to me as I looked for the one man I needed to stay away from. *Fuck, I'm an idiot.* Every instinct in me screamed to turn around and leave. I'd been smart staying away from Enzo. Reaching up, I touched the bandage on my cheek. The rush of emotions was a tornado of confusion and shame. My mother hadn't stopped calling me, but I couldn't talk to her yet.

I spotted Enzo, making my blood pressure shoot through the roof. He walked around the bar with a frown on his face. A man stepped into his path. Enzo reached out, grabbed the man by his collar and yanked him forward until they were face to face. I stalked forward before stopping myself.

What am I doing here? Am I turning into a stalker now?

I needed to turn around and disappear. However, as much as I told myself that, I was still standing there, staring at him as his fist connected with the man's face. Giancarlo pulled him away, making him stumble back. Enzo stared at the man like he was ready to take off his head. As he lunged forward, he turned in my direction and froze.

Shit. Can he see me?

Blu was dark, but it wasn't pitch black. I yanked my hood up over my head and turned away. The part of me that wanted to see Enzo was overruled by logic. I hadn't seen Enzo in what felt like ages. He didn't seem like the kind of man that would forget a slight. What was it he'd said? He always kept a knife on him.

I stumbled out into the darkness, too many drinks in and wobbly. Glancing over my shoulder, I tried to spot him, but he was nowhere in sight. I turned back around and headed for the alleyway like I'd done before. Ducking down one and turning left at another, I exhaled deeply. I'd gotten away. As much as I hated it, Enzo hadn't caught me.

My back slammed against a wall. I blinked. *How much did I have to drink?* A pair of shoes stepped close to me. Confused, I looked up to find Enzo glaring at me, his thick eyebrows pinched. Before I could say a word, his hand wrapped around my throat.

"Why are you here?" he growled.

That voice, mixed with his swirling anger, made every last nerve in my body ignite like Christmas lights. I opened my mouth, but his hand tightened, cutting off my air and ability to speak. Still, I didn't stop him from what he was doing. It felt good dancing on the edge of a live wire, not knowing if he would end it all.

God, I need this.

"You should have stayed away."

I know. Trust me, I know.

My body lifted toward his automatically. Even now, he was too far away. I was desperate to feel his touch, to drown in the way his mouth tasted as the scent of his cologne blanketed me and made me feel... safe. I wanted to laugh. When I was near him, I was both safe and terrified. How was that normal?

Enzo's dark eyes searched my face. I saw something in his eyes, something dangerous and dark. He could kill me. The rage was right there, waiting to be unleashed. But I wasn't ready to die.

His lips crashed against mine, stealing what little air I had left. The world spun, spots of blackness coming and disappearing from my vision. My body shoved forward, seeking him out. *I'm going to pass out if he doesn't let it.* I grabbed his arms and yanked straight down. His grip slipped, and I used the opportunity to raise my knee, driving it into his stomach. I coughed as he recoiled, trying to drag a breath into my tight lungs.

"Shit," I groaned. "Are you trying to kill me?"

"Yes."

I blinked up at him as I doubled over, using my knees for support. "At least you're honest."

He pulled a face. "Last time we were face to face, you practically called me a liar."

I licked my lips and straightened up. "Yeah, I did. I know now that you weren't lying. Chelsea told me all about Brycen."

Enzo's frown deepened. "You're staying with her?"

"No," I said. "That's not the point anyway."

"What is the point?" he countered.

I opened my mouth and snapped it shut again. I didn't have a point.

Enzo closed the space between us in two short strides. His hand went for my throat, but I sidestepped him. Enzo grunted as he stopped himself against the brick wall. He turned, his dark eyes glaring at me.

"You left."

"I told you I had to," I shot back. "You don't listen."

"What part of 'you're mine' didn't you fucking understand?"

Enzo lunged for me, and I was too slow to dodge him. I expected the heavy, hot weight of his hand around my neck. Instead, what I got were his lips on mine. Hard, rough, and sharp, the kiss pushed me to the brink of my sanity and threatened to drop me off the edge.

I *needed* him. Enzo's tongue swiped against the seam of my lips. I groaned, trying to push him away and maintain my strong stance, but he wasn't having it. His hand gripped my cheeks, squeezing them roughly until my lips puckered. Enzo's tongue slipped inside. I tasted whiskey on his mouth, strong and smooth. Something expensive.

Were you drinking because of me?

My cock throbbed in the confines of my jeans. Every inch of me ached for him. The alarm bells in my head rang. No matter how much I knew I should stay away, I burned for Enzo.

He grabbed my arm, turning me around and shoving me against the brick wall. Cool air tickled the back of my neck, sending a shiver down my spine. Enzo's hands were quick, unfastening my pants and tugging them down my hips. He spread my cheeks. My heart jumped into my throat.

Fight back. Don't give in to this.

I shoved back against Enzo. He responded by pushing me forward. I grunted, planting my feet as I tried to wiggle out of his grasp. No matter how much I wanted him, it didn't mean I should go through with it. Enzo was a fresh line of coke, temptation on a plate.

"Enzo," I growled.

"Shut the fuck up," he snapped. "I'm trying my hardest not to fucking kill you right now."

Cold sweat etched its way down my spine. There wasn't a single hint of a lie in his tone. It made me hesitate to move, speak, or even think. Enzo spread my cheeks and spat between them. I pushed away from the wall only to be shoved against it more firmly.

"Did I say move?" Enzo asked. "Keep your ass out."

My cock jumped. For some reason, I did what I was told. The sound of Enzo's zipper in the stillness of the alley was loud. He yanked my hips back before I felt the familiar feeling of his cock sliding against the crack of my ass.

My need for him grew hotter every second. The longer I was forced to wait for Enzo to take me only made me more desperate. "What are you doing? Just put it in," I growled through clenched teeth. "Come on, Enzo. Fuck me. Please, fuck me."

His hand wrapped around my throat, but he didn't squeeze. The wet, slick heat of his cock pressed against my hole. Spit wasn't the same as lube, but my twisted little heart loved that. I wanted it to hurt, to stretch, to blind all of my senses. I wanted Enzo Vitale to make me feel nothing but his brand of possession and control.

"Fuck!"

Enzo slammed inside of me in one fast, sharp stroke. I grabbed the wall, bracing myself as he thrust inside of me. My knees buckled, and it took everything in me to stay upright. My head swam. I reached between my thighs, shoving a hand around my cock and stroking it as he grunted, bottoming out inside of my hole.

Stars burst behind my lids as I pushed back against him. Enzo's grip around my neck tightened. I leaned into his hand, devouring the warmth of his flesh against mine after so many empty, lonely nights. I wanted to grab him, hold him down, and keep him against me. Enzo was the enemy, but I didn't give a damn when every "hero" seemed three times as bad as him.

A kiss, and then teeth tugged on the lobe of my ear. Even with his hand on my neck, there was a plethora of kisses left on my skin. Soft, feathery, but each one more demanding than the next, as if he could force me to stay if he just held me long enough.

God, did I want to crumble. An imaginary life with Enzo was better than a thousand empty nights with people who didn't give a fuck about me.

My throat tightened. Hot, wet tears rolled down my cheeks. I imagined the bandages getting wet on my cheek, soaking into the wound that was more than flesh and blood. I cried out.

"Why are you crying?" Enzo asked.

"Just fuck me," I begged, not giving a damn how pathetic and desperate I sounded. "I need to feel you fuck me."

Enzo paused. His cock throbbed inside of me. For some reason, that stillness pushed me toward the brink. I felt like I was going to break down. Until Enzo slammed inside of me.

"Tex," he whispered against my ear. "It's okay."

Those words almost broke the dam, but I held back. Enzo and I moved together, grunting, groaning, and moaning together as we chased our highs. I felt the familiar swelling in my balls, the tingling along my flesh, and I knew I was blissfully close.

"Enzo!"

I painted the brick with ribbons of my cum as I was flooded with hot, sticky heat. Enzo bucked his hips, rolling and thrusting until he had nothing more to give me. He laid against my back, the soft panting like music to my ears until he broke the silence.

"What happened?" he asked, dragging a finger over my bandage. "Who did this to you?"

I froze. "It's nothing."

"Tell me," he demanded, gripping my arm. "Who hurt you?"

I swallowed thickly. Telling Enzo anything felt like a death sentence for the person I named. However, part of me still wanted to tell him that it was my father so I could watch the man rip him apart.

Slowly, I turned to face Enzo. I dragged my pants up my

hips as warm cum coursed down my thighs. Enzo peered at me, his eyes studying mine like he always did. It was a familiar sight. One I had missed.

"Long story," I said quietly. "Not worth repeating."

"It was your father, wasn't it? You went to visit your parents not long ago. That wasn't there before you went."

My stomach tightened. "Jesus, Enzo. This is why we can't be together."

"Why?" he asked, his eyes growing sad.

"You're following me," I explained. "You know where my parents live. This is too much. How am I supposed to cope when everything I say to you could end up with someone dead?"

"I'm trying to protect you."

I knocked his hand away. "Who asked you to?" I pinched the bridge of my nose. "This is never going to work. I have to get back to my job."

Enzo grabbed my arm, yanking me back to him. "How many times do you think I'm going to let you run away?"

"Let me?" I asked, scoffing. "And I'm not running away. This is me being an adult and doing what needs to be done."

"If you believe that, you're naive," he said evenly.

I pulled away from Enzo. "I have to go."

"Fine." I stopped and glanced back at him. Enzo stuck a cigarette between his lips. He lit up, smoke curling into the night sky. "Don't let me see you again, Tex. I showed mercy this time. Next time? I'll kill you."

Fear trickled down my spine. I didn't doubt him for a second. Rolling my shoulders back, I watched as he walked away, disappearing into the shadows, leaving me utterly and completely alone.

I opened my mouth to beg him to stay, to pretend everything was okay for a little while. But I'd stuck my own foot in my mouth. My heart shattered into a million fucking pieces as I continued to stare down the empty alley. I couldn't see Enzo again.

Not without there being a bloodbath.

Twenty-seven
Enzo

IN MY HEAD WAS THE LAST PLACE I WANTED TO BE. I REPLAYED my recent interaction with Tex, picking it apart piece by piece. How he'd felt pressed against me, or the way his ass had sucked me in and clenched tightly, threatening to never let me go. However, that wasn't the case. Tex ran, and I let him every single time.

I ground my teeth as my fingers curled around the knife in my hand. Muffled screams pulled me back to reality, and I blinked a few times as everything came into view. Gone were Tex's blue eyes and warm touch.

A heavy sigh fell from between my lips as I took in former officer Aaron Chandler. Even while dissociating, I'd made sure to avoid any vital spots. His leg was a carved-up mess. If I squinted and tilted my head slightly to the right, I could make out Tex's name.

I dragged the sharp blade over the torn flesh, and it split

further. Blood ran down the sides and joined the growing puddle.

"We can do this all night," I said.

He shook his head, the cloth in his mouth keeping him from talking. Reaching up, I removed the damp fabric.

"You... you haven't asked me anything."

I blinked. I'd been too deep in thought. Shrugging, I stood up taller and loomed over Chandler. "Why waste my breath? You know why I'm here."

He shook his head. Why did they all want to do it the hard way? Normally, I looked forward to those who could hold out against me. The longer they did, the longer I could enjoy my time holding a knife and watching blood spill. Lately, however, my patience was paper thin.

Any second now, I'd slice his throat. We'd be back at square one, trying to find out who was steadily fucking us out of money and trying to ruin connections.

"Did you think stealing from us would work out for you?"

Chandler shook his head. "No, I would nev—"

I twisted the knife around and brought down the handle on the arch of his nose. The crunch of bone resonated around me like someone chewing on corn nuts. A thick gush of blood followed and splattered on my already blood-soaked hands.

"All lines lead to you," I said.

Rolling my shoulders back, I stared down at him as he turned his head, spitting the blood that dripped into his mouth. The rap of knuckles on a door gave me pause. I looked up just in time as Benito and Giancarlo walked in.

"Anything?" Benito asked.

I shook my head as we all stared down at the man who'd fucked us over. His eyes widened the moment he realized he didn't just have one but all three Vitale brothers there.

"You did a number on my business." Benito pulled out a cigarette and lit it as he brought it to his lips. "I can't help but feel as if you were unhappy with the amount of money you were getting from me."

Chandler coughed. "No. I... I didn't do this. Ramada dragged me in." His eyes pleaded with us to believe him.

Benito blew a puff of smoke out, filling the air with the smell of tobacco. He looked calm, as if the whole ordeal wasn't threatening our very foundation. "And you kept it going?"

Chandler flinched and tugged at his restraints, but he wasn't going anywhere.

"I was going to tell you about it," he cried out.

Benito hummed and nodded at me. "You see, I don't believe that. Why should I trust anything that comes out of your mouth right now?"

I moved toward Chandler and removed the last bit of fabric covering his cock. An undignified squeal came from him as I gripped his cock in one hand and brought my knife to it.

A memory of me doing this very same thing to Tex flashed before my eyes, and heat traveled down my spine, followed quickly by longing. My hold tightened until Chandler screamed out in pain. I loosened my grip slightly and shoved down the memory of Tex. It would only further distract me.

"I'm going to ask some questions, and I want answers, or you can become a dickless man." Benito shrugged. "Up to you."

Chandler was trembling from head to toe. His wild gaze bounced from each of us as if trying to find a lifeline in the room full of monsters. He wasn't going to get any help, not from us.

"We only hit up the suppliers who were going down in busts. It was already a product that was going to end up in evidence." Chandler coughed, making his body jerk and pressing his cock closer to the blade of my knife. "Shit, get that thing away from me!"

Pussy. Tex could handle it. Fuck, he'd even cum for me. I swallowed back the groan and kept my face impassive.

"You're wasting our time. What else?" Gin prompted.

"That was it. I swear, we didn't plan to take any money straight out of your pocket." Chandler cleared his throat, trying to meet our gazes but failing. "It all stopped once Ramada went missing."

Benito blew out a puff of smoke. I applied pressure dragging the blade back and forth, cutting into Chandler's flesh. I had to be careful. Too much pressure would have the knife cutting off his dick like a hot knife through butter. I sawed it instead, forcing him to feel his flesh parting slowly as I cut off his cock.

His screams grew, and he flailed as much as his restraints allowed. His words became intangible as he banged his head back against the table. The stench of urine filled the air, mixing with the metallic scent of blood.

I grimaced as piss cleared some of the blood off my tattooed hands. I gritted my teeth and stopped halfway through his cock.

Giancarlo pushed off the wall, grabbed Chandler's face, and slapped him. The cop's mouth opened and closed before his eyelids fluttered. Blood continued to drip out past my knife.

"You shouldn't lie. Who's all working on this?" Benito asked.

Chandler shook his head, choking on his saliva.

"Man, I've met idiots before, but you're taking the fucking cake here." Giancarlo took a step back, wiping his hand on his pants leg.

Benito didn't need to give me direction. I cut through the remaining piece of flesh. Blood squirted up, and Giancarlo let out a huff of laughter.

"He's not going to hold out," I said. I'd been working Chandler over long before they arrived. It had just slipped my mind to ask questions.

"Doc is already on her way," Benito said.

I grabbed a wad of paper towel from Chandler's kitchen and stuffed it over the bleeding stump where his cock once was.

The room grew quiet as I leaned against the wall. Tension hung heavy in the air. This had been going on far longer than any of us had realized. We were going to need to put the fear of the devil in everyone that was under us.

Benito must have predicted that I was going to go too far too fast. Not even five minutes later, one of our men let the doc through.

Melony's thick curly hair was pinned back in a bun. Her dark brown skin glowed even in the dim lighting of the kitchen. She stepped through, her mouth turned down in a frown, the moment she saw the man on the kitchen table. She stepped around, trying to avoid the puddles of blood as she approached him. "How long?"

Benito stared at the doc. "Long enough to answer my questions."

She shook her head. "It won't be easy." She held her hand up, silencing Benito. She was probably one of the very few women who could, besides our nonna. "Once I'm done, be ready to work quickly." She started setting up, taking some of his blood and testing.

I turned away and moved to the side as we waited for her to bring Aaron Chandler back around. Couldn't get answers if he was knocked out or too close to death.

"When he gives up your boy, I want him dead," Benito said.

I went stiff at the thought of killing Tex. No matter how much I threatened him, if it came down to it, would I be able to pull the trigger?

"He won't," I said through gritted teeth.

Benito didn't look convinced. Giancarlo was quick to jump up before a full-blown argument started again.

"Come on, are we sure he's working with someone?"

"Yes," Benito and I both said in unison.

"There are too many products and too many avenues being fucked with for him to be able to do it alone," Benito said. He put his cigarette out and grabbed another. "Had to have inside information on our shit as well." He eyed me accusingly, and my fist balled up tighter.

It isn't Tex! I kept my mouth closed. I could scream it until I got blue in the face, and my brother still wouldn't believe me. It would take every drop of evidence and then a fucking miracle to convince him otherwise.

"Benito—"

"Shut up, Gin," Benito said. He pointed his cigarette at him. "I know you don't want to go back to prison."

Giancarlo's face twisted in anger before smoothing out. Out of the three of us, he wore his emotions a lot more. He was also the one who hated confined places. Hospitals and jails were all the same to my brother.

"This is different," Gin argued.

"Is it? As far as I'm concerned, this is history repeating

itself." Benito glanced my way. "Only this time, he went straight to the enemy."

It isn't like that. Right? Am I destined to pick between my family or the man I love?

My chest tightened as I realized that I loved Tex. What was I supposed to do now?

"Stop your quarreling. I know you're brothers, but you're going to make me fuck up." Melony pulled back and finished hooking up the IV. "Alright, I say you got another ten, maybe twenty minutes."

She stepped back and packed up her things. She didn't glance back toward the man on the table as she headed toward the door. "Benito, double my fee for tonight. You know how I feel about working on corpses."

He nodded, not arguing with her. To be honest I was certain we'd pay Melony more than a surgeon made if it meant she would be all ours. But she liked running her low-end clinic with her girlfriend. And we weren't going to get in the way. Out of all the people who worked for us Melony came close to being family.

The moment she was gone, I shoved off the wall but Benito was up and shaking his head for me to stay still.

"I don't want you tampering with answers."

I gritted my teeth.

"If he was going to do that, then he would have done it already. Come on, Benito. Enzo has always put the family first."

Benito grunted. I couldn't agree with Giancarlo this time. Not when my heart was still racing with the knowledge that I loved Tex. Fuck, for the first time in my life, I questioned my loyalty to my family.

If Tex's name is listed what am I going to do?

I felt eyes on me and looked up, not remembering when

I'd tilted my head down. Giancarlo stared at me and I couldn't find it in me to reassure him, not yet.

"Time to wake up," Benito said.

He smacked Chandler a few times, but the man only groaned. Benito pinched Chandler's broken nose. His eyes flew open as a nasally shout left him. That was one way to do it.

Clarity was fleeting in his dull-looking eyes.

"How many of you are fucking me out of my money?"

Chandler's head nodded to the side, and Benito slapped him again. "Answer me."

"Th-three... no-now two." His teeth were chattering as he lay there. "C-co-c-cold."

"Who's your new partner?"

My stomach clenched as I waited on bated breath.

"I'm so, so, so cold."

Benito lit a cigarette and sucked in a lungful of smoke before putting out the red cherry against Chandler's flesh. The sizzle crackled in the air before the man screamed.

"There, you're nice and warm now." Benito grabbed Chandler's face and forced him to look up at him. "Name now!"

Every single time his teeth clanged together as he shivered brought more anxiety trickling down my spine.

"R-r-ro-ro... Rourke... Houghton."

My feet were moving before my brain could register it. I stood next to the table as Chandler repeated the name as if it was the only thought going through his head.

I knew it wasn't Tex.

Chandler started to convulse, his body shook, and his eyes rolled to the back of his head. We stood there watching him going into shock, none of us racing to help him or ease his way to death's door.

Time slipped by. What was probably only a matter of minutes passed as Chandler took his last breath. His fingers twitched, and I checked his pulse. I concentrated on the warm flesh as no pulse greeted my fingers. I dropped his bound wrists, and they flopped down lifelessly.

"Leave an example," Benito said.

I grabbed the severed cock and pried open Chandler's mouth. Shoving the limp cock down his throat was messier than I'd assumed. The member squished and folded under my fingers. Blood eased the way as I stuffed him like a Thanksgiving turkey. I grabbed my knife once more and carved the word thief into his flesh.

Blood rolled out slowly, the heart no longer pumping it through his veins. It made cutting him a lot easier. I moved around and shoved him a little way down the table. I traded out my knife for his kitchen meat cleaver. It had a good weight to it as I raised it and brought it down over his wrist with a substantial amount of force.

I hacked away at his wrists two, three, four times before they pulled free.

"Get in here and clean up. Leave the body," I said.

Some of our men moved in with gloves on and went about cleaning up the evidence. All that would be left behind was the body of a thief. No one stole from the Vitale family and lived to see another day.

I washed the blood from my hands before heading out of the house and toward my car. Giancarlo's hand gripped my shoulder, and I stopped. I cocked a brow at my brother as he studied me.

"You seem different."

My natural reaction to tell him he was seeing things didn't come forth. Could I deny it when I felt different?

"Things are changing."

He nodded. "What are you going to do about him?"

Gin didn't have to specify for me to know he was talking about Tex. My heart fluttered, and I absentmindedly rubbed at my chest. "I'm going to drag him home."

Giancarlo's mouth tilted down in a frown. "He's a cop."

"He's the man I love."

We both stood there, Gin's eyes wide as his mouth fell open. Saying it aloud only cemented the feelings.

"Enzo." Gin's voice was sullen.

I pulled free and turned to face my brother. "Tex is mine."

Gin pushed his fingers through his hair. "You know what they say. If you love something, let it free or some shit like that."

I shook my head. "That is ridiculous. It should be, if you love something, lock it away so that it never escapes."

Giancarlo laughed. "Man, I'm starting to feel bad for a cop." He moved past me. "We solve this shit and get things back in order. After that, we'll see about you getting your cop."

"Tex."

Gin cocked a brow at me.

"He is more than a cop. His name is Tex."

Giancarlo laughed and it helped dissipate some of the tension that constantly surrounded me as of late. "Right, a mobster and a cop." More laughter bubbled out of him. "Fuck, you got it bad."

There was no denying that. I loved Tex Caster, and there was a future for us even if I had to clear the way with blood.

Twenty-eight
TEX

"LET'S GO, PEOPLE!" SERGEANT WHITE'S VOICE BROKE OVER the radio. "We need to get into position and fast before the Vitales realize what we're up to."

My chest squeezed so tight I briefly wondered if I should stop and go straight to the hospital. I tugged my bulletproof vest away from my body and groaned. *Stupid thing feels like it's suffocating me.*

"Stop fidgeting," Rourke muttered.

"Can't." I squirmed in my seat.

It was almost time to leave the car, and then the action would start. This was that exact moment that I loved on rollercoasters, that second when the platform shifted, and there was no going back. The truth was that hundreds of feet up in the air, it got my dick so hard I could burst. But now? I shivered. Cold sweat trickled down my back, and I was pretty sure my balls had jumped up inside my body.

"Are you good or not?" Rourke snapped.

His eyebrows pinched together and his mouth turned down into a deep frown, bordering on a scowl.

"Let me get ready my way, and you get ready your way, okay?" I snapped. "What does it matter to you if I can't sit still?"

Rourke's eyes narrowed. "Is there a problem?"

My life is the problem. I wanted to tell him to leave it the fuck alone, but I was done talking. Any second now, we'd be raiding one of the Vitales biggest warehouses. It was the kind of betrayal there was no coming back from. When Enzo found out, we wouldn't be fucking in dark alleys. I'd be dead.

Shadows walked back and forth around the warehouse. There were guards all over. No doubt there were more inside. Every second that ticked by made the hair on my arms raise. I adjusted my vest again, mapping out every scenario that could possibly happen.

I shifted in my seat, and I caught Rourke glaring at me. *Fuck, something bit him on the ass.* To be fair the entire precinct was up in arms after hearing and seeing what had happened to former officer Chandler. My stomach twisted in knots just thinking about it. I'd prided myself on having a strong stomach, but I'd tossed up my entire breakfast after seeing the pictures of his mutilated body.

"What are you going through, Caster?" Rourke asked.

I pressed the back of my hand over my mouth, forcing myself to swallow back the bile. "Nothing. Just remembered the stuff with Aaron Chandler."

Rourke stiffened, and his mouth dipped further in a frown. "A good man tortured like that. Only a monster could do it." He ground his teeth as he stared intently at the warehouse. "Fucking Vitales."

At the mention of them, my heart skipped a beat. *Enzo.* "We don't know it was them." Even as I said it, a part of me knew that was false. It could have very well been Enzo who did it. "He was a dirty cop. I hardly think he qualifies as a good man."

Rourke scoffed and slapped the steering wheel. "Are you sticking up for them now? Do you need to stay back?"

I shook my head.

"Caster, you need to be on the good side. I can't have a partner who doesn't have my back."

He's right. What the hell am I even thinking? I nodded. "I got your back, Rouke."

We stared at each other for another minute before the same old smile appeared on Rouke's face. It was jarring how quickly his facial expressions had changed. "Good, it's you and me." He touched my arm, but it felt off, that same icy feeling permeating my veins.

I nodded, giving the only reaction I could before turning back and watching the warehouse. Buzzing came from Rouke's side, but I knew it wasn't the chief calling or Sarge. They would use the radios for that. I forced myself to relax.

"We should move," Rourke muttered.

I turned to stare at him. "What are you talking about?"

"Everyone else is out front. There's only us and two other guys back here because all the action is going to be up there. Come on, if we get in there we can clear shit out and rub it in their faces."

I blinked at Rourke like he'd lost it. "We barely know how many men are in there. Ten, twenty? But there could be more. We're going to take them all on?"

Rourke gazed at the building. "No. We're going in from the back. They won't even know we're there. Let's go in, start clearing them out, and Sarge will have the rest join us any minute now. But if they get in there and we've already started, guess who ends up looking like big damn heroes? Us."

"Or," I said. "We both lose our jobs. And if the chief is really off, he finds some charge to stick to us so we sit in jail for a while thinking about how fucking stupid we were."

"I thought you wanted to be a detective?" he asked. "Aren't you ready to finally shove it in everyone's face and get there? The chief will promote you so quick your head will spin if you take down the Vitales."

"They're probably not even here," I said, my pulse racing at the thought of finally reaching my dream. It was so close I could taste it.

"But if they are and you arrest them..." Rourke trailed off.

I would get my wish. My mind tried to conjure up images of slapping handcuffs on Enzo's wrists. None of them would go down easy, but I didn't need all three broth-ers. Just one. Besides, Enzo was the one who had threatened to kill me if he saw me again, not the other way around. If he really gave a damn, he wouldn't say crazy shit like that.

"Are we going? Or not?" Rourke snapped.

"Fine," I shot back without thinking. "Okay, fine. Let's do it."

Rourke was out of the car before I could even finish my sentence. I was right after him. The moment my feet hit the pavement, a chill fell over me. *Am I making a mistake?*

"Let's take this backdoor. No one's around. Hurry up," Rourke hissed.

I didn't have time to think. Instead, I moved. We slipped through a gate. The guards that had been there before were nowhere in sight. My gaze swept over the area. It was like they'd disappeared.

"Where is everyone?" I whispered.

"Doesn't matter," Rourke muttered. "Keep going."

Tingling spread through my chest as every step we took brought us closer to the warehouse entrances. Cold dread settled in the pit of my stomach. When we reached the door, I drew my gun and stood on the other side. Rourke looked at me, held up three fingers and started counting down.

Three... two... one...

We moved in unison, pushing into the warehouse. As soon as we did, the fear and worry fell away. This was the part of the job I loved; the adrenaline. It ramped up, and I was ready to go, focused. I could take on anything.

"Get on the ground!" Rourke yelled. "Police, do it!"

To my surprise, some of them listened to him. They laid down, dropping their guns as their eyes darted around like caged animals. *Is this supposed to be so easy?*

"Caster, you paying attention?" Rourke asked.

"I'm right here."

"Then move. We need to get through these guys, and there's an office on the other end. Let's go!"

I moved along with him, something nagging in the back of my brain. We zip-tied the wrists and ankles of those on the ground and kept moving. Gunshots rang out, piercing the quietness around us. Rourke and I split apart, taking cover as the gunshots intensified along with yelling.

"I think they know we're here," Rourke said, a glint in his eye. "Keep pushing!"

"Wait," I said, shaking my head. "Shouldn't we wait for backup? Where is everyone?"

"Fuck that, we're already here. If we turn around, someone else gets all the glory."

I frowned. "Since when do you give a fuck about glory?"

"Come on!"

Groaning, I turned off of the pillar and squeezed off a few quick shots. A man yelled as he went down. I moved around, pushing forward.

There was no going back now. However, that didn't mean I wasn't praying that the Vitales weren't here. More than likely, they were at home. Or off terrorizing someone else. What were the odds that any of them would be here?

"The longer we take," Rourke yelled over the roar of gunfire and yelling. "The greater the chance the Vitales slip away."

I froze. Rourke dropped a man like it was nothing, and I watched as a slow smile appeared on his face. *Is he enjoying this?* Something tugged at me. It was like he knew the Vitales would be here, but how could he know?

"Tex, pay attention!"

I tuned back into things and ducked in time to avoid a bullet. If we were going to get out alive, I had to stay focused.

"Get on the ground!" Rourke yelled.

Some men dropped, but others? They didn't give a damn. Instead of listening, they tried to put a bullet in our brains. I glanced around, but there was no backup. *Does Sarge even know we're in here?* The warehouse was huge. What if they didn't know we were inside?

"Enough!" A voice cut through the chaos. "Are we done shooting? Can we talk?"

I froze. That was a voice I would know anywhere. Benito. I glanced around and saw him standing there, staring in our direction.

"We already know there are cars out front, but it'll be a while before they get in. That door is reinforced, and it's going to take more than a ram to get through it. So, we can talk, or we can go back to shooting at each other."

"There's nothing to talk about," Rourke answered. "Get

on the ground, lay on your stomach, and get cuffed. I've seen enough contraband around here to put all of you away for a long ass time, so do it!"

"I don't get on my belly for anyone," Benito shot back.

"Yeah, I think I'm good on that," Giancarlo chimed in, a grin on his lips. "The only way I'm getting on the ground is if I'm getting fucked."

I glanced over at them. My eyes landed on Enzo. He was silent, his eyes darting around in the dimness of the warehouse. *Is he looking for me?*

"I'm not going to tell you again to get down on the ground!" Rourke yelled. "Last chance!"

"Or what?" Benito chuckled. "You shoot me?"

"Abso-fucking-lutely."

I stared at Rourke. "We need to back down until the others get through."

"Fuck that," he sneered. "I'm sick of these pathetic, criminal assholes getting away with shit. We take them down, and we get the fuck out of here."

"Rourke."

"Don't be a pussy, Tex," he hissed at me. "Who gives a fuck if a couple of scumbag mobsters die?"

I care! I fucking care!

No matter how badly I wanted to be detective, I wasn't willing to murder them just because of who they were. It didn't feel right.

"We're doing this right," I snapped. "Arrest them."

"Do they look like they want to be arrested?" he shot back. "These fuckers will put us in the ground!"

"What the hell Rourke? This wasn't the plan."

Rourke rolled his eyes. "Stay there and piss your pants, Caster. I'm taking these monsters down." He shook his head. "Thought you were going to be better than your old man."

"Fuck you," I growled.

If Rourke wasn't going to listen to reason, I had to take care of it myself. The Vitale brothers were criminals, but they were still human. Whatever had gotten into Rourke had made him crazy. He was so eager to kill, and I had never seen that side of him before.

"Put the weapons down," I called as I stepped out of cover. "Enzo, get them to listen. I don't want this to end badly."

Enzo's dark eyes focused on me. "Tex."

"Yeah," I said. "It's me. Don't do this. I don't want to be the reason you die."

The moment the words left my lips, I felt lighter. What I'd said was a truth that I had buried deep inside of myself for what felt like centuries. I *couldn't* be the reason Enzo died. No matter what he and his family had done, I wouldn't be the person who killed him.

"He's slaughtered more people than you know," Rourke spat. "Who gives a fuck if he dies?"

"I do," I said. "This isn't how we do this, Rourke."

"He's a fucking parasite! Just because you fucked him doesn't mean he'll hesitate to kill you."

My stomach tightened. I kept my hand wrapped around my gun as my heart plummeted to my stomach. I knew who Enzo was. But there were still some things I didn't want to believe.

Enzo scoffed. "Me? Why don't you tell Tex who's been stealing our products and selling them? Or who's been orchestrating turning our men to his side?"

I glanced at Rourke. "What is he talking about?"

"I don't know," my partner bit back. "He's pulling stuff out of his ass."

"No," Enzo said, shaking his head. "You know me, Tex. I

take my time and calculate everything. Rourke has been dipping his fingers into our business and profiting. Didn't you find it odd you reached us so quickly? We knew there were more rats." Enzo's gaze flickered to Rourke. "Just like I'm sure one of those rats tipped him off that we were here tonight. He's a part of this."

I stared at Rourke as my body went cold. "Tell me he's lying."

"Come on," Rourke growled. "They're doing this to get into our heads. It's a game so they can kill us."

I frowned. "If they wanted us dead, we would have been already." I lowered my gun. "What the hell are we doing here?"

Rourke stared at me. His eyes searched mine, but I had no idea what he was looking for. I hoped he would turn around, and I would follow him. We could forget about what we were doing, what was going on, and go back to the way things were. However, deep down I knew the truth. There was no going back.

Rourke's gaze darkened when I didn't say anything. "Fuck this. If you can't do it, you can join them."

What? Before I could question my partner, my friend, someone I trusted, Rourke's fingers curled around my collar, and he yanked me back. The gun slipped from my hand and clanged to the floor as I was dragged closer to him. He moved us from behind the small shelter. My blood rushed as I was faced with not one but three guns trained on me.

Scratch that, four. The warm press of Rourke's gun tapped my temple as he shielded his body with mine.

"Don't shoot," Enzo said. His voice cutting through the fog of confusion taking up residence in my brain.

Rourke laughed. "Shit, you know I thought you'd been pulling my leg that you were fucking this low life."

Benito and Giancarlo kept their guns aimed our way. I hadn't been this close to death in a long fucking time.

"Put the guns down now, or I'll blow your fuck toy's brains out." His hot breath fanned against my ear, and he lowered his voice so that I was the only one to hear him. "Don't worry. No one at the precinct will know you spread your legs for a bunch of monsters. You'll die a hero instead of the failure you really are," he spat. "Let's be honest, the only reason the chief gave you this fucking task force in the first place is because you're daddy's special boy. It's bullshit," he spat. "I've worked my ass off for years, and you waltz in, some pathetic drug addict and get all the praise because of who your father is. I'm fucking sick of it."

I twisted in Rourke's grasp as his words hit me in the chest like a sledgehammer. What friendship I thought we had never existed, did it? My brain suddenly clicked, and I realized why I'd felt that nagging feeling this whole time. Rourke *knew* where everyone was. He'd known the layout of this place. Rourke had been here who knew how many times.

"You're doing this because you're jealous?" I scoffed. "What the fuck is wrong with you?"

"Shut up," Rourke snapped, his hold tightening. "You don't know what it's like trying to work your way up from nothing. They handed you this job, the best assignments like it was nothing. Fuck you and your asshole father."

Enzo lowered his gun and stepped forward.

"What the hell are you doing?" I demanded. "Enzo, move!"

He didn't say a word. Everything moved at a snail's pace, and I was left helpless as I watched. Rourke leveled his gun, squeezed the trigger and horror shot through my veins. I stared, wide-eyed and open-mouthed, as the bullet tore through Enzo's body. He wheeled back, his eyes opening to the size of saucers.

My ears rang, and I heard nothing else as Rourke's finger curved around the trigger. Heart racing, I threw myself on him. We went down in a heap, a ball of flailing limbs and pounding fists. My knuckles split on one of his teeth, blood gushing onto his face. Everything was a blur around me as my instincts took over, and I fought with Rourke. My back hit the unforgiving ground. Pain rattled up and down my spine, but I continued to swing. My limbs grew heavy as Rourke's hands wrapped around my throat and squeezed. Air became scarce, and spots danced in my vision.

"Get off him!"

I blinked as a blur shot past me and tackled Rourke to the ground. My throat ached, raw and throbbing as I choked and tried to drag air into my lungs. I looked up and watched as Enzo and Giancarlo stomped on Rourke's head. My partner tried to reach for his gun, only for Benito to crush that hand beneath his shoes.

"Tex," Rourke called out.

I stared at the man I'd spent so much time with. How many nights had we sat together at some dingy bar, destressing after the horrors of work? How many times had we called each other late at night just to vent? How many beers had we shared, cups of coffee, fucked up home life stories? And he was willing to kill me.

My body stayed glued to the spot as they turned him into something that didn't even resemble a human being anymore. I couldn't turn away, no matter how much my brain screamed for me to do just that.

Enzo grunted, his knees hitting the ground. That shook me from my stupor. I was up on my feet and over to him before I could think about what I was doing. There was blood on his once-clean shirt, and his eyes were unfocused.

Boom!

"Shit, they're trying to get through," Giancarlo muttered. "You okay, Enzo?"

I crouched down and brought Enzo to his feet, using my shoulder to support him. "I've got him. How do we get out of here?"

"You disappear, and they're going to have some questions for you, kid," Benito said.

"I don't give a fuck! I'm not leaving him," I snapped. "Enzo isn't looking good and he's losing blood. We need to get out of here. Now."

Don't ask me to lose anyone else tonight. I can't.

"Follow me," Benito said. "Move fast. Help him, Gin."

Together with Giancarlo, we moved Enzo through the warehouse. Benito moved one of the huge boxes and pointed at a trapdoor in the floor.

"Go. They'll lead us outside."

Nodding, I moved out of the way as they wrestled with the heavy door. My eyes went to Rourke. He stayed on the ground, a crumpled, bloody mess. All of his limbs were at odd angles. The whites of his eyes stood stark against all the blood, staring up at the ceiling.

My stomach turned. He'd been close to killing me, and I still couldn't hate him. Why? I wanted to shake him and ask why the fuck he'd betray me like this. Had it always been there, his hate? Or did it develop slowly when I wasn't looking? My throat clogged, but there were no tears. I recognized the shock that had settled over me, turning me cold. Later, I knew there was a floodgate waiting. One that would break as I mourned the man I thought I knew.

"Tex."

My attention snapped back to Enzo. His eyes were glazed, and he looked pale, like he was going to pass out. I couldn't even tell where the blood was coming from. My heart sped up, everything else forgotten except for him.

"I'm right here. Enzo, I've got you."

He held onto me as we descended the stairs. Above, I could hear the voice of my Sargeant. However, I wasn't going to turn back. I'd made my decision.

Enzo was the most important thing in my life. I only wanted to focus on him.

Twenty-nine
TEX

I ripped open Enzo's shirt and searched for the wound. There was so much blood it was like a curtain, obscuring my view and hiding where he was injured. Frustration fueled my irritation, and I looked more closely.

"Do you know what you're doing?" Benito asked.

"Fuck off!" I snapped.

Benito's eyes darkened. "Watch yourself."

"You think I give a fuck about what you can do to me right now?" I stared through Benito like he was nothing. I'd never shaken so badly in my life. The only thing I gave a damn about was Enzo. "I just had my friend, a good friend, threaten to fucking kill me. He put a gun up to my head." I shivered. "Now he's dead..."

Emotions stole my next words, clogging up my throat as tears spilled down my cheeks. The shock was still there, keeping me safe from the reality of the situation. But I could feel it coming on, that nasty truth that was waiting to rip me open and tear me into tiny little shreds.

"The only thing I give a fuck about right now is him," I said, nodding to Enzo. "He's all I've got left."

The world hammered at my door; my friend had been stomped to death, my job was more than likely gone, and Enzo was bleeding on the expensive, dark leather of his brother's imported goddamn car. It was like I was living in some fucked up nightmare.

"I'm o-okay." Enzo grabbed my hand and squeezed. "It's not so bad."

"Shut up," I snapped at him. "Just shut up before you fucking bleed out on my leg."

Enzo smiled at me, and I almost fell apart. My heart squeezed. He was an idiot. Why the hell had he taken a bullet for me? This was the guy who swore he would murder me if we ever crossed paths again more than once. And yet he'd dove in the way of Rourke's rage as if it was nothing.

I found the wound and shoved my hand against it. Shifting Enzo slightly, I made sure the bullet had entered and exited. Once I was certain that it had, I sighed in relief. At least it wasn't lodged in his body. That would be a kind of horror I couldn't take right now.

Benito and Giancarlo didn't exist for me. All I could focus on was Enzo. He reached out, his hand gripping mine so tightly it could break. Or maybe I was just more aware of every sensation right now. His hand felt like lead on mine, and the air in the car was stifling with the scent of blood and gunsmoke.

"Stop," Enzo muttered at me. "You look like shit when you cry."

I burst out laughing. It was such an unexpected thing to

say it took me off guard. The laughter died, and I cried harder. My life was falling apart. The only one that had ever truly seen me was a criminal. I had no idea what anything was anymore.

Enzo's hand brushed against my cheek. "Breathe," he said. "It's okay."

"Shouldn't I be telling you that?" I muttered.

"Stop being so fucking stubborn."

I wanted to wrap my arms around Enzo and never let him go. Even when he was in obvious pain, I could feel how much he worried about me. The crazy, housebreaking, stalking piece of shit *cared* about me.

Giancarlo moved over and helped me apply pressure. We locked eyes, and he nodded but kept quiet. I wanted to thank him for that. Right now, I couldn't take anything more than what was in front of me.

"Tex?"

"Yeah?" I asked, clearing my throat so I didn't sound like such a little bitch.

"We're almost home."

Home. Enzo said it so casually as if it meant nothing, but it meant the world to me. My eyes clouded again, and I wanted to curl up on myself and sob where no one could see me. I knew it was part of being in shock, but goddamn, did it hurt.

"Yeah," I whispered.

I looked out the window of the car as the streets rolled by. We really were heading for his place. I gazed at his brothers. Neither seemed alarmed, and I assumed they'd made medical arrangements.

"We're almost home," I whispered back. I gazed up at his brothers again. "I need something I can wrap around his wound."

Benito took off his jacket and passed it over wordlessly. I tied it around Enzo's body, pulling it tightly. The smile fell from his face, and a hiss slipped past his lips instead. He narrowed his eyes at me.

"Don't glare at me. I'm doing the best I can."

Enzo grunted as the car came to a stop. The brothers disembarked before Benito turned around and held out his arms.

"Give him to me. I'll carry him up."

"No." I shifted out of the car. "I'll carry him."

Benito growled. "You're really pushing me."

"I said I'm going to carry him." I stepped closer to him. "Get out of my way."

"Come on, Benito. We're wasting time," Giancarlo said.

I turned back to Enzo. The two of them could argue over bullshit. I needed to get Enzo up to his place. He leaned against the car, his skin pale and his breathing heavy. I crouched down.

"Get on my back."

Enzo, to my surprise, didn't argue. He wrapped his arms around my neck, groaned, and laid on me. I wrapped my arms around his legs and hoisted him into position. Standing up, I made sure he was balanced on my back. We took the service elevator up to his place.

"There you all are," a woman said as she stood at the door, frowning. "He looks terrible. Get him inside and on a bed. Downstairs."

I didn't ask questions. Moving into the guest room, I carefully unloaded Enzo from my back. Every pained intake of breath put me on edge.

"Let me get to work." The woman laid a hand on my back when I wouldn't move. "Get out of the way, or I can't save him, honey. Move."

I shifted out of the way but not too far. Pressing my back into the corner of the room, I watched her work. *If she fucks up, I'll shoot her.* The thought was so sudden I jolted, but it was exactly how I felt. I would kill her without blinking an eye if Enzo died.

Enzo's laughter made me look at him. "Stop glaring at the doc," he said, shaking his head. "Melony is good at her job."

"Awww, thank you," she cooed. "Now, hold still and focus on yourself."

Enzo winked at me before his face contorted in pain, and he swore. I stepped forward, but a sharp whistle cut through the air.

"Back off," Benito said. "Let her do her damn job."

I want to shoot him next.

I stopped myself from pacing. Eventually, Melony stepped back and let out a heavy sigh. She peeled her blood-slicked gloves off.

"Those stitches will hold," Melony said. "Just be careful, and you'll be okay. Here." She dug into her bag and pulled out a bottle of pills. "Take one of these every eight hours to kill the pain. It's good shit."

I took the bottle from her. "I'll give them to him."

"He should have someone here to look after him. I'm guessing that's you?"

"Yeah," I nodded. "I'm not going anywhere."

"Lots of rest, water, and feed him before the medicine," she said, checking her phone. "I have a shift in a few hours. I need to get out of here. I'll come back to check on you after work, Enzo."

"Thanks," he groaned. "Pill."

"She said I should feed you first," I said, stepping closer to him. "Let me make something."

He waved a hand. "Pill."

"I know you're in pain, but—"

"Give him the pill," Gin groaned. "If he pukes, he pukes."

I sighed. "Fine. I'll get some water." I laid a hand on Enzo's leg. "I'll be right back."

He nodded. I stared at him. His shirt had been cut away, and his chest was bandaged up. I could see spots of blood trying to appear through the wrapping. Yeah, I wasn't going anywhere because I needed to be the one to change them. It was my fault he'd been shot in the first place. He was right; I was naive.

I made my way to the kitchen, leaving him alone with his brothers. My hands were still shaky, but not as much as before. Some of the shock had worn off, but it was replaced with exhaustion. I couldn't deal with Rourke's death, not tonight. Tomorrow, however, I knew it would hit me like a ten-ton truck.

Cold water spilled over my hand, waking me up. I shut off the faucet and quickly returned to Enzo. The room was empty now besides him.

"Where did your brothers go?"

"Told them to give us some space." He raised himself up on one elbow. "Let me get that pill."

"Right." I placed a pill on his tongue, washing it down with the water. He swallowed it and plopped back onto the bed. "I'm sure it'll kick in soon."

"Hmm," he grunted, his hand grabbing mine. "Get in."

I frowned. "I don't want to hurt you."

Enzo tugged, and I toppled into the bed. "Hey, careful!" I growled. I sat the glass on the nightstand. "You're going to hurt yourself if you do shit like that."

"Don't care," he mumbled. Enzo tugged me closer, burying his face into my neck. "Are you okay?"

"You're the one who got shot," I pointed out.

"So what? You saw your friend die tonight. And we weren't nice about it." He turned my head so I couldn't look away. "Are you okay?"

"No," I answered honestly.

Enzo nodded. "I didn't think so." He laid his arm over me, holding me tightly as silence stretched between us. My body grew heavy, my eyelids drooping. "Tex?"

"Yeah," I muttered.

"I love you."

My eyes snapped right back open. "What?"

Enzo's eyes were starting to close, the medicine kicking in. "I love you," he slurred slightly. "Stay with me."

My heart raced. *Did I just hear that?* Enzo searched my face, his tired eyes looking for something. I licked my lips.

"Fuck. I think I love you too," I whispered.

A smile took over his lips as his eyes closed one last time and stayed closed. The soft, even breathing against my ear made my chest tighten. I stared at Enzo for what felt like ages, watching his chest rise and fall as he held onto me.

I love you more than I've ever loved another human being in my life.

Thirty
Enzo

LYING AROUND AND HEALING WAS FOR THE WEAK. THERE WERE better things I could be doing with my time. Like reminding a certain cop exactly what I was capable of.

I slipped from the bed and moved around the guest room without making a single sound. Tex was in the living room, fixing and placing books back on the shelf. After two days of being out of it, confined to the bed, I noticed Tex had kept himself busy. The piles of unfinished projects that had decorated most of my place were cleared away.

A part of me thought Tex would be gone. I fought the drowsiness of the pills, but they dragged me down to darkness each time. Waiting for me was the worry I'd open my eyes and Tex wouldn't be there. *I need to make sure he never tries to leave again.*

My chest tightened. I squinted to see if he'd put them in the order I'd shown him the first time. A few were out of place, but it surprisingly didn't bother me. I leaned against the wall and watched him for another ten minutes. He moved around, but it was like no one was home. His blue eyes were vacant.

I moved swiftly across the living room with light steps. Tex turned but it was too late. I had him in my trap already. I slammed him against the wall, face forward. He grunted, and I groaned, being pressed so close to him.

"You're supposed to be resting!"

I ground my cock against his firm ass. I cursed the fabric between us. A shiver of pleasure coated me from head to toe. The pain was little more than an annoyance. Something I could easily ignore for him.

"Mmm, is that right?" I wove my hand around Tex's waist and pushed past the elastic band of his sweats. Hot flesh greeted my fingertips and went further until I had Tex's cock in my hand.

Tex sucked in a sharp breath as he pushed back against me. He was in need, and what kind of person would I be to ignore the man that had my mind, body, and black soul in the palm of his hands? I'd be worse than a monster.

My lips brushed along his ear. "Say it again."

I wanted to hear those sweet words, the ones that carved deeper into me than any knife or bullet ever had. I craved them like I craved Tex's flesh.

"What?" Tex groaned. He shook his head and tried to pull away from me without hurting me. "Enzo, you need to be in bed."

I tightened my fist around his cock and stroked it just how I knew he liked it. The whimper that tumbled free of Tex was like finding a gold mine.

"That's not it." I pressed firmly against him, closing my eyes for a moment and breathing him in.

"What—" His words broke off into a gasp as I swiped my thumb over the head of his cock.

"Enzo."

The way he said my name only spurred me on further. My blood boiled, and every inch of my body was on high alert, all focused on Tex.

I pulled back and turned Tex around. His back hit the wall. Before he could stop me, I dropped to my knees and yanked his sweats down. His cock was hard, and a pearl of precum greeted me.

The smirk on my face was impossible to contain. Tex needed this just as badly as I did. We'd been without each other for far too long. I could see in his beautiful blue eyes that he was one second away from shattering.

"Enzo, you shouldn't—"

"Hands behind your head," I demanded.

Tex hesitated for a second, staring into my eyes. He slowly raised his hands and intertwined his fingers before placing them behind his head.

"You listen so well." I ran my tongue up the length of his cock. "When you want to."

Tex's teeth bit down on his bottom lip as he stared down at me. Concern and desire played havoc in his gaze. I could tell he wanted to both stop and beg me to do more.

He's so precious and all mine.

I cupped his balls as I blew a breath over the head of his cock. Tex's hips moved forward, and I slammed them back against the wall. I held him firmly there. His eyes widened, but it was the moan that spoke volumes.

"There is only one thing I want to hear come out of your mouth besides my name." Parting my lips, I took the head of his cock into my mouth. I swirled my tongue around the tip, teasing and watching Tex's reactions.

"Ugh, you're insane and need to be strapped to a hospital bed," Tex said.

I cocked a brow at him, and he smirked down at me. I slammed forward, taking his cock to the back of my throat. The smile fell away and was replaced with one of shock and euphoria. I swallowed around the head of his cock, making sure to keep my throat relaxed.

"Shit, you're too good at this." Tex's legs trembled, and his cock pulsed against my tongue.

I pulled back before he could cum and covered the slit with my thumb. A whimper echoed around me and filled my dark soul far more than the pleas of a dying man.

"Enzo, come on, why did you stop?"

"Say it," I demanded.

Tex's eyes were wild as his mouth opened and closed like a fish. "What do you want me to say?"

I swallowed his cock back down, pressing my nose against his pelvis. I pulled more moans from him as he struggled to form a coherent sentence. I hallowed my cheeks as I moved back and ran my tongue over the slit collecting the precum that dripped freely.

"Fuck me!" Tex's chest rose with every labored breath as he struggled to keep his hands behind his head. "Stop fucking stopping."

I smirked and took his balls in my mouth while I lazily stroked his cock. His length felt heavy in my hand, and I wanted nothing more than to have him back in my mouth. "You can't cum until you say it."

Tex shouted but stayed firmly against the wall. His gaze swept over my face, and I knew the moment it dawned on him. The blush on his cheeks deepened, and his mouth opened. I released his balls and took his cock back into my mouth.

I moaned around his thick length. Tex swore, his head banging against the wall as his hands fell away and his fingers tangled in my thick dark brown hair. I kept my eyes open as I swallowed around him.

Tex looked so good when he was wrapped tightly in pleasure. He shoved his cock further down my throat, and I relaxed, accepting it all.

Our eyes locked in an intense hold that felt ironclad. Not even Satan himself could break it. The world fell away, and it was just us, how it was meant to be.

"Enzo, I hate that I love you," Tex said.

His fingers untangled from my hair and cupped my face. There was a gentleness to his touch regardless of what we were doing.

"I love you so fucking much... that it scares me."

His hips stuttered, and he went to pull away. I locked my arms around his hips and kept him in place as Tex climaxed. Hot splashes of cum filled my mouth, and I greedily swallowed it down like a fine wine.

I released his cock with a pop. Tex sagged against the wall as I stood up. I grabbed his face and pressed both sides of his cheeks, forcing his mouth open. I fed him back the few drops of cum I hadn't swallowed.

"I hope you don't think we're done."

"Enzo." Tex audibly swallowed. "You're the devil."

I kissed him again. It was as if I couldn't get enough. "But I'm your devil."

"Fuck me. Now." Tex pulled me close. His fingers danced along my waist, pulling at the silk pajama bottoms I was wearing.

"I plan to do more than fuck you, Tex." He stopped to stare into my eyes. I wasn't sure what he saw, but fear flashed in his eyes. Laughter bubbled out of me, and I kissed him again. "I love you, and yes, I plan on destroying you."

Tex's breath hitched, and desire rushed through me. I pulled back and dragged him to the guest room. I couldn't wait to go back upstairs to our room, but I didn't have the patience at the moment. I needed every ounce of energy I had right now.

Clothes fell away as we got on the bed. Our mouths locked together in a never-ending kiss.

"We need to be careful," Tex said.

I shoved him into the bed. "There will be nothing gentle about this."

"Enzo, you're injured."

I climbed into the bed behind him, grabbed a cheek in each hand, and squeezed. They were firm globes that fit perfectly against my palms.

"Tell me more."

Before Tex could utter a word, I dove in like a starving man. My tongue thrashed against his hole. His moans bounced off the walls as I feasted on him. I licked and nipped at the puckered flesh.

Tex's hips wiggled, and I groaned as I pushed my tongue inside of him. He was so hot I swore I'd get burned. But not an inch of me wanted to stop. If anything, I fell deeper into the hunger that clawed inside of me just for Tex.

I worked a finger alongside my tongue, stretching Tex and teasing him.

"Ah, fuck," Tex moaned.

I pulled back in time to catch him tugging on his pierced nipples. I licked my lips greedily as he turned his head to look at me.

His face was flushed, and his cock hung heavily between his legs like he hadn't just cum moments ago. I draped myself over his back as I grabbed the lube I placed under the pillow.

"Had it all planned," Tex muttered.

I shrugged. "Can't go hunting unprepared."

Tex scoffed and shook his head. I lubed up his hole further and slathered the rest on my cock before tossing the bottle to the side.

Draping myself over Tex, I crowded him. Making sure all he could hear, smell, feel, see, and taste was me.

"I'm not prey," Tex growled.

"Oh?" I rested the tip of my cock against his hole, pressing against it but not enough to enter him. "Then I should stop."

"Don't even think about it." Tex reached back and pulled me forward.

My cock was instantly encased in heat that bordered on too hot. Pleasure ignited inside of me and took hold.

Everything disappeared, and all that was left was Tex. I pulled back and plunged into him again. Our flesh clashed together, creating a symphony along with our groans and moans.

I can't get enough. One taste was never going to be enough. I wanted to laugh at my past self for thinking I could have let someone like Tex go.

My tongue danced along Tex's ear before I bit it. "Go ahead and fall apart."

Tex shook his head, but I gripped his chin as I snapped my hips forward. His mouth dropped open as his eyes rolled back.

Perfection.

"You trust me, don't you?"

Tex whimpered but nodded.

"Not good enough. I want to hear it." Heat radiated

down my spine, and my toes curled as the pleasure built to new heights.

"I... I trust... you." Tex's words were slurred as I continued to own every inch of him.

A smile graced my face, and I felt lighter than ever. As if I could take on a thousand bullets and still live. Irrational, but maybe that was what love did to people.

I closed my eyes, basking in the feeling of Tex. In everything that he was. "Then trust I will put you back together."

As if my words were a wrecking ball, the dam broke, and tears slid down Tex's cheeks. He took in a shuddering breath before a scream left him. I tightened my arms around Tex and continued to thrust. Tex's fingers curled around my forearms as if he was holding on for dear life. I didn't stop, and he didn't ask me to. His tears fell freely, and I gave him the moment to do so.

Piece by piece, he shattered in my arms. His cries became hoarse, and his body went lax.

Tex was an ugly crier but when I was the cause of his tears, it was the sexiest thing I'd ever witnessed. He tried to hide his face, but I wasn't having any of that.

I kissed him and pressed our foreheads together before pulling back and grabbing his hips in a bruising grip. Pain trickled in where my bullet wound lay. I promptly ignored it. Nothing in this world could get me to stop. I picked up the pace and changed the angle just slightly. Tex's hoarse moans filled the room. I pounded into him. Making sure his mind, body, soul, and heart knew I owned all of Tex.

"Cum for me," I demanded as ecstasy licked up my spine.

Tex's body tightened around me, sucking me in further, making it harder to pull out. I groaned as he dragged out my climax. I buried myself as deep as I could, wanting to mark every inch of Tex.

Spots danced in my vision as I remembered how to breathe. Bliss tried to drag me down, but I pushed through. My cock slipped free of Tex, and he fell face-first into the bed. I turned him over, still riding the high of my climax. I kissed each of his eyes and then his forehead.

I had no words that would make everything right. I couldn't tell him to get over seeing his friend die or even the betrayal. Everyone processed things differently. However, what I could do was be there every time he needed to break apart.

"I love you."

Tex blinked up at me, and I wiped some of the tears away. "Yeah? Will you still love me when I fuck up?"

There was no need to think about it. "I thought I made myself clear." I wrapped one hand around his throat and the other around his cock.

Tex sucked in a breath through clenched teeth, no doubt sensitive after cumming back to back.

"You're mine. You've had your moment of freedom. You will never escape me again."

Tex stared at me for a long while before his lips tilted up in a smile. "Freedom? I was on the fucking run."

I hummed and let him go. My arms fell to my side as I took in a slow, measured breath. The pleasure and need for Tex overruled everything, but now the pain was slowly trickling in. There was warmth where my bullet wound lay that I knew wasn't sweat.

"What's wrong?" Tex asked.

How had he known? I normally didn't let anything show on my face. Pain shot through me, and all other thoughts slipped away.

"Idiot," Tex growled as he moved closer to inspect the blood seeping through the bandages.

Cupping his face, I smoothed out the tension between his brows. "I'm fine."

Tex rolled his eyes. "I'm calling Melony now."

I grabbed him and pulled him forward until he fell back on top of me. "No need." I buried my face in his neck and sighed as every muscle in my body relaxed. "I have you."

"Sweet but stupid. You were shot."

"Great observational skills. No wonder you became a cop."

"Enzo." Tex pulled himself up. "Now isn't the time to make stupid jokes, you asshole. At least take off the bandage and let me see."

I didn't get the sense I was going to get out of it. I slipped free from the bed and headed toward the bathroom with Tex two steps behind me.

Ringing pierced the air, and Tex glanced at his phone. His shoulders bunched, and a look of dread came over his face.

"Answer it tomorrow."

Tex shook his head. "I can't. It's already been two days. A text isn't exactly excusable."

His eyes were red and puffy from crying, and he wanted to go to work. They were going to eat him alive. I'd be damned if I allowed anyone to hurt what was mine.

"Tomorrow morning," I said.

Tex looked up from the phone but before he could argue, I grabbed him and yanked him close. His hand collided with the bullet wound, and I hissed in pain but didn't allow him to pull back.

"I will not share you with anyone. Right now, you're all

mine. Tomorrow you can go to work and bring Penelope home."

Tex's shoulders dropped. "I should at least send a message."

I shook my head and snatched the phone away. "You told them you were lying low to hide from the Vitales. What's another day?"

"Okay."

Tex let out a shuddering breath. I wanted nothing more than to hide him away from the world. If I did that, I risked losing what made Tex him.

The trickle of blood down my torso let me know the wound had opened up. I groaned and grabbed my phone.

"What are you doing?" Tex asked.

"Calling Melony."

He pulled back, and his eyes widened at the sight of the blood-soaked bandages. "Idiot, I knew it."

I tuned Tex out as he started to curse at me. His hands waved around as he pointed out how stupid I was. My lips twitched as I fought back a smile.

"Wow, that's a record, Enzo. Normally, it's Giancarlo I have to visit multiple times for an injury. Can it wait, or you need me now?"

Tex yanked the phone out of my hand before I could answer.

"This dumbass opened it up. The bandages are soaked." Tex left the bathroom, talking to Melony. He poked his head back into the bathroom. "Sit the hell down."

I didn't argue. It felt nice to be taken care of. I sat down and relaxed as Tex grabbed whatever Melony told him to. My eyes closed for a second. Warm fingers brushed along my flesh, drawing me out of the bliss I was basking in.

Blinking, I found Tex wiping away the blood around my

wound. His brows were furrowed as he concentrated. "Melony said you opened it a little, but there's no need for her to restitch it."

I gave a curt nod and let him continue to clean the blood up and rebandage me.

"Need a pain pill?"

"Maybe later." I stood up once he was done, watching him as he cleaned up. He even grabbed the sanitized wipes and wiped everything down.

"I'll order us something to eat unless you want my cooking."

"Your cooking is far deadlier than any bullet wound." Tex could make a sandwich, but anything else was a toss-up.

Laughter filled the room as Tex pushed me toward the bed. "Yeah, I know."

I got into the bed and groaned as the ache settled in further. Tex's mouth opened before he closed it.

"What?" I asked.

"You missed Pen too?"

I grunted and got comfortable. The fur ball was important to Tex. And I might have missed hearing his bell or even the resounding purr he let out anytime he sat on Tex's chest. Or when I pet him the way he was *supposed* to be petted. Tex was much too gentle. Pen enjoyed it when I didn't hold back, rubbing up against me and looking up at me with those big, soft eyes.

"Go get food."

Tex's face lit up. "Oh, you did. I can't wait to tell him."

"Just bring him home." If Penelope was there, I knew for certain Tex wasn't going anywhere.

Thirty-one
TEX

Enzo was still asleep by the time I stepped out the door. I made sure he was nestled up with Pen, a smile on my lips as I thought about the two of them cuddling. He liked to pretend he only enjoyed Pen's company so-so. Strange that ever since Chelsea had dropped him off, the two of them had been more cuddled up than I was with Pen.

He loves that orange menace.

I pulled my phone from my chest and stared at the screen. *Focus.* I needed to get this shit over with. I'd had time to think. Enzo had broken me out of that cold, frozen place. I was ready to move on with my life. For now. I had no idea when it would all come crashing down again. My mind would be flooded with those horrible memories, but I couldn't stay locked away forever.

My fingers hovered over the screen before I sucked

down a deep breath and called my boss. The phone rang a few times before it was picked up.

"Caster? Where the hell are you?"

"I'm fine," I said, not exactly answering Sergeant White's question. "I need to—"

"The chief wants to talk to you too. Hold on."

"Wait, Sarge. Sarge?"

The sounds of the precinct filled the phone, but she clearly wasn't paying any attention. I sagged against the hallway, pinching the bridge of my nose. Great.

"Okay, Tex, you're on with both of us."

"Where the hell are you, Caster?" Chief Hawkins asked. "I understand you saw some horrible shit," he said solemnly. "Especially with Houghton."

I tensed up. The whole reason they'd let me off the hook was because of how Rourke had died. I'd told them I was shaken up and hiding from the Vitales. They understood it immediately because who wouldn't after seeing the wreck that was Rourke's body?

"He was working with one of the recently fired cops," I said, keeping my voice steady. "And they were both stealing from the Vitales. They didn't like that." *That's an understatement.* "I have evidence to turn over for that case; some of my own, some from a consultant. I'll have it on your desk tomorrow. I just need one more day."

"You take the time you need, son," the chief grunted. "That bust was as successful as it could be, considering Rourke screwed it up on his end. We want you back working on the Vitales' case."

My throat tightened. "I can't."

"Not as an officer," he continued. "As a detective."

I felt like I couldn't breathe. He was offering me my dream job. Since the moment I'd sobered up and knew I would be heading for the academy for training, that was my goal. Now, the word detective sent ice down my spine. I couldn't imagine relying on someone after Rourke's betrayal, which was a big part of the job.

"No," I said more firmly. "No, thank you, sir. I'm done. I'll return my gun and badge and finish the appropriate paperwork tomorrow after I turn over the evidence."

The phone went quiet. Sarge's voice eventually came through. "Are you sure, Tex?"

"More than sure," I said quickly. "This isn't what I want to do for work anymore. Thanks for the opportunity, but no thanks." It went quiet again. "I need to go. I'll be in early."

I hung up before either of them could say anything. My dream was no longer to compete with my father. I didn't give a damn if he was upset when he heard about it, either. I had my whole life ahead of me. I wouldn't spend it doing a job I no longer felt any passion for, trying to impress people I didn't want to be around. *Time to move on.*

What am I going to do now, though?

No immediate jobs popped up in my head that I wanted to do. I tried to think of something, anything, but all I pulled were blanks. Sighing, I ran a hand down my face. *I'm still not ready to think about anything else right now.* I needed more time to heal.

"At least I have a rich boyfriend who will support me until I can figure it out," I mumbled, relief spreading through me as I smiled at myself.

"Tex? Tex!"

I pushed off the wall and let myself back into the apartment. "I'm right here."

Enzo stormed to the entryway, Penelope tucked under his arm. His hair was wild, all over his head, like he'd just woken up. And his eyes were huge.

I burst out laughing. The last bit of a lump that had been stuck in my throat since I quit disappeared as I lost my shit over Enzo's insane appearance. He glared at me when I straightened up, trying to suppress my laughter.

"Tex," he growled.

I pressed my lips together. "Yeah?"

He narrowed his eyes. "Where were you?"

"Outside. I had a phone call to make." I moved over to him and snagged Pen out of his arm. I kissed his nose. "I quit my job."

Enzo stopped glaring at me. "You did?"

"Isn't that what you wanted me to do?" I asked, looking at him curiously.

Enzo shrugged. "I wasn't going to make you quit if you didn't want to. Do I prefer it, though? Yes. I don't like the idea of you playing both sides. All it ever does is get people hurt. Or worse." He pulled me into his arms. "What are you going to do now?"

I leaned against his warm chest. "No idea. I was thinking I'd laze around at my rich boyfriend's place for a while until I figure out what the fuck I want to do with my life."

He ran a hand up and down my back. "You can do whatever the hell you want. As long as it doesn't involve you leaving."

I chuckled and pushed back. "You psycho." Straightening up, I kissed his lips. "I'm not going anywhere. You know that." I checked the time on my phone. "I'm supposed to be meeting my mother in a little while. You can stay and rest."

"I'm going with you."

A shiver worked its way up my spine. "No way in hell. My father knows what you look like. It's bad enough that I quit today. You want me to reveal I'm dating a Vitale?" I shook my head. "His head would fucking explode."

"Good."

"Enzo," I warned. "No."

He held up his hands. "I'm not actually going to explode his head. Too easy."

I groaned. "Jesus. Don't make me regret this."

Enzo grinned, and my world lit right up. "You called me your boyfriend."

My face heated. "I did."

"I'm your boyfriend?"

"Oh my god," I said, burying my face in my hands after dropping Pen. "Don't make it a huge thing."

"Am I?"

"Yes!" I yelled, pulling my hands away to glare daggers at him. "Happy?"

Enzo's smile grew, bordering on insanity. "Happier than I've ever been."

My heart skipped a beat, and I gripped my shirt. The man who loved to kill looked like a child who had just received the best Christmas present ever. He was so unlike anything I'd expect from a dangerous man like himself, but I loved that about him. Enzo Vitale was complex, crazy, and mine. All goddamn mine.

"We should go on a date," he blurted out.

I blinked at him. "What?"

"Boyfriends go on dates." He frowned. "I don't want to be together only in the house."

I thought about his last relationship. Right, they'd always stayed in the house. He didn't want to feel like I was treating him the same way Brycen had. Even though I'd never do that shit in a million years. Enzo deserved so much more than to be treated like a bottomless wallet with a dick.

Smiling, I reached out, caressing his cheek softly. "I would love that. Where are we going?"

"I'll make the arrangements."

My hand slid down his body, coming to rest on the clean bandages I'd fixed not long ago. "And what about your wound? Are you sure you're good to be going out?"

"I'll take it easy. I promise."

I scoffed. "You don't listen well enough to take it easy," I said, shaking my head. "But if you sit down and it's something like dinner, fine. I won't bitch too much about it."

He grinned and kissed me. "Minimal bitching is all I can ask for."

I slapped his chest. Enzo grunted. Laughing, I walked into the kitchen as my phone buzzed. I stared at the screen before tucking my phone away again.

"Who was that?" Enzo asked.

"My mom."

"You're not going to answer it?"

I shook my head. "Not yet. She can wait until we meet up." Hopefully, without my father. I still wasn't sure if I wanted to go. I sent her back a quick message letting her know I was alive but nothing more. "You and your brothers talk about everything, don't you?"

"Pretty much," Enzo said. "You have to in this life. Secrets can get everyone killed."

"I could have gotten you all killed," I pointed out. "You still kept me a secret, didn't you?"

He walked over and wrapped his arms around me, leaning his chin into the crook of my neck. "Yes, I did. It was a stupid decision. Benito's probably still irritated with me."

"What about Giancarlo?"

"He gets over things pretty quickly. Most things." He kissed my ear. "I need you to get along with them."

Groaning, I turned around and pushed the hair out of his face. "Fine. I'll try."

"They're just like me."

"I'm not in love with them," I pointed out. "And Benito's an ass."

Enzo burst out laughing. "Yes, Benito *is* an ass, but he's family. You are too now if you're with me. Just like he looks out for us, he'll be looking out for you too."

Great. I'd gone from cop to affiliated with criminals overnight. I looked at the pleading expression on Enzo's face and deflated right away. Enzo was no better than the rest of them, that's what I had to come to terms with. If I was in love with him, then I had to at least try to get along with his brothers. Maybe it wouldn't come overnight, but it would eventually.

I hoped.

"Alright," I said. "If it's going to make you happy, I'll do it. That's all I care about."

He smiled, relief smoothing the lines on his forehead. "Does this mean I get to meet your parents?"

"No way!" I laughed. "My dad, remember?"

"Your dad who hits you."

I tensed. "I don't want to talk about that right now, okay?" I wrapped my arms around his neck. "All I want to do is spend time with you, eat, and then maybe we can sit on the couch. You can read, and I can watch the game."

Enzo's lips brushed over mine. "My boyfriend, the game watcher." He chuckled.

I poked him in the ribs. "Shut up."

Our lips pressed together. The rest of the world melted away as I held onto Enzo, melting against his body. I never wanted to let him go.

"Meow!"

I stepped back. "Alright, food's coming."

"I bought him one of those automatic feeders like the ones in your place. It should be here today." When I stared at Enzo, he rolled his eyes. "You don't wake up early enough to feed him, and he whines about it and steps all on me."

"You love him," I teased.

"Whatever. I love both of you."

My heart squeezed. "Say it again."

Enzo groaned. "I love both of you!" he snapped.

"Good boy."

"Just because there's a hole in me doesn't mean I won't kick your ass."

I grinned. "Bring it on, baby."

Thirty-two
Enzo

"Wow, I know for certain it takes months to get reservations here," Tex said. His gaze bounced all over the room. The floor was cleared of the usual tables, and only one sat in the middle. The lights were dimmed, and the only people there were the band, a waiter, and the chefs.

"This way, Mr. Vitale," our waiter said.

"You rented out the entire place?" Tex asked.

I gestured for him to sit, and we took our seats. His head turned every which way, still admiring the place. A huge chandelier hung from the ceiling above our table. White pillars were wrapped in black silk and adorned with silver tulle. The beautiful sounds of the cello and violin wrapped around the room.

"When you said you would make arrangements, I didn't know you meant this."

"Do you like it?" I asked.

Tex finally met my gaze as he nodded. "Yeah, no one has ever done something like this for me."

My shoulders eased, and tension seeped out of my muscles. I'd been nervous for the past few days about the date. My mind had been a mess. Would the things I enjoyed really work for Tex?

He shrugged. "I would have been fine going to Chili's."

I shuddered at the thought. "Why must you ruin a good moment?"

Soft laughter bubbled out of Tex. "Excuse me, not everyone can afford five-course meals. Half-price appetizers and happy hour can be romantic."

"How so? It's noisy, crowded, and not to mention the multitude of smells." There was no way it could be romantic, let alone enjoyable.

Tex's head tilted as he stared at me. "Well, yeah, but it's a great discount. I'm going to take you one day. It's good to expand your horizons."

"I'd rather eat at home where we can relax."

"Well, you're cooking is freaking good, so I guess that makes sense."

The waiter sat bread at our table and made himself scarce.

"So I guess every date you go on, you've done something like this, huh? Kind of makes it hard for people to get over you if this is how you date them."

"I've never been on a date," I said.

Tex stilled a piece of bread halfway to his mouth. "I'm sorry, can you repeat that? You're thirty-three!" He rubbed his ears as if they were clogged.

"Dating seemed to be a waste of time. I had far more important things to do."

Tex's mouth dropped open. He stared at me as if I'd grown another head. "But it was your idea to go on a date."

I nodded. "You're the most important thing to me."

He shut his mouth, and his cheeks went red. Tex stood up just as the waiter held the bottle of wine over his glass. They collided. Almost in slow motion, the bottle of wine slipped from the waiter's hands and hit the table, breaking and pouring all over Tex in the process.

"I am so sorry," the waiter said. His nervous gaze moved over to me, but I stared at Tex.

"It's okay. It was my fault." He groaned and stared at his clothes. His shoulders slumped forward.

Getting him cleaned up and changed was my first thought. I snapped my fingers, and a few more people came to the table. "Towels."

I got out of my seat and pulled Tex out of his seat. He didn't meet my gaze. I gripped his chin and forced him to. "We can go home now—"

"No, I... I'd like to stay. It's our first date."

I nodded.

"Here you are, sir," a woman said, holding more towels.

Tex took them. "I'm going to clean up what I can."

I nodded and kissed him. I smiled at him. "Everything will be ready once you return."

"Okay."

The table was fixed, and all the glass was cleaned up.

"Again, sir, we deeply apologize."

"It is fine."

When had I become so patient? Yes, they had dumped wine all over my man, but I wasn't ready to rip anyone's head off. Was this Tex's doing? Was he changing me?

"Your meal will be on us," the chief said.

"It's fine," I repeated. "Just make sure there are no more issues." I waved them away just as Tex came out.

"It wasn't their fault. I wasn't paying attention." Tex sat back down, and I reached for his hand over the table.

"Why did you get up so fast?"

"Um, you said I was important."

My head tilted. "You are."

Tex looked up and finally met my eyes. "You know, you're oddly romantic."

Am I? I was simply telling him the truth.

"Sorry I made a mess on your first official date," Tex said.

"There is nothing to be sorry for. As long as you're not harmed, everything else can be replaced."

"Yeah, but I know how you feel about messes."

He pays too close attention to me.

"When I'm outside of my home, they don't bother me nearly as much."

Tex's shoulders finally eased as he relaxed. I hadn't known he was so nervous; it was interesting. Tex always seemed so confident when we left our home. I realized I liked this side of him too.

The food came out shortly after. I ate, but mostly, I watched Tex. The way he enjoyed food could drive any man crazy. Before I knew it, we were leaving the restaurant, and the valet handed the keys over.

"Dinner was nice, except for the part where I spilled an entire bottle of wine." Tex groaned as he stared down at his stained suit.

"The date isn't over."

"It's not?"

I shook my head and took his hand in mine. I placed a

chase kiss on the back of it. A tempting blush crept up Tex's neck and colored his cheeks.

"One more place. The premiere of The Last Candidate is tonight." Some spy movie Tex had brought up a few times. We still had two hours before the movie started.

"You know, we can watch it at home," Tex said.

Warmth flooded my chest. I didn't like movie theaters because they could be too loud and crowded. Still, I'd made arrangements for that as well. I did everything to ensure Tex and I had a perfect date.

"It's the premiere. This time you will see it before others spoil it for you."

Tex groaned. "It's annoying as hell, people who see the movie freaking post about it right after ruining it for the rest of us."

It was a familiar complaint I had heard from him. As always, I let him rant away about how people were inconsiderate. Watching him get worked up was like listening to my own personal ASMR. I relaxed and pulled him close, ignoring the wine soaked into his clothing.

"I need to get changed then." He pulled at the ruined suit. Tex pulled away from me and hopped into the car. "Come on."

"There is a shopping district—"

"No, thanks," Tex said, cutting me off.

I started the car and pulled out into traffic. "I can buy you something new."

Tex rolled his eyes. "Why when my apartment is just around the corner? I can change there."

My molars ground together as my fingers tightened around the steering wheel. Tex's hand rested on my thigh, calming the rage inside me. We said nothing, but I'd made it clear I wanted him to stay with me. Not that I was giving him any choice. I wouldn't allow Tex to go back to his place away from me, and he knew that.

I relaxed and pulled into the parking spot right outside his old apartment. "Pack up everything you feel is important."

Tex paused halfway out of the car and glanced over his shoulder at me. "We don't have time for that. We're still on a date."

I didn't want him to have any other place but mine to go to. His gaze met mine, searching for who knew what. He sighed.

"Enzo, we can come back and get the rest another time. I'm just here to change clothes."

"Fine."

He squinted at me. "I'm serious, Enzo. Don't hire someone to move me. I will get my shit and say goodbye to this place when I'm ready."

The creaking of the steering wheel penetrated the fog clouding my mind. I released it and nodded. He had no more than a month to get all of his shit out of there, or I'd take matters into my own hands. I turned the car off and hopped out behind him.

"What are you doing?" Tex asked.

I cocked a brow at him. It was obvious, was it not? Tex shook his head and placed his big hands on my chest. Even through the suit, his warmth touched my soul.

"No, you don't. You come in, and instead of getting clothes on, I'll be bent over."

I stepped closer to him, gripping his chin to look at me. "And what is wrong with that?"

Tex's tongue swiped over his bottom lip as his pupils dilated. "We're on a date. Not to mention, I really want to see the movie."

I forced myself to let him go. "You have twenty minutes to get cleaned up. If you aren't out here by then, I'm coming in."

Tex smirked. "Yeah, and what will you do, clean up?"

I grinned at him. "I will destroy you."

His Adam's apple bobbed as he took a few more steps back. "You know, when you say it with a straight face like that, it sounds more like murder."

"Your time is ticking away."

"Bastard." Tex turned on his heels. "Give me thirty. I want to shower."

I tapped the watch on my wrist. Tex groaned as he ran up to his apartment.

I headed back toward the car and reached for a pack of cigarettes. Tex's phone buzzed and rattled in the cupholder, stopping me in my tracks. A single glance at the screen showed his father's name.

Anger blossomed in the middle of my chest and seeped to my fingertips. If there was a man I wanted to hurt more than anything in this world, it was Henry Caster. He'd played a hand in nearly bringing my family to ruins two years ago. Benito had forced Gin and me not to return the favor. He could easily be forgotten as an old man forced to retire and live out his days in agonizing pain and always wondering if we would come back for him after the bullet in his leg. It was punishment enough, but that wasn't his only crime. The one that was above all was the harm he'd done to Tex.

The phone vibrated in my hand. I was oblivious to the fact I'd picked it up in the first place. I hit the green button. Air clogged my throat, making it impossible to talk as I brought it to my ear.

"Boy, you have lost your damn mind." What sounded

like a woman in the background pleaded for him not to get angry. Something about his blood pressure getting too high.

"Kate, let me handle this," Henry growled.

I picked out the sounds of an engine and knew they were in the car.

"Are you high again?"

My stomach twisted

"Gregor called, said you quit. There you go fucking up a good thing. Everything has been handed to you, and you continue to mess it all up. The fact that the Chief of Police offered you detective was your one moment of luck, and you pissed on it." He cleared his throat. "Anything to say for yourself?"

I looked up in time to see an old burgundy Cadillac had pulled into the parking lot. As clear as day was Henry Caster with the phone to his ear and a woman beside him, crying.

"You're doing that shit again, aren't you?" he growled over the line. "You made your mother cry. We aren't going through this shit again."

I said nothing. He hadn't noticed me yet. I slipped the rest of the way out of the car and gently closed the door. I kept the phone close to my ear, listening to him.

"Nothing to say for yourself? Well, I'm here. If I have to beat it into you, I'll straighten you out like I should have done when you were a kid."

"Henry, he's tired. It was a hard case," Tex's mother pleaded.

"You don't know what it's like! The boy needs to toughen up. I saw ten times the amount of shit he did." The door of his car swung open, and he angrily got out. He wobbled with his cane, not finding good purchase on the gravel.

I hung Tex's phone up. Before Henry could so much as

take a single step toward the building, I stepped behind him and caught his gaze in his side mirror.

He had the same blue eyes as Tex, but his were far duller. They widened, and his face went ashen. The passenger side door opened.

"Kate, stay in the car!"

She glanced over at us, wiping at her face. I smiled at her.

"I'm an old acquaintance, and seeing Henry again, I couldn't help but come over."

She looked at her husband again. "Oh, um—"

"Kate, get in the car," Henry said through clenched teeth.

Her face reddened, but she followed his instructions.

"Are you here for my family?" Henry asked.

I closed the car door and walked around him. I made my way toward the back of the small building in case Tex came out earlier. Henry Caster followed behind me, limping as he made his way to the back. He attempted the tough guy act but old age and time off the force made him soft in certain areas. Fear peeked through the cracks, but it wasn't enough for me.

"You'll let my wife go," Henry said.

With a single step forward, I snatched the cane up. He staggered but caught himself and leaned against the wall. Good enough. I inspected it. Of course, he'd cleaned Tex's blood off of it. Good thing, I don't think I could have held back if I'd seen it.

His mouth opened to spew something I had no time to hear. Before so much as a syllable could be uttered, I whipped the cane around, and it smacked against his cheek.

I tisked. It wasn't the exact same. Henry crumbled down to the ground, groaning in pain.

"Stand up."

The old man wheezed as blood dripped down his cheek. His eyes were unfocused as he continued to lie on the ground.

"I said get up."

Henry attempted to get up twice, his leg giving out on him each time. I watched, unmoving. There was so much I wanted to do to him. I could easily spend weeks torturing him, bringing him nothing but suffering and it would still be only a drop of the anguish he'd caused Tex.

"If you're going to kill me, get it over with," Henry spat.

"If I was going to kill you, we'd be somewhere I could have fun." I stepped closer to him. He was more than likely taller than me in his prime. However, with his hunched-over posture as he fought to stand up, I dwarfed him. "This is personal."

His eyes flicked around me, and I brought the cane back down. It cut through the air, making a soft whistling sound. The hardwood against flesh echoed around us. Henry crashed to the ground, scrapping the other side of his face.

"Uh, fuck."

I grabbed a fistful of his hair and held his head up, inspecting it. It mirrored the cut I'd found on Tex's face perfectly. Killing him would anger Tex. Although I knew Henry Caster deserved it, I couldn't.

Henry groaned as I helped him up, too dazed to pull away. I handed his cane back. His fingers shook as he took it away from me and leaned heavily on it.

He blinked rapidly as he stared at me. "What makes this personal?"

I tapped his cheek, pressing against the wounds there. He winced. I wiped his blood from my fingers onto his checkered button-up.

"Know any time you hurt him, I will return the favor to you."

"Who?" Henry asked. His head snapped up before I could speak. "Tex? What does this have to do with my son?"

"He's mine."

I could practically see the wheels turning in his head as my words settled in his mind. A look of distraught morphed into one of anger. His face reddened as he bared his teeth at me.

"Being with you, he's going to end up just like Brycen Grennan." Henry shook his head. "That boy—"

I took a step closer, and his mouth snapped shut. "Respect him, or I'll make it so he will never have to hear disrespect come out of your mouth again." Cutting out his tongue wouldn't kill him.

"You will stay away—"

I cut off his pathetic attempt at a demand. I needed to wrap things up. I had a date to continue. "This stays between us. I'd hate for you to meet your end in some tragic accident. Freeing your wife and son of the plague that is you."

The idea sounded more pleasing the longer I thought about it.

"You're not a cop anymore. Stop with the heroism. We both know you're no warrior of justice."

Henry glared at me. "I still have connections."

"The last time you came after us didn't work out so well, did it?" I pointed to his leg. "Do I make myself clear?"

Henry ground his teeth. "Crystal."

There was still a visible fight in his eyes that I planned on snuffing out. I gestured for us to go back toward the cars. He leaned heavily on his cane as he headed toward the parking lot.

"Tex is nothing like Brycen." I didn't look at him as I spoke. I owed this man nothing, and neither did Tex. But I found my lips moving on their own. "He is loyal, head-strong, ambitious, and a far better man than you."

Henry scuffed. "He is a drug addict who made nothing but messes for me to clean up."

"It's a shame that is all you see out of him when I see someone who, regardless of their hardships and shortcomings, has made something of themselves. Could you say you'd be able to do the same in his shoes?"

Henry was silent next to me as we approached the cars.

"He still ended up with a murderer."

I caught his gaze. "Don't worry. You're safe from me for now. We're going to be family."

"Everyone knows I wouldn't have anything to do with you or that vile family of yours," Henry spat.

"It would be a simple task to change that opinion. The headlines would read: Hero cop, crooked and corrupt. All his achievements connected back to the mafia."

Henry went stock still.

"Just as you have connections in the NYPD, so do I."

I opened the car door and stared at Henry as he moved toward it. He glanced at the building as if hoping Tex would come down. A man like Henry Caster was all about his reputation. On paper, he was the perfect man; a hero, a family man, and an all-around good samaritan. To have that tarnished would ruin everything he held dear.

"I look forward to meeting you on more official terms as Tex's partner."

Henry visibly bristled as he slipped into the car. He attempted to yank it closed, but I held it firmly.

"Henry, oh my goodness, your face. What happened?" Kate reached out to her husband.

he batted her hand away, never taking his gaze away from me. "I'm fine. Slipped."

Henry cleared his throat and tugged at the door handle. I let it go, sufficiently happy that the last bit of spark in his eyes was gone. He knew I'd follow through. I'd do anything to protect Tex. Henry pulled out of the parking spot and was gone in a matter of seconds.

I think I handled that well. Tex's father was still alive, and I managed to return the favor.

I deleted the call history from Tex's phone and placed his phone back in the cup holder. The cigarettes were crumbled, and there wasn't one I could salvage. The door opened, and Tex stepped out, drawing my attention.

He smiled the moment our eyes met, and he raced down to meet me. "I didn't like the suit, so I went with a plain button-up and slacks. Fancy enough?"

He looked good enough to eat. I snatched up his wrist and yanked him close. I smoothed my thumb over the scar left on Tex's cheek.

"What?"

"I'd kill for you."

Tex stared at me. Silence blanketed us for a few heartbeats. "I know, but I don't want you to."

I brought our lips together, and our tongues tangled in what I could only describe as perfection. Tex tasted divine. I wanted to take him back home and taste every inch of him. To own every inch of him.

"From now on, I'm the only one allowed to hurt you or make you cry. Every inch of you belongs to me." I bit his lip. "Even your life."

Tex groaned. "Yeah. Where do I sign, Satan?"

Epilogue
TEX

Twenty-nine and a half days later

GIANCARLO GRUNTED, RISING TO HIS FEET WITH ONE OF MY boxes. I looked at what was written on top. Enzo had insisted on labeling everything while we packed, unlike my system of tossing crap into a box and having a headache when I had to put it all away.

"Upstairs in the bedroom. You can actually put it in the closet."

"Alright," he groaned. "What the fuck is in here?"

I shrugged. "No idea. I had to move fast because your brother is a nutcase."

"Hey," Enzo called.

"It's the truth," I muttered, walking over to Benito. "Those can go to the bookshelf. I don't have a ton of books, but I'm sure someone will want them there."

Benito nodded. We still weren't BFFs forever or anything, but we were at least on speaking terms. The conversation we'd had a few weeks ago got rid of most of our irritation, and we'd both come to the same conclusion; Enzo was more important than any hurt feelings between us.

"Ooh, let me have these!" Chelsea called, pulling out some old firecrackers I forgot I even had. "We can light them up."

"No," Enzo answered.

"After we finish moving," I said, winking at Chelsea. Enzo moved away from the truck, and I glared at him. "You get back there and stay back there."

"Keep it up," Enzo warned.

I raised a brow and grinned at him. Enzo had to know by now that I wasn't afraid of him. He'd take it out on my ass later, but at least I could ride him and make him relax. Moving heavy boxes was strictly forbidden until Melony cleared him. He was a lot better than before, but I wanted him to stay that way, not backslide.

"Stay, boy," I ordered. "Sit."

Enzo's hand turned into a tight fist as he growled at me. Chelsea and I exchanged a look and burst into laughter.

"You're going to get in trouble later," she sang.

"God, I hope so."

"Disgusting," Chelsea groaned. "Give me some good luck so I can find some of that."

We chuckled, glancing up only to look at Enzo. He was still glaring daggers, making me snicker. Chelsea cleared her throat, calming down.

"Hey, he's dating you. He might still kill me."

I rolled my eyes. "Yeah, right. If he did that, he'd be a dead man himself."

"What are you two talking about?" Enzo asked.

"Nothing!" I called. I grinned as I saw a familiar face approaching us. "Melony, how are you?"

"Fabulous as always." She walked over to me, and her smile faltered before she cleared her throat. "And who is this?"

I glanced at Chelsea. "Oh, this is my good friend Chelsea or Chels. This is Melony."

"Hi," Melony said.

"Um, hi," Chelsea mumbled. "I, uh, what—"

"Chelsea's tired," I said quickly. "We've been moving stuff all day. Can you check Enzo out to make sure he's okay? I won't let him move until we're sure."

"Right, I should do that." She took a few steps back, her eyes still lingering on Chelsea. "Nice to meet you."

"Yeah, you too."

Melony turned on her heels, a visible pep in her step as she bounced over to Enzo. Chelsea's eyes ran up her long legs. She whistled.

"She single?"

"I think she has a girlfriend," I said.

"Are they serious?"

I elbowed her. "Chelsea! Bad girl, down."

She groaned. "It's like she walked right out of my dreams."

I shook my head. "Are you going to move boxes or daydream?"

"Daydream?"

My elbow collided with her side again. She hissed at me, but one glance from Melony made her scramble from the back of the truck. Chelsea picked up a box, propped it onto her shoulder, and made her way to the apartment.

I shook my head. "Show off."

"Shhh!"

We carried the boxes in while Melony and Enzo broke off to the guest room. It was the one place that wasn't stuffed full of boxes. I navigated a few stacks. Penelope meowed at me from his spot on the wall perch Enzo had built for him. I reached up, scratched between his fluffy ears, and kept going up the stairs.

Smoke filled the air. I waved a hand through it, narrowing my eyes at Giancarlo and Benito. Both of them paused, blowing smoke out of the window and looking as if they were kids who had been caught sneaking into the cookie jar.

"I thought you two were helping," I said as I put a box down.

"Busted." Gin grinned, walking over to throw an arm around my neck. "We're having a smoke break. Want one?"

I peeled his arm off. "Nope. I'll be out of breath. And don't let Enzo see you touching me."

"Right. I keep forgetting he's crazy these days." Gin laughed. "We're practically brothers now. He'll have to get over it."

"Don't start shit," Benito warned his brother. "I'm not cleaning up anyone's blood."

Gin threw his hands up. "Nobody knows how to have any fun around here."

"We clearly have very different definitions of fun." I shoved Chelsea's box on top. She made herself scarce, not used to Benito's withering gazes. It still got to me sometimes, but I felt safe because of Enzo. "I think we're almost done."

Benito grunted. "And you're sure this is the right decision for you two?"

I nodded, meeting his gaze head-on. "Yeah. I love him. I don't want to be anywhere else but with him."

Giancarlo awwed. "You two are disgusting together."

"Now you sound like Chelsea." I grinned.

He grinned right back. "Don't break my brother's fucking heart, or I'll rip yours out while you watch."

Cold shot through me. I blinked. Giancarlo was still smiling, looking just as carefree and laid back as before. *Did I make that up? Did he actually say that?*

"I feel the same way," Benito added, and I knew I hadn't misheard a damn thing. "What do you plan to do now? I don't want another freeloader bringing him down."

"Enzo and I have talked about things. When he's feeling one hundred percent, and I'm not having night-mares of my partner's head being turned into a red pulp, I'll look into school again. I'll find something I want to do."

"Sorry about that," Gin said. "We might have anger issues."

"Might?"

"Okay, fine," he groaned. "We definitely have anger issues."

I shook my head. He was right about that. Not one Vitale seemed to be able to control their tempers. Even Enzo, who could be very level-headed, had a monster simmering under his skin, waiting to be released.

"We better get back to it before Enzo thinks we're torturing you," Benito said.

I nodded. As we walked to the door, I stopped with the knob still in my hand. I turned back toward them.

"You two know he's autistic, right?"

"We don't talk about it," Benito muttered. "The way our family back home is—"

"One hundred percent." Giancarlo laughed. "Known it since forever. We're so used to it I think we honestly forget."

"We don't talk about it," Benito repeated, giving Gin a pointed glare. "Shut up."

"I'm just saying!" Gin shrugged. "There's nothing wrong with it."

"According to us. Not to the rest of the family."

"Right." Giancarlo scratched the back of his head and shrugged. "Anyway, it doesn't matter.   Enzo's just Enzo. We love him, same as you."

"Not the same," Benito clarified.

I grinned between the two of them. Benito almost seemed jealous. It made sense; I'd come out of nowhere and stolen his little brother from him. I wanted to tell Benito I was never going to hurt him, but my words didn't mean shit. All I could do was show him.

"What the fuck are you three doing up here?" Enzo growled as he wrenched the door open. His eyes narrowed. "What's going on?"

"Nothing," I said, reaching out to wrap my arms around his body. "What did Melony say?"

Enzo looked at his brothers before his gaze wandered back to me. "She says I'm fine. I can move stuff if it's not too heavy."

I nodded. "I still think you should take it easy."

He gave me an exhausted look. "I had the doctor check me out, and you're still bitching?"

"Get over it."

Enzo grabbed a handful of my hair. His nails dug in, scraping over my scalp as he dragged me into a deep kiss. When he pulled back, he growled at me.

"I already told you to watch it."

My heart pounded, all the blood rushing right to my cock. That was what I was looking for, that dangerous edge that made my heart go pitter-fucking-patter. I left a kiss on the tip of his nose, making him let out an exasperated sigh.

"We better get this stuff moved before Chelsea steals your doctor."

Benito brushed past us. "I've seen more than enough of that," he muttered.

"I'm with him." Gin jogged down the stairs. "I'll stop Chelsea."

I didn't know what it was about those two, but he and Chelsea were actually starting to get along. She was still nervous, especially when he let something crazy leave his lips, but they had things in common. Like being completely unhinged. I had the distinct feeling he was on his way to encourage her debauchery.

"What were you three talking about?" Enzo asked once everyone was gone.

I waved a hand. "Nothing important," I said, reaching out to brush my fingers through his hair. "You have good brothers."

He nodded. "We'd do anything for each other."

"I believe it." I leaned down to capture his lips once more. Enzo's warm tongue slipped into my mouth. I groaned, shoving him against a wall as my body ached for him. "Would it be rude to disappear for a little while?"

"What's a little while?" Enzo asked.

"Ten minutes."

"We both know it'll take longer than that." Enzo's hand slipped into my pants, wrapping around my cock. "I plan to take my time."

I licked my lips. "Fuck."

"Yep." Enzo bit my bottom lip.

"Stop being whores and help!" Chelsea called up the stairs. "We're not getting paid for this!"

I groaned as Enzo pulled away. He caressed my cheek, brushing his thumb over my skin before dragging it across my bottom lip. My tongue darted out, lapping at it.

"You'll pay for teasing me."

"I sure as fuck hope so," I muttered. I laughed as I turned, only to have my wrist grabbed, and I was turned back to face him. Enzo's face had suddenly gone serious. "What? What's wrong?"

"I love you so damn much."

I desperately tried to swallow around the lump in my throat. "I love you too."

Our lips met, and I never wanted to pull away from him again. No matter what shit we had to go through, we would face it together because I knew one thing for sure. Being with Enzo Vitale was the best decision I'd ever made.

AUTHORS NOTE

Enzo and Tex's story came to us one pineapple and Bacardi filled night. The moment the characters came alive in our heads we ran with it. Best fucking decision yet. This love story came from the deepest parts of our black souls and we hope you could feel that as you read.

We hope you're excited for the next book Paid In Full!!! You are in for an epic treat.

We would greatly appreciate if you would take the time out of your day and leave a review informing other readers on your thoughts about Take Me Apart.

VITALE BROTHERS

Take Me Apart

Paid in Full

Say I do

Never Say Never

End It All

ABOUT BREA ALEPOÚ

Keep updated on what Brea Alepoú is working on,
Subscribe to her **Newsletter.**

Brea Alepoú realized her dream was to write and tell stories
after spending five years in college getting a degree. She has
since been writing and letting her imagination free. She
thought she would only write contemporary at first but soon
found her love for making worlds. So now she rights it all.
With her wild imagination, expect lots of different stories,
from fairies ruling, to vampires killing everyone, to the
sweet loving between two men, passion between two fierce
women, or the love of multiple partners. She believes that
everyone deserves love even if not all of her characters get it
right away. Love is passionate, hot, needy, confusing,
painful, draining, fulfilling, and all-consuming.

*M/M & F/F Romance: Paranormal, Dark, Fantasy, Shifter
Mpreg, Shifter Fpreg, & Harem
There will be a book for everyone.*

Insanity is Contagious. Brea Alepoú

Brea.alepou@gmail.com

ALSO BY BREA ALEPOÚ

Blood Series (M/M/M/M+)

(Dark Paranormal Romance)

More Than Blood [Audio]

Holiday Blood (Short)

Spooky Blood (Short)

Their Blood

Addicted to His Blood

Our Blood

Trading in Blood

Paranormal Delights (M/M/M/M+)

(Dark Gay Harem Paranormal Romance)

Mafia Prince

Dragon Boss

Heartless Assassin (coming soon)

ABOUT SKYLER SNOW

Skyler Snow is the author of kinky, steamy MM books. Whether contemporary or paranormal you'll always find angst, kink and a love that conquers all.

Skyler started off writing from a young age. When faced with the choice chef or author, author won hands down. They're big into musicals, true crime shows, reality TV madness and good books whether light and fluffy or dark and twisted. When they're not writing you can find them playing roleplaying games and hanging out with their kids.

— Skyler Snow

ALSO BY SKYLER SNOW

MAFIA DADDIES SERIES

(Contemporary Daddy Romance)

Break Me Daddy

Fight Me Daddy

Watch Me Daddy

Obey me Daddy

Paranormal Delights

MM+ Paranormal Romance

Mafia Prince

Dragon Boss

Heartless Assassin (coming soon)

Made in United States
Troutdale, OR
09/17/2024

22919570R00213